Uncharted Journey

Uncharted Journey

by

Harold G. Ross

SUNFLOWER UNIVERSITY PRESS®
1531 Yuma • P.O. Box 1009 • Manhattan, Kansas 66505-1009 USA

Printed in the United States of America on acid-free paper.

Cover by Tom Bookwalter, Olsburg, Kansas.

ISBN 0-89745-277-1

Sunflower University Press is a wholly-owned subsidiary
of the non-profit 501(c)3 Journal of the West, Inc.

To
Jesus, the Christ,
Who, by love and grace,
answered all my prayers.

I left Mosswood after Ma and Pa were killed, with pain in my nine-year-old heart and flint in my jaw. I was on an uncharted journey to wherever life might take me. . . . But I was determined I would survive . . . for I was the proud son of Robert and Elizabeth Sinclair. . . . And courage and bravery ran deep in my blood.

One

THE EARLY MORNING sun was golden through the lace curtains of my bedroom, when I heard the shouting of angry men. In moments, the deafening blasts of gunfire racketed throughout the house.

Ma rushed in, closed the door, and quickly pulled me from my bed. Grabbing hold of my Bible, clothes, and shoes, she shoved me through the hidden door in the west wall, following me into the dark cavity and closing behind us the opening that had been concealed within the shelving of my books. She held my hand as we went down abrupt, narrow steps to a landing, then to more shaky treads, into a darker place.

It was a room I'd been in before, but Ma could tell I was frightened this time, and she put her arms around me as she whispered, *"It'll be all right, Sean . . . everything'll be all right!"*

Ma felt her way along the wall, then stopped to light a match that snapped into brilliant colors, as she lifted the chimney of a kerosene lamp.

It was June 17, 1860. Two days earlier I'd had my ninth

birthday. A lot of what I remember of that painful morning when Pa was killed is sketchy.

We lived in the Mississippi River delta, some thirty miles southeast of New Orleans, near Breton Sound, which linked to the Gulf of Mexico. From the grounds of Mosswood, our plantation, you could see the ocean and when the wind was right could hear the waves breaking fast to the shore. Our land was located on valued fertile soil, in an area of giant oak covered with hanging festoons of gray-green Spanish moss. To the rear of the large house in the bayou were enormous, tall cypress trees, their toughened, bald knees rising from the swamp water.

My Pa was a kind man — not the scoundrel that certain others had tried to bandy around in whispers. He had long been a sea Captain of his own ship, and had made a great amount of money — not always gained from the work of his hands, I knew, for some of his dealings had seen clandestine exchange of goods with countries America then held no trade agreements. But Pa operated in the long-ago tradition of a privateer on the high seas who'd defended his ship when challenged, and took the spoils of any conquest when left to him. I'd seen his recent treasure with my own eyes, as it had been hauled to shore, before he had cached it somewhere in the swamp.

It was from Pa that I'd learned the valued things of life — especially in the year he had let me sail the seas with him. And this past year, with the three of us together at home, was the happiest, days of pleasures and luxury.

But I remember Pa's appreciation of his prosperity as well.

"Be thankful, son, in what you have, because nothing's for long, even life on earth."

I recollected Pa's words as Ma and I huddled close in the small secret room, within the halo of lamplight and its shadow. A table with four chairs had been placed near the stairway, and a cupboard stood along the east wall. Against the north, several boxes of clothing were stacked. Nothing else was in the dank chamber.

It wasn't long before Ma and I smelled smoke working its way below grade into our refuge. I could see the fear in Ma's face. She hurried to the left side of the cupboard and swung it out, revealing an even darker tunnel. My eyes must have widened. The unknown before me was frightening, but I realized we had a burst of new air and it was refreshing.

After we had entered the passage, Ma quickly pulled the cupboard back into place. Some five hundred feet later, the tunnel met daylight along the bank of the wetland marsh. The outside entrance was encased with brush, so that there was no way to see the opening, unless you were far into the swamp — and even from there you probably couldn't make it out.

That instant, I heard Ma moan — a brief cry of pain, mingled with apparent exhaustion — and I sat down with her near the cave entrance. It alarmed me as she held me tight and began to silently weep, and I became teary-eyed too. But I wouldn't let the tears be seen. I knew I needed to be strong for her. I could tell in the dim glow of night that Ma didn't look good, and on the ground beside her was some blood. I realized then that she had been shot.

Ma closed her eyes and began to turn grave and sorrowful. Haltingly, as if that effort was almost too much, she worked at drawing a map of where Pa's treasure had been buried. I sat with her, quietly, trying not to show my fear; it was then that she pulled me closer and gave me her instructions.

"My dearest little Sean, I am sorry . . . so sorry." Her voice caught and tears spilled down her cheeks before she could continue. ". . . I fear you will be on your own, Sean — you must make do for yourself, for I don't believe . . . I don't believe I'm going to be with you much longer, son."

I nodded as Ma continued. "Cousin Mary Latimore is in St. Louis, Sean . . . you recall me speaking of her? . . . You must take a piece of the treasure to her . . . tell her it's for your keep . . . and your schooling. And when sold, she'll have more than enough to pay for it."

I listened carefully to what Ma had to say, hiding my own tears from her, until we were suddenly interrupted by thundering, running sounds coming from above. We listened as an angry voice cut the quiet of the morning.

". . . *At least we got that devil Sinclair. . . . But even so, he's managed to kill Logan and Rupert.*

"*Where Elizabeth and her young cub have gone is the problem! I saw her on the stairway . . . I'm sure she's been hit!*"

The voice stopped for a moment, then continued, irritated but resigned. "*Well, we searched before we torched the place, so she and the boy have either disappeared, or they're a pile of ashes, like Sinclair.*"

Just then we heard another voice . . . a woman, chewing on one of the men pretty heavy.

"*Can't you do anything right, Daniel? . . . You know we can't afford for any of them to get away if we want the property. Once we have the place will be time enough to find the treasure! . . .*

"Now go on back to the house and make sure no one's hiding there; you can see no one's down here in the swamp!"

The voice that must have been Daniel's acknowledged his orders. "*All right! . . . They've got to be inside that house somewhere — there's no way they could have gotten out!*"

The woman still had scolding on her mind. "*. . . And, Daniel!*" she shouted. "*I know I have to explain this to you again! . . . . Don't do anything foolish like returning to this place once we're gone. We don't want anyone knowing we've been here. After the fire's discovered and the authorities have investigated, we can find out what's going on from the papers, and then we'll see about claiming the land as our own.*"

The voices were silent; we figured they'd left.

Ma was breathing heavy, but was determined to explain to me what she had on her mind.

"You need to know what's happening, Sean. . . . It's terrible family troubles. Your Pa, until this morning, had four stepbrothers and two stepsisters — his only living kin. That was Daniel talking, your father's stepbrother, and Lucia, his stepsister, the eldest of the living Champlains. The two that Pa killed were their brothers.

"The remaining brother, the second oldest, is Terrill. He always liked your father, and I'd guess knows nothing of what's happening here. The younger sister is Julia. But, as a warning, son, I'd stay wary of the three — Daniel, Lucia, and Julia.

"After your grandfather Sinclair died, your grandmother had married Maurice Champlain, a decent man, when your father was just fourteen. But owing to his notorious stepbrothers and sisters, your father ran off from home in two years, and would have nothing to do with them — except, of course, for Terrill, who in truth had always played and marched to his own drum. Your grandmother and Maurice have been dead some fifteen years now . . . and your father had always suspected they'd been poisoned."

I was perplexed. I never had an inkling of these troubles before.

Ma continued, and I tried to follow the winding family history as best I could.

"Lucia rules the family, and has the traits of her own Grandmother Susette. She was a Jamaican — and into voodoo, and the worst of evils she could conjure up to get her way. Susette's father was a prominent Creole gentleman, and her mother was a beauty — a lovely black quadroon. . . ."

Ma sighed deeply. "Both fine parents to their children, but for some reason a part of their offspring turned to the wicked.

"The Champlains, except for Terrill who's in New Orleans, live at Blackstone, a large plantation northwest of there. Yet they've envied your father for many, many years, coveting his worth . . . but we never thought they'd stoop to *murder!*"

Ma was now almost breathless, whispering so faintly that I could barely hear her.

"Sean . . . you must be wary, for if the three should find out that you're alive, they'll stop at nothing to be rid of you. And I'm not really so sure that Terrill should be trusted, if all be considered, unless things should turn especially desperate."

Earlier Ma had taken with her the pen and paper from the cupboard, as we'd left the underground room. Now, trembling and seeming to be getting weaker, she was trying to write several notes, including a letter to her cousin Mary. Handing me the paper, she told me to give it to Mary. "It explains everything," she said. Then she wrote another message, re-read what she had written, and handed it likewise to me.

"Take this," she said. "Read it later. Memorize it. Then destroy it."

My mind was beginning to fog so badly I could hardly concentrate on what Ma was telling me to do. Fear and grief were intermittently taking over my thoughts, though I could hear her implore me to keep reading the King James as I continued on in life. It was then that the full realization came to me — I was going to be alone, forevermore.

An hour later Ma died, our arms wrapped around each other as we lay in the cave's damp night air. At that moment I became distraught and frightened. I started to sob, until in time, spent of tears and settled somewhat, I sternly told myself, "*I am Sean Sinclair, the son of Robert and Elizabeth Sinclair . . . . My ancestors were from the snows of Norway and the glens of Scotland. . . . And courage and bravery run deep and heavy in my blood.*"

I cried no more.

I slept near the cave entrance, and when I awoke thought all that had gone on before had been a bad dream. Then I saw Ma lying across from me. I sat up and looked at her beautiful face and long, dark auburn hair. The present came back in an instant. I remembered the fateful happenings of the night before, and I felt a burden of melancholy weighing on me. But I forced myself to take charge of my fears and do what had to be done.

Crawling through the bayou brush along a tunnel-like game trail, I came out into the open along the bank of the marsh. The sun was in the west, and looking in the distance, I could tell that the Champlains were gone. I crept up to our house that now lay in ashes, except for the heavy timbers that had fallen and were lifting smoke. I could see the outbuilding where we'd kept our horses was intact, but the animals had been brutally shot.

In the stable I found a shovel, and cautiously, watching for unwanted visitors, over the rest of that day and night I dug a grave large enough for Ma — and for Pa, when I would find him — beneath a giant oak northeast of what had been our home.

Ma was a small, delicate woman, and I was a strong lad, yet she was still too much for me to carry, and so I'd found a canvas tarp and rolled her body onto it. It took me a good hour, but I'd managed to pull the canvas to the grave.

I stayed near her burial site and the ruins of our house for three days after the fire. I had finally found Pa's remains in the debris, along with the two others in the ashes, and I buried him, next to Ma, close together, beneath the oak. I knew it was Pa from the flat ruby ring on his finger.

I'd been to only one funeral in my short life, but I knew you were supposed to say a prayer for the dead. And though I couldn't remember anything in particular at that painful moment, I simply beseeched the Almighty.

> *Dear God . . . if you love my father, Robert, and my dear mother, Elizabeth, as much as I do, then I won't worry; I'll know they'll be safe in Heaven. . . . I love you, Jesus. . . . Amen.*

I pitied away the rest of the day, crying and feeling sorry for myself, until I remembered what Pa had told me about handling adversity.

"You can't change what is, and if it has turned your life upside-down, use it as a prod to make yourself a stronger person. Strive forward . . . and don't look back. It's done."

On my fourth day alone, I returned to the underground room heavy with the smell of smoke. Nothing had been burned down there, and I managed to salvage some necessities from the cupboard, mostly food. I found a pack made of canvas, with straps, and, heeding Ma's words, stowed my King James Bible as well as a rope, needles, thread, matches, canned peaches, green beans, and carrots, and a packet of beef jerky.

I was about to leave when for some reason I had decided to look on the top shelf. Pushed to the back was a sheathed bowie knife, a .44 Remington pistol, and what must have been a hundred rounds of ammunition. I put them in my pack, knowing their worth might be made known to me another day.

I'd decided to leave for St. Louis and Cousin Mary, but not before I went to Pa's treasure. It was hidden in the swamp, and the thought of finding my way, for a mile in and then back out of that wet nightmare of creeping alligators and poisonous snakes, gave me the jitters. I looked at one of the notes Ma had written her last night with me:

> *Sean,*
>
> *From the treasure take the brooch with the emerald and diamonds. It's worth is some $20,000 — maybe more. And take a few gold coins, but not so many you cannnot hide them easily. Give the brooch to Mary, for she will know a jeweler in St. Louis. That will be the money she receives for your keep and education.*
>
> *The coins are for you; but keep them hidden and tell no one, not even Mary. The gold is for dire need, should you find it necessary.*
>
> *When you're older will be time enough to return for the remainder of the treasure.*
>
> *God bless you, Sean. I love you,*
>
> *Your Mother*

Ma had also written me another note, along with the map, describing exactly where Pa's treasure was located. I had no trouble finding it. Though I had only three years of formal schooling, Ma had given me grown-up reading from her *Harper's Weekly* and the *Frank Leslie's Illustrated*, as well as books from her library, all by the time I was seven. I understood well what she had written. And that day, as she'd instructed, I burned her notes and the map, except for the letter to Mary.

I wasn't prepared for all that lay before me, except for what Pa had now and then tried to tell me of life; sooner than I expected, I knew I'd need to put myself to the test of surviving on my own.

A week had passed since the fire, and just after daybreak I was walking northwest on the wagon road to New Orleans. I'd found some clothes in one of the boxes stored in the basement room, and put another set in my pack. I had no coin but a gold piece in my pocket, and sixteen others I had crudely sewn into the bottom of the pockets of my two pair of pants. As I walked, I was wishing for some silver, for I knew that a gold piece, when cashed, was liable to create some unwanted attention.

In a mist of blue haze the sun came up a glowing red over my right shoulder. I walked a hard-packed earth, with the Mississippi River on my left, now and then passing others treading that way on foot. The blasts of the river's barge horns kept me company as I continued on, wary of the Champlains and cautious of any strangers. It was at that time in life that I became much more aware of my surroundings — not only of man, but of nature.

The Louisiana land around me was rich with growth of trees and wildlife. Game birds and song birds abounded in the marsh and along the river, and they lifted my wounded spirit as I listened to their music and journeyed along my way. Still, now and then, my eyes would fill for but a moment if I'd let myself think about Ma and Pa.

That night I slept out of sight along the Mississippi, beneath an old keelboat hull half buried in the granules of a sandbar, hidden from the roadway by a patch of willow trees. While lying on my ground sheet I thought back to the terrible day of the fire. I had salvaged Pa's ruby ring, and Ma had asked me to take her own diamond from her finger, as well as the gold watch she wore on a chain around her neck. I held them that night, closing my palm around them, as if to bring Ma and Pa close to me. Ma's watch had a picture of the two of them inside the cover, a picture of lives that were no longer a living part of mine.

I listened to the river and gave in to sleep.

The morning was gray when I awoke and watched the current flowing its last few miles to the ocean. I was hungry and opened some of the peaches and beef jerky I had brought. Feeling better, I listened to the roar of the river and prepared for my hike into the French Quarter. I was by then a full participant in my adventure, on the unstoppable wheel of time, and I prepared myself to meet the world. I wasn't forgetting, though, that I'd found how cruel life could be.

I don't know why, maybe it was Pa reminding me from Heaven to be wary, but I'd decided to arm myself. I took the pistol and knife from my pack, putting them out of sight beneath my jacket. The gun in my belt was loaded and ready to fire, for I was not alien to guns, since Pa had worked with me many times in their use and care. I could hit the target Pa'd put up at fifty feet — not the bull's-eye like he could, but a target, nevertheless, a lot smaller than a man. If presented the opportunity, I was certain I could hit a Champlain, should any of them show their faces.

Two

WHEN THE SUN was high and a golden globe in the cerulean sky, I walked lonely into the teeming city of New Orleans. Two blocks west of the riverfront docks I'd trekked down Royal Street on a narrow cobblestone way looking at the elegant buildings before me. Foot traffic on St. Philip Street had pulled me east a block to Bourbon, where loitered what appeared to be the usual wide-ranging mix of the Louisiana populace. New Orleans was a town said to have quartered more free men of color than bonded since the very early 1800s.

The French Quarter was a new experience for me, however, and curiosity filled my eyes, with the shops, the street people, and the painted pastel-colored stucco buildings. The structures mostly were one and a half to two stories tall, with their common fronts flush along the walkway. Their flat tile roofs, hanging out over the walks, formed a canopy as far out as the street. And ornamental balconies of iron had been cast in elaborate patterns.

I would learn that the retail owners often lived above their stores, and the houses to the rear of the shops had been built around open courtyards, with handsome moldings and elegant cornices.

As I continued down Bourbon Street that day, I was ever so fearful, yet stricken with wonder at the busy scene before me. But the locals seemed to pay me no mind, and maybe it was because of the many other youngsters on the street — some, too, left homeless . . . by the cholera and yellow fever taking parents from them. Nevertheless, I was cautious, for I had met no friendly faces.

I was hungry, but figured to save what I had in my pack, and so standing taller and more confident, I walked through a wide, opened doorway into a dingy-looking tavern and sat down at a near table. The room was dark, but my eyes soon accustomed to it and I could see more than a few patrons. Two shared a bottle of rum nearby, and scattered throughout the place were others at drink or eat, all men . . . all with unfriendly eyes on me. I knew it was not usual for a young boy to be out dining alone, and I could sense a potential for trouble. But I was determined not to get up and leave.

I was put somewhat at ease when the server walked over and asked what I would like.

"Well, . . . something to eat," I'd told her.

"You'll need cash . . . as much as twenty cents," she explained, "dependin' on your choice."

"I have it," I answered, in as grown-up a voice as I could muster.

She nodded, then told me they had corn-meal fried and crawfish for fifteen cents, or shrimp and potatoes for twenty.

I'd decided on the shrimp, and as she gave me her prettiest smile, she walked off to the kitchen.

I carefully glanced around the room, and could see a man deep to the back in the darkness who seemed to be watching me with interest — then another, a couple tables away. The closer of the two, with a slight smile, spoke.

"My name's Clyde Radford, young man."

". . . Nice to meet you, Mr. Radford; I'm Sean."

"Just Sean?" he asked with amusement.

His question alerted my senses, and I quickly blurted, "Blackstone . . . Sean Blackstone."

I didn't want the Sinclair name to be out and about, for it might start a scoundrel wondering. I knew word of my father's demise could have been afoot by then.

The server brought my food and nothing more was said, except as she handed it to me she quietly told me to be careful if I was traveling alone.

I was grateful for her concern, but it had added a new level of fear to my situation.

I quickly finished my meal and paid the barkeep with a gold piece. He looked at the coin, then asked if I had anything smaller. As I shook my head, he went into his money drawer, and by that time I was truly nervous, for all eyes in the place seemed to be watching me.

Once outside, I could feel my heart pounding, but was relieved to be away from there and on my way again. I figured I would need to find a path to the river, so decided to walk to the docks, in the hopes of getting a boat to St. Louis.

I hadn't gone a block when Clyde Radford caught up with me. He'd wanted to help, he'd said, and I trustingly told him I was looking to find transportation north.

He looked at me askance. "You got the money?"

I didn't know how to answer. But he seemed reliable enough, so I took a chance, nodding, "I have enough for the fare."

"Well, follow me; I know just the boat. It's headin' for St. Louis in the morning."

After ten minutes trailing behind Radford, we seemed to be leaving all civilization and making our way down a tenuous, narrow walk along the river. It made me uneasy, with the brooch and money I was carrying, and I finally spoke up.

"I'm not going any farther; I'm heading back to find a boat on my own!"

Radford obviously didn't like what I'd said, and while pulling a knife he replied angrily, "No! You're not headin' back, kid. I want your pack. Hand it over and I'll let you go; otherwise you're alligator meat."

I backed away as he came closer, and in an instant pulled the .44 Remington. The surprised ruffian's eyes turned angrier. I knew I couldn't run, for he'd catch me in a few steps. He came at me, and I pulled the trigger. The bullet hit him in the belly, and it stopped him. He looked down at the blood dripping from his shirt, and realizing he had a fatal wound, furiously shouted what must have been his last. "*You bastard of a whelp! . . .You're dead!*"

He lunged forward, falling on top of me, just as a shot rang out. It was he who was dead, his knife falling harmlessly away.

I looked up, stunned to see the man who had been sitting at the back of the tavern. He had shot Clyde in the head. He spoke as he pulled the hoodlum off of me.

"You had him all right, son; the only problem was it could take him the rest of the day to die. When you shoot a man," he instructed, "you need to hit him in the head or the heart, someplace that'll put him out of commission."

I started to cry. I was finally overwhelmed with all that had happened the past week, and I sobbed for some time with the stranger holding me in his arms.

"It'll be all right," he told me . . . and I remembered those were the very same words that Ma had said, when Pa'd been killed.

Before we left the river bank, James Malone had introduced himself. Then he picked up the ruffian and threw him in the river. There were no witnesses, and as we walked back to town I told him my name — my real name. Why? I don't know for sure, but I think it was because he had saved my life, and I trusted him.

God was surely watching over me that day along the waterfront, and I asked Malone how it happened that he had followed Radford to the river.

He explained, "I knew he was riff-raff and a thief, and when he went outside after you, I knew it was trouble."

I spent more than a week with Malone in New Orleans. He told me he gambled, but beyond that I hadn't a clue what he did to earn a living. I had to be a burden on him, but for reasons of his own he took a liking to me and became my protector. We stayed at the elegant Saint Louis Hotel, where he always stopped when he was in New Orleans, he said. At night, after dinner, he'd leave the room around nine and not return until close to three in the morning.

In one of our talks he confided to having enemies that had wanted to do him in, and so all his daily movements were made with caution. I noticed, as well, that the management at the hotel always treated Malone with the utmost esteem, like he was an important personage — or maybe they were just afraid of him.

I liked Malone; he took me in without a question and treated me like an equal. He went out of his way to explain the pitfalls encountered in the cities. And in a lot of ways, he reminded me of Pa.

Early that July, on a bright Monday morning, Malone and I walked up the gangplank of the steamboat *Tennessee*. On deck we found our stateroom with the name Virginia above the door. I had told Malone I needed to go to St. Louis, to find my mother's cousin, explaining that the Latimores hopefully would make a home for me.

He had been needing to go to St. Louis himself, he said. "I've property just north of town."

Malone didn't say, but I think he would've stayed longer in New Orleans if not for me — though I don't think it really mattered to him just where he put his hat. I knew one thing; I felt safe when Malone was around, and from appearances, it looked to me like only an idiot would ever cross the man.

A golden sunlight was picking sparkles off the Mississippi as the blast from the sternwheeler's horn shouted its warning of departure. I stood by the rail and watched the paddlewheels churn as the boat picked up speed. In no time the riverfront, stacked with bales of cotton, and the busy streets of New Orleans lay silent in the distance.

Except for all that had happened in the past two weeks, I felt an exhilaration in my heart at the new adventure pressing upon me. Now and again, when I thought of Ma and Pa, there would come a sadness in my heart.

As I watched the river, Malone stepped up to the railing; he knew I could read well, and handed me two issues of the New Orleans *Times-Picayune*.

"Sean, these are last week's papers. There's some articles I thought you might be interested in."

He continued, "There's a card game today in the Alabama stateroom, and I've been invited to play. It'll take up most of my day. . . . I think you might want to stay close to the cabin; there're some rough characters on board."

Malone always wore a cartridge belt and six-gun, but this time he carried no weapon.

"Malone," I asked, "shouldn't you get your six-gun?"

"No," he told me, ". . . I'm wearing my sleeve gun."

Patting his right forearm he confided, "Sometimes it's better if a gun's not showing." I told Malone I'd go to the cabin and read the newspapers, then as I turned to walk away, he cautioned, "Sean, keep the door locked, and open it for no one but me."

I was taken aback by his warning. I couldn't figure out why he was suddenly wanting me to be extra careful . . . but I would soon find out. It was not ten minutes later, when I was in our cabin, leafing through the July 3rd issue of the New Orleans paper, that I saw on the inside page a short column with the headline: "*Sinclair Plantation House, Mosswood, Burns.*" The article told the story.

> *. . . A neighbor, Jacob Thornton, riding by the property discovered the catastrophe last week and reported it to the authorities. Two unrecognizable bodies were found in the ashes, thought to be that of Robert and Elizabeth Sinclair. Mr. Thornton told the authorities the Sinclairs had a young son, Sean, thought to be eight to ten years of age. After another search through the ashes and remaining debris, no remains were found of the boy.*

I anxiously picked up the July 7th issue Malone had given me, and near the bottom of the front page read, "*Sean Sinclair, Missing.*"

> *The recent Sinclair fire remains a mystery. Authorities searching the grounds found a fresh grave with two bodies, one a woman, the other unidentifiable. The corpses were thought to be Robert and Elizabeth Sinclair. Strangely the woman's body had not been in the fire and had died from a bullet wound. The question remains as to who buried them.*
>
> *Thornton, the neighbor, replaced the bodies where they had been buried and told the sheriff he would likely put up a tombstone. The two bodies found in the ashes of the house are unidentified.*
>
> *Local authorities had first thought the fire was accidental, but without finding the young boy's remains, and finding Mrs. Sinclair shot, they figure foul play with kidnaping to be a possibility. The sheriff has asked everyone to be on the lookout for a homeless nine-year-old boy.*

Malone had never asked me why I was on the streets of New Orleans, and I had never told him; he just took me in without question. But he knew my real name, and now, from the newspaper, he knew the whole story.

I never heard Malone when he came to bed, but it had to be after midnight. When I awoke the sun was coming in the east porthole. Malone was sitting at the small table counting bills he'd put in stacks. I lay there watching as he slid most of the money in a belt, along with gold coin. The rest he stuffed in his pocket. Malone glanced over and saw I was awake.

"Well, Sean, it looks like we'll be able to eat. I won two thousand last night, and a good thing, for I was getting a little low on cash. Now we can forget business and enjoy the rest of the trip."

After I had dressed I told Malone I'd read the newspaper stories, then explained to him everything that had happened since the fire, and the Champlains' involvement in the murder of my Ma and Pa. When I started to tell him of the treasure, he stopped me.

"Sean, tell me no more. I don't want to know about it. Even I might not be able to resist the temptation of cheating you out of it!" he laughed.

"But I trust you, Malone. You're my best friend."

He gently pulled me to him and gave me a hug. "And you're my best friend too, Sean; but tell no one about the treasure, or where it's cached, not even the Latimores."

I took the brooch from my pack and showed Malone. He softly whistled as he shook his head.

"And show *that* to no one, Sean! I can only hope for your sake that the Latimores are honest people."

Malone and I walked the deck that evening with the steamboat continuing to churn water upstream. A silver moon rose above the tall cottonwoods, as it sailed by a fishing craft moored along the east bank, streaming a silver light across the river and the deck of our boat.

I was surprised that night when Malone told me he had once met my father in New Orleans, some six years earlier, when Pa was working the seas. They'd had some kind of dealing together, but he went into no details of their venture, except to suggest that Pa's ship was used to bring in some goods then considered contraband. Malone paused for a moment and added.

"Your father was a tough man, Sean, though a person had to be in his business. But he was a fair man. And I liked him. The Champlains, however, have a wide reputation as scoundrels. I've heard one of the women practices voodoo, and works with poisons, and from what you've told me, your mother was right that they won't be satisfied until you're dead."

I was surprised Malone knew so much about my folks and the Champlains, then I asked, "No card game tonight?"

"Yes, there's a game. But I don't need the money, and I'm not in the mood. The night's too beautiful to waste my time on cards, and I have someone to meet."

We walked to the stern and standing there was the most beautiful lady I'd ever seen, except for Ma. She had blonde hair that hung in ringlets along her face, and when she smiled, even I was smitten. I was staring into her deep blue eyes when she spoke.

"James, what a handsome child. Is the boy related?" she queried, and held out her delicate hand.

I shook her hand and proudly announced, "My name's Sean."

"What a beautiful name," she exclaimed. "I'm Sarah . . . Sarah Jones."

Malone never responded to Sarah's question, and told me I might go to our room. I thought it strange that he hadn't told Sarah I wasn't related, but figured he might have said so later.

Some hours past, when I was awakened by scuffling and shouts outside the cabin. . . . "Gi'me your money! Now! . . . Now, or I'll blow your head off!"

"He means it! Hand it over! . . . All of it!" came a second voice.

I heard Malone speak. "It's not your money. I watched you palming cards during the game and said nothing. You should be pleased I didn't call you on it last night in front of the others. You had it coming, and I meted out justice."

A moment later pistol shots split the night, followed by the sound of tumbling movement. I heard a splash from the river . . . then another.

I was shaking, but grabbed my six-gun, fearful that something had happened to Malone. Before I could get to the door, I heard the lock turn and he stepped inside. He peered at the gun in my hand and ruffled my hair.

"It's okay, Sean; just some disgruntled card players who'd lost money the other night. They were cheating, so I turned the tables on them."

By that time we could hear footsteps outside our room and excited voices asking others about the gunfire. Then silence returned, and Malone fell asleep. I wondered myself as I lay abed, how it was that two ruffians couldn't handle Malone, especially when they had the drop on him. He was one tough man . . . but still I worried for his safety.

It wasn't long before we docked in St. Louis. Malone took me by the shoulders and looked me in the eye. "Sean I need to talk with you before you go to the Latimores. . . .

"You know that no one will treat you like your own parents did, and if things don't work out there, you might again be left on your own.

". . . I'm making you an offer here . . . . You could stay at my place north of town for a few months, and I'd work with you some more on the handling of guns and defending yourself. I just hate to turn you loose yet, Sean."

My heart was pounding. I was excited with the opportunity to stay with Malone. I didn't need to think it over.

"I'd like that, Malone! I'll stay with you and not even go to the Latimores!"

"No," he laughed. "It's best you go, in time, and get an education. I only want to make sure you're ready to face some of the dangers when necessary."

The plan was decided. I was happy.

I never saw Sarah after that night on the boat. It was as if she had disappeared. I was disappointed, for I liked her a lot, and Malone never explained.

Three

ST. LOUIS lay on the west bank of the Mississippi — the gateway to the West they called it — at the confluence of the Mississippi and Missouri Rivers. The sternwheeler *Tennessee* docked at the riverfront just as an east sun was gleaming a golden light across the wide expanse and into our eyes when we walked out of our cabin with our packs. I stopped for a moment to look at the flow of glittering water, where the sun was busy picking thousands of diamonds from off the surface.

We were slow in leaving the boat and all the other passengers were gone when we walked the gangplank down to the dock. Malone stopped at a livery stable, and after a friendly exchange with the hostler, we rode out the barn doors. I'd been riding horses since I was four, and it came easy for me.

We moved north, then some three miles later we turned east down a private road toward a timber of large oak. Inside the park-like setting of oak we came to a stone archway. Malone unlocked the ornate iron gate and swung it wide, then closed it behind us. The lane turned north, and ahead was a two-story plantation house surrounded by more large oak for shade. The home sat on a high plateau with a panoramic view of the Mississippi. Behind the house were the stables, with a sixty-acre holding pasture, and all around the dwelling were elaborate gardens of colorful flowers and green foliage.

We rode to the stables, dismounted, and cared for our horses. Malone showed me the feed and grooming storage, then we went out two wide swinging doors into the corral. I could see horses in the pasture, as we climbed the fence for a better look. Of the eight, the one that caught my eye was a palomino, a four-year-old gelding, not quite the hands tall as the horse Malone had ridden from St. Louis. I said nothing, but I caught Malone watching me out of the corner of his eye.

After stepping down off the fence we went to the house. Malone opened the front door and we walked into a beautiful marbled entry with a massive curving stairway to the second floor.

"Come on, Sean," he said, as we walked into the parlor. I admired the room's large fireplace along the north wall. Then from behind me came the sweetest voice a body would ever want to hear. "Hello, Sean."

"Sarah!"

"Welcome to White Oaks," Sarah said, as she wrapped her arms around me. I'm so glad that James brought you here where you'll be safe."

I tried to stop the tears, and I did, but not before Sarah noticed a few spilling down my cheeks.

"Sean," she said, looking into my eyes, "everything *will* be all right."

That was the third time I'd heard those words, and her voice sounded so familiar I had to look again to make sure it wasn't Ma.

"I'm a Sinclair," I told her, "and our men don't cry."

She sympathized. "Well, it's all right if men cry sometimes, Sean. I think it makes them *more* of a man."

When Sarah and I rode out into the countryside, I was always on the palomino that Malone had given me. The gelding and I had become almost inseparable. On one particular trip, Malone had been gone for two days, off somewhere taking care of business. What errand I never knew for sure, for again, like Pa, he was a person of many mysteries — as was Sarah, in fact, an equal puzzle. But Malone would be gone for weeks at a time. Occasionally Sarah might be away one or two days, but hardly ever more. At times, they would leave together, but when they did, they'd almost always return that same evening.

It was when Malone and Sarah were gone that I'd gotten well acquainted with the live-in help. Henry Ducette was a light-skinned Creole who had worked for Sarah's family over thirty years, and he'd been with Malone and Sarah after that. He was like Sarah's shadow, and hardly ever let her out of his sight, unless Malone was around. He had to be nearly sixty, but he was extremely strong. He carried a bowie knife under his shirt, and I pitied the man that ever tried to interfere with Sarah's well-being. On one occasion, when Henry was showing me the bowie, he suddenly threw the knife at least fifty feet, driving the blade almost through a post. There was no equal to his strength.

The women that cared for the house at White Oaks were Marie, Henry's daughter, and Esther, his granddaughter. The grounds man was Joseph, Marie's husband. Esther, Marie's daughter, was eighteen, and seemed like a sister to Sarah. The domestics all appeared to be more like family than servants, with Sarah the head of the clan.

The Ducette family spent their days joyfully attending to what needed to be done, with neither instruction nor command — at least I was aware of none. They were always close by. And it was always a treat to hear the family singing of an evening, after their White Oaks duties had been finished for the day. I well remember the haunting Ethiopian melody of "Old Folks at Home," as Marie and Esther would harmonize.

"All the world am sad and dreary, everywhere I roam . . . Oh, how my heart grows weary, far from the old folks at home. . . ."

The melancholy words especially touched my still raw and tender heart.

While I was at White Oaks, whenever Malone was around we'd ride out together, and hour upon hour we'd spend at the art of self-defense — not only with guns, but with staff, rapier, and knives. By that fall, I could hit any bull's-eye with rifle or handgun, and throw a man to the ground four times my size.

But there was a lot I didn't know while I lived with Malone . . . like what was Malone's and Sarah's relationship? They seemed close, but Malone and I slept in the west end of the house, separate from the main part. Many times we ate and spent our evenings with Sarah in the large dining room and parlor; other times we ate in the large room off of our bedrooms, where Esther brought us our food. It was a room rich of decor and elegant cherry wood. Bookshelves covered the north wall, except for another large fireplace. When Malone wasn't around, I spent many leisure hours reading the fine books in the stately room. Malone had said the library had come with the house.

One evening Malone confided to me that he was thirty-two, and then told me how he'd come to own White Oaks — the house and the thousand acres. He'd won the plantation, five years earlier, in a card game with Tyrone Billings, a gambling businessman who'd been cheating good and honest people out of their money for years. Billings was president of a St. Louis bank, and was just the kind of man Malone liked to get into a poker game.

Their game was five-card stud, and Malone said he had intentionally lost to Billings the first time they'd played together, to the tune of twenty thousand dollars. Their second game, a few weeks later, was with four men — a St. Louis attorney, Jeffrey Amos; a trader, George Ellis; Malone; and Billings. After four hours, only Malone and Billings were left at the table. By eleven that night, Malone had won more than a hundred thousand dollars. But Billings still had ten thousand left that he could bet in the table stakes game.

Malone said he'd dealt the cards and Billings picked up three Aces, a nine, and a Jack. Malone had a possible three-card straight. Billings bet the ten thousand he had in front of him, and Malone called. Both drew two cards, and Billings got the fourth Ace and a King.

Malone said he knew he would best the man. Billings nervously wrote out an I.O.U. for one hundred thousand, betting the amount Malone had on the table. But Malone refused the paper, insisting on cash or hard collateral. Billings was angry, but those were the house rules.

Billings was certain he'd had a cinch hand and wanted desperately to win back the money he'd lost earlier. And so it was that he agreed to put up the White Oaks plantation he had recently foreclosed upon. Malone had attorney Amos write out a deed, Billings signed, and Ellis witnessed it.

Billings pushed the document to the center of the table, laid down four Aces, and gloated. Malone laid down a straight diamond flush. Billings's face turned white, Malone said, and he started cursing and ranting like a madman. He told Malone to come by the bank the next day and he'd give him the hundred thousand for the deed. But Malone refused.

"No, I'll keep the deed."

"But the plantation's worth ten times that bet!" Billings argued.

Malone responded, "No, your deed went against my hundred thousand."

Billings turned a furious red from the neck up and accused Malone of cheating, then made finger-pointing threats as he stomped from the room.

"You're a dead man, Malone, and I won't rest until you're six-foot under!"

All in the room were glad to see Billings get his comeuppance, Malone said, and the attorney, expressed their feelings on the situation.

"For once Billings got what he deserved," he reassured Malone, "and I think I speak for all who've played the man in saying it's about time; we've been trying to beat him, but he always came up with the cards to win."

Malone nodded, paused a moment, and explained.

"He's won because he's been cheating. He's slick at it, and I almost didn't catch the way he'd marked the cards."

Malone told Amos and Ellis to reclaim their starting money from the table, and after they had happily retrieved their cash, Malone had taken in nearly sixty thousand dollars and a plantation.

I asked Malone, "Did you have to cheat to win?"

Malone smiled that handsome smile. "Sean! You know I wouldn't cheat a pillar of the community like Billings."

"I didn't know he was a pillar of the community."

"Well, he's not; I was being facetious. He's nothing but a cheat. Sometimes so-called respected citizens are worse than the bandits of the land. At least outlaws don't deny what they do. Men in esteemed professions sometimes hide behind respectability."

My curiosity got the better of me and I asked, "Malone, what exactly does facetious mean?"

"It means I was not being serious."

Malone had told me the rest of the story — that Tyrone Billings had later hired thugs to murder him, after the card game, and for four years he had put up with an unwanted cat and mouse game, escaping attempt after attempt on his life. Tired of watching shadows, in 1858 Malone arranged a meeting with Billings, prepared to kill him if it was a trap he walked into; but it went well. He left the bank feeling maybe he had accomplished an end to any more efforts on his life. But he'd told Billings that if there were any more ambuscades by his henchmen, he would personally hold him responsible — and if it did happen again, he assured Billings that he had better arm himself — Malone would come looking for him.

Malone still didn't trust Billings, and said he had moved about wary; but two years had gone by, and there'd been no more attempts on his life. Then, one day in September, while I was living there at White Oaks, Malone received a note from Billings to meet him at eight that evening, at an address on the riverfront. The message implied it was a business opportunity that could benefit them both.

Malone figured it was a trap and arrived before dark to look things over. The dock was clear, except for the bales of cotton stacked nearby. If it was an ambush, the only place someone could hide would be behind them, and Malone could see no one was there.

He waited, and by fifteen past eight Billings was a no-show. A light was on in the warehouse, but nothing moved outside. Malone wondered if maybe the banker had arrived early, so he left his safe place and approached the doorway, next to the stacked bales. As he neared, the bales were suddenly ripped open by four gunmen inside.

It didn't take Malone but an instant to respond. His six-gun thumbed repeated hot explosions of fire. When the smoke cleared, he didn't know for sure if the four would-be killers were dead, but he could see each laid out, not moving. He'd been hard hit, too, though, and was losing blood.

Around ten that night, Malone came riding home lying over in his saddle, looking shot to pieces. Inside the house, Henry was awake, and rushing outside, he was able to catch Malone as he all but fell off his horse. Henry removed two lodged bullets, then cleaned and bandaged seven different wounds with his herb and plant medications.

"It's up to God now," Henry told us. "By rights he shouldn't be livin' with all the lead he'd caught, 'specially the two in the stomach. But Malone be a strong-willed man," Henry declared, "and with prayer I'm believin' he has a chance."

We all prayed for Malone's recovery. I think Sarah was on her knees most of the time, as was I. Over the next four days we never knew if he'd make it or not. Then on the fifth morning, Sarah, who'd been by his side all night, came out of his room with a smile and gave me a hug.

Excitedly she declared, "His fever subsided this morning, and he's sleeping. Thank God, Sean, I think he's going to be all right."

Malone had told me a little about Sarah — at least what caused her to be living at White Oaks. She was at the time twenty, the only daughter of a wealthy family from Savannah, in the shipping business. Her father had taken his stepsister's no-account son into the company as a favor, and in error gave the boy too much power. He had managed to get Sarah's father to sign papers giving him controlling stock of the firm if he were deceased — a document he had shuffled in along with other legitimate papers. Young Fred then had Sarah's father murdered, and in July of 1858 he'd taken control of the company.

Earlier, in '57, Malone had met Sarah while in Savannah on business with her father and had judged him a fair man. When Malone learned Sarah's father had been swindled, he went to Georgia, arriving just as Sarah, with nothing left but her thirty percent of stock in trust, had been forced to move out, with no place to go. Concerned for her life, Malone quietly moved her to St. Louis and White Oaks.

After seeing for myself that Malone was going to recover, I found the place along the river where I liked to be alone with God. Along the high bank I could sit and watch the flowing water. Sometimes I'd lie in a meadow of thick native grass, absorbing the sun's warmth and inhaling the smell of plants and earth. It reminded me of my home in Louisiana, and of Ma and Pa, as did the other times when I leisured there beneath a canopy of oak and surrounded by wildflowers. I often went to that place, along the powerful Mississippi, to give my thanks for Malone's healing. I'd found it was there, in my sanctuary along the river, where God was always present. After hours of meditation I'd go back to the house, with a renewed feeling of contentment.

On this day, I knew Malone would live and I was happy, but in my bones I felt sorry for what no doubt would happen to Tyrone Billings.

In October, Malone and I were at our place amidst the beauty of the eastern Missouri landscape, where he'd been training me in the art of self-defense. It was an open area of grassland, a mile north of the house, with a backdrop of dogwood and blackjack oak. We practiced in the warm and fragrant grass, still blossoming with flowers of yellow foxglove, blue aster, and pink bouncing bet. In no time I'd become skilled with my Remington handgun and Malone's .44 Henry rifle.

By then, Malone had fully recovered from his wounds, and the day was exhilarating — just the joy of our being together in the wilderness silence . . . a silence that included the tenor of songbirds, the chatter of a squirrel scolding its mate, the faint humming of the river, the octave of an eagle in the sky, and the rustling of sturdy oak leaves in the wind.

At noon, we sat in the grass and ate a lunch Marie had prepared for us. It was then, beneath a blue and cloudless sky, that Malone had confided to me a few of the details of his and Sarah's arrangement.

Together — but mostly Malone — they had been laying the ground work for Sarah to get the shipping company back, a property that was rightfully hers. Malone was confident he'd soon have it in Sarah's hands once again.

I could see that Malone attacked the problem the best he knew how — by using his strength and finding his opponent's weakness. From his spies, Malone knew the young nephew loved to gamble. But he always played his game of high table stakes poker with cronies of his own, men he knew well. And it was for that reason he usually won.

Several times Malone had done business with the man, and twice after closing a deal Malone had made subtle overtures to entice him into a game by showing a willingness to play but feigning poor knowledge of the cards.

Malone acknowledged, "It takes patience. I've been casting out the bait for two years to catch Mr. Brown. Sooner or later he'll ask me to play in his game of chance. . . and the reason I know he will is his greed. The carrot I'll dangle will be too much for the thief to turn down."

A week later, Malone left for Memphis. Four days after that, on a Sunday, he returned to White Oaks. I could not help but notice, the day before, in the *Globe-Democrat*, a picture of Tyrone Billings had been featured, along with the caption that read:

> *St. Louis banker killed near his home on the north side in what appeared to be a shoot-out; one bullet had been fired from his*

handgun. Neighbors heard two shots but saw no one. Whoever the gunman was, he disappeared.

Malone glanced at the paper, nodded, and laid it aside.

Four

BY MAY OF 1861 I was still at White Oaks. The past year had been happy, except for all that had happened at Mosswood. I never once reminded Malone about my going to Ma's cousin, and I'd hoped he had forgotten. I didn't want to leave Malone and Sarah.

My day clouded over when he told me it was almost time for me to make the change.

"Sean, I've taught you all you need to know. Keep practicing, and you'll only get better. But you're now ready to defend yourself under most circumstances, and except for your youth and lack of experience, you're as good as I am with guns, knives, or fists. It'll soon be time for you to go to the Latimores."

"I'd rather stay . . ." I told him.

"I don't want you to go, Sean, but you're a smart lad and you need schooling."

"Well, how about I give you the brooch and you see to my education? Anyway, I owe you for my keep."

Malone smiled. "No, Sean, you owe me nothing. You've been a big help here at White Oaks. Henry tells me you've been helping him around the stables and with the horses. . . . But we don't have to decide on your leaving today."

Nearly a month later, as we sat in the comfortable chairs of Malone's library before bedtime, he asked if I remembered his friend Jeffrey Amos.

I nodded. "Yes . . . the attorney. I met him once when we were in town."

Malone continued. "Some time ago I told him about your place in Louisiana, that I'd been concerned the Champlains might try to claim the inheritance, and that you were the son of the late Robert Sinclair and rightful owner. Amos has an attorney friend, Louis Dumont, in New Orleans, who looked into the matter, Sean.

"It turns out that Daniel, Lucia, and Julia Champlain did file claim for the property, maintaining they were the closest of kin. But Dumont put a stop to their claim, pointing out to the court that he represented you, who as the closest of kin should inherit. And I believe that we should have the court assign Dumont as the conservator of your estate; I will be happy to be on the record as guardian if you so choose.

"Dumont has sent the papers — and an affidavit you'll have to sign and send back to the court. That'll stop the Champlains from confiscating the property . . . but it will also let the them know you're alive, and living in St. Louis.

"You'll have to spend your days and nights alert to all happenings around you, Sean, for this is a dirty business they are about. Sources familiar with the Champlains confirm that your life will certainly be in danger. And I believe, now, that you'll have to forget the Latimores and leave the St. Louis area.

"But even before all this came about, Sean, I had decided you shouldn't go to the Latimores. I've checked on the family; Mary's not known to be a reliable sort, and her husband's thought to be an alcoholic."

As I listened to Malone, I began to feel as if I were in that same fog that had settled in on me the day Ma died. A twinge of fear of the uncertainty nagged at my mind, but I listened carefully to what Malone was saying. I trusted him. I knew he would do what was best for me.

". . . I've made arrangements for you to attend school in Kansas, Sean, in a new town, just founded in '55. It's called Manhattan, and it's pretty remote. You should be safe there . . . but, no matter, you still must stay wary. You can board with a trusted friend of mine, Travis McClusky, who owns a hotel and saloon there, on First Street."

I finally was able to gather my thoughts enough to ask Malone, "Why Kansas?"

"Well, one reason, it's out in the middle of nowhere, and the last place the Champlains would suspect. And it just recently has been granted statehood — a good sign.

"Oh, and before I forget, Sean, that affidavit will need to be renewed and signed every ten years, in New Orleans, proving you're alive, so that Dumont can protect your property claim."

It sounded more and more complicated to me. "Maybe I should just make out a will leaving it all to you; that way if something happens, the Champlains can't get it."

"Your're a smart young man, Sean. That's a good idea, only why don't you make Sarah the beneficiary; I think I'm too much of a risk."

I agreed, and told Malone we should sign all the papers. Then I hastened to add, as I reached in my pocket and handed him the brooch, "I want you to sell this to pay for my schooling."

Malone nodded in agreement. "Fine . . . but what cash is left over when you return will be yours.

"Also, Sean, for safety's sake, to throw the Champlains off the trail, you'd best use an alias for your surname."

I looked at him. "How 'bout Malone? . . . Sean Malone," I replied.

With a twinkle in his eye, Malone confirmed, "Sean Malone it is. I'll fill out your papers of introduction."

I was proud to have the name of the man I so greatly admired — even if just for a while. Then, with our conversation finished regarding my life and problems, in a serious voice Malone brought up the storm clouds of war then swirling . . . a war that long had been brewing between the states.

"It looks like there'll be an all-out confrontation, Sean. South Carolina has already seceded from the Union, and in January, another five had done so, including your own Louisiana. And the Confederacy was formed in March to fight against the Union. Northern forces are even now preparing to invade Virginia, and it could happen any day.

"I might tell you that after you leave for school, if it looks like war's a certainty, there's a possibility I'll be heading for Virginia to enlist, for that was my home state."

I acknowledged that I'd had no idea things were so bad. "I'd heard rumors, but it seemed so senseless. We'll all be fighting our own!"

Malone nodded. "I wish they could have settled it all in Congress."

The June sunlight had the color of summer in the air when I rode to the train station, on my way to Kansas. Malone tooled the buckboard up to the hitching rail and tied the pair of blacks to the railing. We stepped down out of the buggy and walked into the depot. We were an hour early, and I felt anxious as we sat on a bench watching other passengers milling around the room.

The teletype was busy clicking away, with incoming and outgoing messages. Then I heard the shrill blast of a whistle, and in minutes the westbound train pulled in and slowly rolled to a stop. The engine puffed and gasped for air as white steam rolled out from along the iron wheels of the railcars.

I started to get up, when Malone said, "That's not your train, Sean; there's been a change of plans. I didn't want to worry you at the last minute, but I've arranged for you to attend a well-established private school back East, in New Jersey. I'd hoped it might not be as disrupted by this civil unrest . . . and I've also learned that Daniel and Lucia have been here in St. Louis the past month looking for you. Someone broke into Amos's office, and he has papers missing — one which lists your new address in Kansas."

I was surprised — and worried. Malone then handed me a letter.

"Read this when you're on the train, Sean; it will explain what you need to do and who to see once you get to the town of Princeton. You'll be all right; you'll be safe."

Thirty minutes later I was on an eastbound, heading inland of the Atlantic coast, and still bewildered at the change of plans. I was disappointed, for I'd prepared myself for the excitement of the lawless frontier of Kansas. But I concluded this was just another indication of how circumstance and events can affect your life . . . events over which you have no control.

On June 15th of 1869 I had turned eighteen, and my second year at Princeton University was behind me. I'd been away from St. Louis eight years, except for two summer visits in '63 and '66. I'd spent six of those years in the strict military school Malone had chosen, before I enrolled at the University.

I still didn't know what I wanted to do in life, but with my education I knew I might try about anything. Though I was now older and independent, I still missed Sarah and Malone. I felt like they were the only family I had left in the world. I surely never considered the Champlains as family, at least those of them that had wanted to see me dead. Though I still would have liked to meet Terrill, for I had heard some good things about him as well as the questionable. And I remembered that Pa had liked him.

While I'd been away, Malone had joined the Confederate Army in 1861, and by war's end he held the rank of Colonel, surrendering with Lee at Appomattox in April of '65. I'd received letters from him usually one every three months, until '68, but none since. I had already about decided to go to St. Louis, and then I heard from Sarah. After reading her letter, it made up my mind.

> *Dear Sean,*
>
> *I thought you should know I've not heard from James for over a year. It's unlike him to not write or contact me some way in his travels. He leads such a dangerous life, I'm concerned something may have happened to him. I thought maybe you had received word from him, and if so, please let me know.*
>
> *You have nearly $8,000 left in the account that belongs to you. Please write if you want me to send the University money for the coming year.*
>
> *Love, Sarah*

I immediately sent Sarah a telegram.

> *Haven't heard from Malone.*
> *I'll be there within a week.*
> *Sean*

July was around the corner when I stepped off the train in St. Louis, and an hour later I was at White Oaks. Sarah and I were both happy to see each other, and we spent an enjoyable day visiting. It was evening before she spoke of her fears for Malone. Comfortable in her parlor chair, she began her story.

"While in Kansas City, James had won some mining shares in a poker game. The player had put up the shares to call a mere fifty-dollar bet. After the game, the man told Malone that as far as he was concerned, the shares were probably worthless — five hundred shares, fifty percent ownership in the Aetna Mine near Georgetown, Colorado. He was a banker and in '65 he had backed the two other stockholders, who were miners there, with ten thousand dollars in exchange for half ownership in the mine. But he'd received no return on his investment, nor had he ever seen the place. He told Malone he'd heard rumors that a lot of gold was being removed, yet his two partners continually claimed they were barely making ends meet.

"The banker sent an investigator to Colorado to see what was taking place at the mine, but the man never returned. Then, in April of '68, last year, James left for Denver and Georgetown."

"And you've heard nothing?" I asked.

"Nothing!" Sarah replied.

For the next couple weeks I relaxed at White Oaks, and off and on worked around the place with Henry. I'd missed the old man while I was away, and I swear he hadn't aged a day in those eight years. The gentle Creole looked just as he had when nine-year-old eyes looked upon him many years earlier. I'd gotten efficient with the bowie knife over the years, but I still had a lot to learn when I watched what Henry could do with it.

One day, working in the stables, Henry wanted to talk; he seemed to have a lot on his mind.

"Missy not happy," he told me. "An' Henry not happy. Malone gone too long. I worry."

I sympathized with him. "I know, Henry, and I'm not happy either; but I'll be leaving soon to find him. There's a reason he's not returned home. You can bank on it; I'll find him. God will lead me to him."

Sarah told me that Malone had managed to get the Jones Shipping Company back for her in '66, and her father's loyal former employee now was running the company for her. In appreciation of Malone's efforts, she gave half the company stock to him. He had characteristically balked at first, but she told him she loved him and wanted him to have the shares.

Nevertheless, the only way Malone would take the stock would be for her to accept half ownership in White Oaks — and thus Sarah accepted.

For two years Sarah and Malone spent winters in Savannah at Sarah's family home, and then summers at White Oaks. Sarah admitted she had pressured Malone to settle down and stop living the dangerous life, but after a time she could tell being tied down was eating at his soul. He had lived on the edge too long.

When Malone got a letter of invitation to a poker game in Kansas City, Sarah had told him to go ahead, "Go to Kansas City. It will do you good."

I acknowledged that it was considerate of her to encourage Malone in what he really loved, adding, "But like you, I was hoping he'd adopt a somewhat calmer life."

Sarah smiled. "Yes . . . but would you ask a rose not to blossom? I know he loves me . . . and I hope there comes a day when he'll want a different life, but it's something that can't be forced upon him. Something happened early on to make him the way he is. He's never told me, but I've wondered if it was not too far from what happened to you — why he cares for you so much. It may have been that he had no one to come along to help him . . . and that's why he's been so protective of you. Whatever it was has molded his nature.

No one can care more than he does for those he loves; yet within him is something powerfully vicious for those that work against him."

That winter, while I was at White Oaks, my palomino died from pneumonia, and Sarah told me to pick any horse I wanted. I chose a four-year-old blue-roan gelding I called Genius. He was the smartest, strongest, and fastest horse I'd ever been around, and right away we hit it off.

As the days moved along into January of 1870, I purchased a new .44 Remington handgun, holster, and cartridge belt, and a .44 Winchester rifle. I practiced almost every day until they seemed a part of me.

I stayed a year at White Oaks, as did Sarah . . . a pleasant year of working around the place helping Henry, riding out with Sarah, and going to my special vista at the river's edge. All those many months I'd expected any day to see Malone ride through the gate in his nonchalant way with that special smile. . . . But it never happened.

Five

THE OVERCAST SKY in the late spring of 1870 was misting the swampland and cypress trees standing in the waters north of the Champlain plantation house and outbuildings. Everything was sorely in need of repair. The decaying house had been white when the elder Champlains were living there, but the paint had peeled away, except for a few scaly patches amidst the gray patina. Weeds and native brush had taken over the once elegant, cared-for yard and long roadway arched with oak trees to the house . . . a house guarded with four round weathered pillars at its front entrance.

Daniel rode his gelding up the lane, dismounted, and walked the steps to the door. He stepped inside to a dark, gloomy entry. The shutters and curtains were pulled tight. In the parlor sat Lucia, then thirty-eight, the oldest of the family. Her clothes matched the dismal but ornate furniture and surroundings, as did her mood.

"Well . . . ," she caustically demanded, "what did you find out?"

"Not much," Daniel responded. "Sean left Princeton last year, but I don't know for sure where he is now."

"My God, Daniel!" she swore. "We're no closer to obtaining that property than we were eight years ago. That affidavit he signed killed our chances, and now we've got to find the boy and do away with him . . . before he marries and has other heirs! And what about the treasure? . . . Have you been able to search the property?"

Julia walked in and sat on the sofa next to Lucia. At twenty-nine, she was the youngest of the clan, and simply went along with whatever Lucia and Daniel wanted.

"*No!* . . . I haven't been able to get near the property!" Lucia's questions angered him. "That damned attorney Dumont has leased it to John Harmon, and he's there most of the time."

"I should've known that would happen," Lucia smirked. "But who'd have thought he'd do it so soon? First to Thornton and now Harmon!"

"You want me to get rid of Harmon too?" Daniel asked.

"*No!* You fool! The authorities are already suspicious; they've been keeping an eye on us since you eliminated Thornton."

"Well, it's paid off, hasn't it? We bought his place last year for a little of nothing. It just hasn't worked out, our locatin' the treasure, with the swamp between the two places."

Julia broke in and asked, "Are we going to kill Dumont?"

Lucia quickly responded. "Julia, we can't go on killing people close to the case. We'll all end up in prison. . . . No, we have to find Sean — and Daniel, if you don't come up with him soon, I'll go after him myself!"

"Well, I do know that Sean left Princeton for St. Louis," Daniel said, and hastened to add, "Oh . . . I forgot to tell you, he's changed his last name to Malone."

". . . Changed his name! Why didn't you say so to start with!" Lucia was at first irritated, then smiled . . . a look that changed her scornful face into the beautiful woman she was.

"Now we're getting somewhere," she acknowledged. "Daniel, I want you in St. Louis before the week's out, and for God's sake don't mess it up — find the lad and kill him!"

That June of 1870 I would be nineteen. I lingered in my room at White Oaks, looking in the mirror, a young man, full grown, almost six-foot, some one hundred eighty pounds. Peering back at me seemed to be an average-looking man with light-brown hair, and with the blue eyes of a nine-year-old waif who had come a long way from the Mississippi delta.

I threw on my cartridge belt and six-gun, then walked outside and down the steps. Henry was holding onto Genius, standing alongside Sarah. He already had strapped on my bed roll and put my Winchester in the saddle boot. Sarah handed me my saddlebags filled with food and then gave me a kiss on the cheek.

"Be careful, Sean; and if you don't find James, you come back. This is your home too."

"I'll find him, Sarah. God answers prayer; some just take longer than others. I don't know why we haven't heard from him, but I know in my heart he's alive."

Henry was kicking the dirt with his shoe, and looked up for just an instant as he muttered, "Bye Sean, I wish I be goin' with ya."

"Thank you, Henry; I just wish you could," I answered.

I mounted Genius and rode down the lane toward St. Louis. Before I was out of sight, I turned and looked back. Sarah and Henry were still standing in front of the house, and when I raised my arm, they waved.

Though Henry had wanted to go with me, he knew his place was to protect Sarah — especially since she had regained the shipping company and the loser was probably not a happy man. Malone had told Henry that the thieving nephew was furious the day he and Sarah walked into his office and fired him. He had threatened to kill them both. You just never knew how a vindictive man might rationalize his own act of defrauding, yet when he was the one hoodwinked, that seemed a different matter.

An hour later I was at the St. Louis depot. The train was waiting, and I walked Genius up the ramp into the stock car. Then, with my saddlebags over my shoulder, I hitched up my gun belt and stepped in with the passengers. I figured that where I was going I'd better be armed, heeding all Malone's warnings.

The car held a surprising number of people — five couples, besides myself, plus two single women that sat together and four single men. I'd no sooner sat down, off to myself, when I heard the conductor's shout.

"All *aboard! . . . Last call! . . .* All *aboard!*"

The train's whistle wailed as the railcars moved to a jolting start and then into a smooth roll while the train picked up speed. Near the edge of town, looking out of the passenger car window I saw a solitary traveler on a roan gelding enter the city, a man dressed in black. As I watched him disappear in the distance, I thought he surely gave the appearance of evil, and I pitied his victim.

I didn't know at the time that the sacrifice the villain looked for was me.

As the countryside flashed by, I thought of my schooling at Princeton, wondering what I would eventually do in life. I was certain that money would be no problem, with the treasure patiently waiting in the swamps of Louisiana, and the nearly eight thousand dollars I had recently transferred to Wells Fargo. And with my six earlier years of military school, I could probably enlist in the Army as an officer. From my University work, I figured I could apprentice a lawyer, or banker, as some of my classmates had done — yet neither occupation piqued my interest.

For now, I was just anxious to find Malone; my vocation must wait. In time, God would surely guide me to my calling.

My musing finished, I looked around at the passengers. A dark, handsome middle-aged cowboy across the aisle and two rows ahead appeared to be watching me with interest. On a second glance, I decided I'd been wrong about his being a cowboy, for I figured he most certainly was a gambler. I had noticed the man before, when he'd boarded the train. His apparel also was black, except for a well-pressed white shirt. He had on a frock coat, flat crowned hat, quite elaborately tooled boots, and black cartridge belt with tied-down holsters and six-guns.

A few of the passengers were watching the countryside slither past, and others slept in their seats. When I again peered back at the dark figure, he smiled. Then he stood up, and as the train swayed, he ambled across the aisle.

I was completely disarmed when he said, ". . . Hello, Sean, I'm John Terrill Champlain. . . . You mind if I sit a spell?"

I stammered, " I don't mind . . . have a seat." I was nearly in a state of shock, and momentarily fearful.

"How did you know who I was?" I asked, as Terrill lowered himself across from me. He hitched up his gun belt, settled in, and responded.

"It wasn't hard; you're wearing your father's ruby ring that I've admired many times. You've also inherited your father's rugged handsome features — and your mother's good looks I might add."

"I see," I replied. I didn't know how to take his compliments; I found it difficult to forget he was a Champlain.

I had started wearing Pa's ring a year earlier on an evening at White Oaks, when I was going through the memorabilia I had brought from

Louisiana. I was intent on looking at the locket watch with Ma and Pa's picture, but then tried on the ring. It fit perfectly, and I never took it off.

Terrill and I visited for a time, but there was something about him that hit me wrong and burred my neck, as when he asked, "What are you doing heading West when you own property in Louisiana? . . .You're not running from anything are you?"

His taunting smile ruffled my temper and I blurted, "I could ask you the same question, Terill."

His eyes narrowed for a moment, then he laughed. "I didn't mean to pry. I was only curious, seeing as we're related.

"I like the far West. Mostly summertimes, whenever I'm bored and want a little action, I head for the Kansas plains and the Colorado mountains. I check out the gambling saloons in Kansas at Manhattan and Junction City, Abilene, Council Grove, Ellsworth . . . Dodge City. Then it's to Denver, Black Hawk, Central City, Idaho Springs, and Georgetown. . . . I pick up a lot of money in the mining towns."

I knew nothing for certain about Terrill, but I could see he'd be a tough man if it came to a showdown. He had the looks of someone who could handle a six-gun with ease. I didn't know if I should trust the Creole or not. Pa had always said he was the best of the Champlains, but that might not mean much. And Malone had told me to trust no one; then if it turns out they are reliable, you still haven't lost anything.

Terrill had laid out his reasons for going West, so I did the same. "I'm planning to stop in Manhattan, to see what I can find out about James Malone. If he's not there, I'll travel West until I can pick up his trail. He's been gone for two years, and his friends in St. Louis are worried about him."

Terrill peered at me with a puzzled look. "I saw Malone last summer in Abilene. He was playing poker at the Alamo. I never get in games with Malone; he's too good, and for some reason lately, he's turned disagreeable. Malone was always a tough man to tangle with, but he's gotten worse. I heard he'd killed one of the card players who'd accused him of cheating — though the victim was a no-account bum, and even the Marshal seemed relieved he was dead!

"But I'd stay away from the man if I was you."

"No . . ." I told him, "Malone's okay. He took care of me when I needed help, and if he's alive, I'll find him."

Then I asked, "At the Alamo Saloon . . . did Malone recognize you?"

"Well . . . now that you mention it, I don't think he did. It seemed a bit strange, for he looked right at me. But he never nodded or spoke, and for years we've known of each other — not acquainted personally, but from a distance. . . . It was as if he looked right through me."

We talked no more for a time, and I began to think something must have happened to Malone; it was as though he'd lost his memory. . . . Maybe that was it.

I peered out of the window and looked at the vast Missouri Valley with its huge rock bluffs topped by a forest of oaks. They seemed to be racing to keep up with the train, only to fall behind in the dusty haze of distance.

When I next looked at Terrill, he was studying me with interest. It made me uneasy, but I faintly tried to smile, and he looked away. Then he looked back.

"Malone's a dangerous man," he warned. "Why would you want to find him?"

I paused before answering, then told him, "I'll tell you why. . . .He saved my life, and cared for me when the Champlains were trying to find and kill me!"

Terrill could see I was angry, and he leaned back in his seat. "I see. I had suspicioned my kinfolk were behind Robert and Elizabeth's killing, but I'd hoped it wasn't so.

"But why didn't you come to me after your parents were killed?" he asked.

I was surprised, and somewhat irritated that the obvious hadn't dawned on him. I rather angrily shot back at him. "Well, I didn't know but what you were trying to have me killed too . . . and if truth be told, I still don't know!"

For an instant Terrill looked at me with hard, smoldering eyes. He curtly responded. "For the record, Sean, I was *not* involved. I thought a lot of your Pa and Ma. . . . And you shouldn't make accusations of murder; it could get you in a lot of trouble. I've killed others for saying less . . . . But we're relation, and I'll overlook it this time."

I'd noticed he put an emphasis on this time, and I explained, "I didn't accuse you of murder, Terrill; I just said I didn't know if you were involved."

He seemed to accept my explanation, and we quickly talked of other things. I soon learned — if he wasn't bragging — that he'd had three duels in Louisiana, and a half dozen gunfights in the West. He apparently carried with him some renown. He didn't have to tell me who'd won the shootouts, for I didn't doubt for a minute he was fast with a gun.

Terrill invited me to trail along with him, so we could get to know each other better, but I turned him down. Much as I wanted to, I couldn't completely trust the man. He seemed somewhat disappointed, then hastened to add, " By the way . . . I saw you particularly noticing the man on the roan gelding riding into St. Louis as we were leaving."

I nodded. "Yes, the man in black. There was something about him that made me uneasy. Do you know him?"

Terrill's smile was rather unsettling. "That was my brother . . . Daniel. Seemed like he was looking for someone.

"Would that someone be you, Sean?" He grinned, like maybe he was playing with my mind.

But I wouldn't give him the satisfaction of knowing I was shaken.

"I don't know," I replied. "At least, for both our sakes, I hope not."

I thought to myself that knowing what Daniel looked like was now my advantage. Nothing more was said, and Terrill leaned back, closing his eyes like he was asleep. But I wondered.

It was evening when several sharp blasts of the train whistle woke me as we pulled into Kansas City. I looked over at Terrill who was for certain then heavy with sleep. He was a handsome man, as were all the Champlains, according to Pa. I just wished I knew for sure about his sincerity, for at times his eyes shone cold and hard. I peered at the two handguns resting in their holsters and wondered, if it came to a showdown, whether I could outdraw the gunman. Malone had always told me that I was fast, and I'd practiced many years since I'd left White Oaks for school.

Terrill looked innocent enough as he slept, but I'd hoped that between us it would never come to a confrontation. I thought it would surely be a benefit to have at least one kinfolk that I could trust.

Six

SUNLIGHT WAS SHINING in the east window of the passenger car when the train pulled into the Manhattan depot. I felt like I'd entered a new world as I stepped off the train, into a country of endless horizons, beneath an unbelievable, vast blue sky. Beyond the village I peered around at a wholesome countryside of gray-green prairie grass blowing in the breeze, accented by tall cottonwood and walnut trees along the creeks and rivers.

The sleepy town lay at the confluence of the Kansas and Big Blue Rivers in a vast basin circled by far hills diffused with erosion-split canyons. The depot, chattering a busy teletype, stood indifferent a few hundred feet away from the banks of the Big Blue. Just south of the depot I could see a well-weathered sign, "McClusky Hotel and Saloon." It was where I'd go later in the day to check on Malone.

I went to the stock car and unloaded Genius. He was impatient to run after the long ride, and I decided to give the gelding a workout. I reined him west up the main street of town that they called Military Road, a part of the trail from Fort Leavenworth to Fort Riley, the frontier military outposts. Looking east, a Concord stagecoach was being ferried across the Big Blue. The following year, in 1871, a wagon bridge would be built just north of the ferry.

At a gallop, I rode northwest to look at a tall building set on a plateau of low hills, well above the bottomland of the town. Later I was told it was the State Agricultural College, one of the country's new land-grant schools from the recent Morrill Act.

It was coming onto noon when I stopped at Platt's Stable. After caring for Genius, I walked down the street to the newly opened Adams House Hotel, located a block north and one west of the depot. At the top of six steps, I opened the door and walked to the desk located in a large entryway. A wide stairway to the second floor rose upward at the south. To the east were two large opened doors to the dining room.

I laid my saddlebags and bed roll on the floor and asked the clerk for a room.

"We have several," he responded. "I have one on the second floor, with a window to the street, for a dollar fifty a night, or I have some cheaper, as low as a dollar."

I took the one with a window.

"Room 204," the clerk said, and pushed forward the register for me to sign.

Upstairs, I found a large quarter, with a dresser and wardrobe along the east wall. Against the west wall was a well-made bed. Before the front window, waiting patiently for an occupant, were a table, two straight chairs, and an arm chair. On the dresser was a white porcelain bowl and pitcher filled with water.

I washed up, looked in the mirror, and went downstairs to the dining room. I noticed eight of the guests were scattered about the room, as I found a table along the east wall. I seemed to be the cause of interest, however, as I waited for my meal of steak, but I realized it was obvious I was an outsider, and from the East by the clothes I wore. I figured right then that I'd need to buy something different if I was going to fit in, and so after finishing my meal, I went to the General Store.

I found a gray flat-crowned hat, dark jeans, gray shirt, blue kerchief, and western-style boots. That evening, after supper, wearing my new garb, I went to McClusky's Saloon.

Looking at it later, I thought I probably should have washed my clothes before wearing them; they'd not have looked so new. But at least my six-gun and cartridge belt were obviously well used.

When I stepped out of the hotel, a wind flurry picked up dust and deposited it farther on down the street. Reaching McClusky's, I pushed through the swinging doors and walked over to the bar. A large man with huge crossed arms and flaming red hair stood waiting. I figured it was McClusky, but hadn't realized he'd be such a bear of a man. He was one barkeep who'd need no bouncer, for anybody would be a fool to tangle with him.

Ten customers sat about the large room. And it didn't surprise me to see Terrill among them, playing cards with four others, just west of the bar. I greeted McClusky with my hand out, announcing, "I'm Malone."

Everyone but Terrill turned to look when I said "Malone." Concerned at the effect of the name on the patrons, I then drawled softly to the barkeep, "Sean Malone."

"Aye," he said. "Travis McClusky here."

We shook hands, mine almost lost in his big paw. "I know about ye, Sean; James had told me your story many years back."

As McClusky and I talked, two in the room continued to watch me with interest.

"What's with the customers?" I asked. "They seemed to alert when I introduced myself."

McClusky nodded. "It's the name; everybody's on edge with Malone. He's a tough man to tangle with . . . though in the past, a gentleman. But I'll tell ye, lad, of late it seems he's suddenly gone sour."

McClusky couldn't help me in locating Malone, for he hadn't seen him the past six months; but he had friends around the country, and said he'd see if he could find out where he might be hanging out. It'd take time, he'd said, and so I decided to stay in Manhattan for a while.

I couldn't help but notice the two men still watching me from a table in the far corner, whispering as they shared their bottle, continually glancing my way.

At around nine, I decided to return to the Adams House. The two restless thugs had left a few minutes before, and their departure for some reason had made me uneasy. When I stepped out the swinging doors, I moved quickly to my right into the shadows along the building. That same instant, gunfire blazed red from the darkness, and a bullet grazed past my left arm.

My gun was in my hand before I even had to think, firing away at the two dark shapes. Then all was quiet. The bushwhackers had only managed to get off one shot apiece.

I saw McClusky race outside with a twelve-gauge shotgun, then walk over to the two dark figures lying in the street. Both were dead. He sent for Marshal Emmons, who looked at the men, then shook his head in dismay as I explained the shootout.

The Marshal was amazed. "It's hard to believe you came out of that with just a scratch." Then, to my relief, he added, ". . . Looks like there'll be no charges; it surely was self-defense. And unless I miss my guess, you did the state a service. I'm positive I've seen posters on 'em. If it's who I think they are, they're wanted for robbery and murder.

"What's your name, son?" he asked.

When I said "Malone," the Marshal was at first somewhat startled, but his demeanor calmed as I told him I was from Louisiana.

"Well, you surprised me for a minute, lad, though I soon realized you were too young to be James Malone. . . . Far as I know, he's not wanted for anything, but many of his gunfights are close to outright murder nowdays. Seems lately he's been carryin' a chip on his shoulder. . . not usual for Malone."

Emmons paused, rubbed his whiskers with his right hand, and murmured. "I still don't know how ya did it, kid . . . how ya managed to kill both of 'em when they had the drop on ya."

"Well, I had a good teacher," I explained. "It was James Malone."

Emmons acknowledged, "Well he's good, and if you're as fast as he is with a gun, you'll do all right. Still I'd like to give ya a little fatherly advice. Don't push too hard for a showdown; there's always someone better or a fighter who won't give up.

"Five years ago, at a shootout in Council Grove, a man took six bullets before he killed his adversary. He wasn't as fast as his foe, but he'd stayed on his feet, kept takin' lead, and put two bullets in the gunman where they counted."

"It sounds like good advice, Marshal. I won't start a fight, but I don't plan on running from one either. . . .What happened to the man that took six bullets?"

"You're lookin' at him!" Then Emmons asked, "You kin to Malone?"

"Not by blood," I replied, "but he took me in when I was nine, and he's been like a father to me."

Emmons nodded, as if he understood. "Well, I may have to look at Malone in a different light. I wasn't sure he had a decent bone in his body anymore." The Marshal nodded a good-bye as he walked north toward the depot.

At that same instant a voice from behind me spoke up.

"Nice job, Sean. . . .You're fast all right, and on the mark!"

I turned. It was Terrill. He had a smile on his face when he asked, "You're sure you don't want to team up? We'd be invincible, the two of us together."

I didn't want to offend him, for after all, he might be sincere; but I just couldn't get myself to put my trust in him, especially if it came to a showdown with his blood kin. I told him I didn't mean to be disrespectful, "But for the time being I need to go it alone."

Terrill nodded. "Have it your way." He walked back into the saloon.

I'd been in Manhattan two weeks and McClusky had heard nothing about Malone from his friends. I spent most of my time riding out over the plush valleys and steep verdant hills of the beautiful countryside thereabouts.

It was nearly six in the evening when I reached the rimrock overlooking Manhattan far and away below me. I'd spent the day riding the Council Grove trail south some twenty miles, and was just then returning. At places I rode a divide where a body could see unending distances in all directions. It was a broken land of steep canyons and spectacular views, particularly into the far valleys of river and creek bottoms, with their waters looping and twisting throughout rich bluestem grass, like a precious blue necklace. Yet above the rimrock was a rolling countryside of different levels and higher isolated hillocks, with mounds of tall tawny grass, turning green, like herds of giant resting buffalo with dark shadowed flanks.

At the base of the steep hill into town I looked at a massive swelling sea of grass. It reminded me of when I was seven, the year I spent aboard ship with Pa, a time I'll never forget. Ma hadn't wanted me to go, but Pa'd insisted; he thought it was an experience I needed, and as I look back upon it, he was right. We were together day and night, and I came to know my father well. Little did we realize what life had in store for him and Ma in but two short years.

Pa was a tough man, yet he couldn't have been a better father, and from that voyage he prepared me for life. I'd thought about it since, and I'd realized he gave me the greatest gift a father can give his son.

I loved the open sea and the endless horizons — the plowing through gigantic waves with rough seas running, the salt water spraying across the bow, the mystery surrounding far ports of call. It turned out a blessing, our sharing together, for after the voyage he'd sailed no more.

The following week I moved from the Adams House to McClusky's. He fixed me a pleasant room on the second floor where I had a view to the street, the depot, and the swift-flowing Kansas River.

It was the first of June, and I'd stayed longer in Manhattan than I'd intended. Earlier in the day I'd ridden up along the Blue River, across a beautiful, rugged country with its plush valleys, abrupt slopes, curving river bends, and high-shouldered hills. On that ride I came to the realization I was getting nowhere in finding Malone, and I made up my mind to leave for Junction City the next morning. I would work my way west and find out what I could firsthand.

When I walked into McClusky's later that day, the sun lay halfway below the far western hills, painting a pink ribbon on ashen clouds. My purple shadow cast long across the red-glowing sunlit street. McClusky was waiting for me when I came through the gray swinging doors.

"Sean!" he'd called. "I've heard from one of my contacts that Malone left Denver yesterday, headin' east, probably for Abilene . . . maybe Council Grove."

The news was welcome. I thanked him. "That's what I been waiting to hear!"

I felt better now that Malone had been sighted. I knew it was only a matter of time until I caught up with him.

The sun was high when I rode Genius out of the livery's double doors and reined him west. The hue of afternoon was painting shadows east of the trees as I crossed the Republican River. Genius seemed to like the cool water and hardly strained a muscle when his feet went out from under him in the deep area near the west bank. That horse took well to swimming, and in minutes he was wading out and shaking off on the west shore.

A half hour later I rode down the main street of Junction City and pulled the gelding to a stop at the livery. A young man sat on a straight chair by the double doors. He'd never said a word when I dismounted and tied Genius to the hitching rail.

"You the proprietor?" I asked.

He peered up at me a moment, and sternly answered, "I am." Then, with the attitude of a grizzly bear, he told me his name was Spencer Jones.

"Nice to know you," I said, trying to be friendly. "How about stabling my horse for a day or two?"

He told me to help myself, pointing inside the barn. "Twenty-five cents a day, and you pitch him his own hay. If ya want to feed him a bait of corn it's ten cents extra. The corn's in a barrel in the store room."

After letting Genius drink his fill from the horse tank, I picked out a clean stall, removed the bridle and saddle, and curried him down, talking to him all the while. I crawled the ladder to the loft through a square opening in the floor, took the pitchfork standing in the stack, and, as I looked down on my horse from above, tossed him some hay. I climbed back down the ladder, then went to the store room for a can of corn and after feeding it to the blue-roan, I whispered in his ear. When I exited the stall, Spencer was standing by the double doors watching me.

"You're spoilin' that horse," he told me.

"No," I replied, "we understand each other."

Spencer looked skeptical. "I see. . . . Well, I heard ya call him Genius. That's an odd name for a horse. Is that why ya talk to him?" he asked, apparently serious.

I laughed. "Like I say, we understand each other. Right away, from our first ride, we hit it off. He seems to anticipate my every move. Mornings he'd be waiting for me inside the corral. And if I went to do something, it wouldn't be long before he'd be following me around the place. I'd check, and sure enough the corral gate would be swung open.

"I was puzzled as to how he was getting out of the pen, so one morning I hid behind the house where I could watch. After the horse had spotted me and I'd left his sight, he trotted to his gate, put his nose under the bar, and pushed, swinging it open. That was when I decided to call him Genius."

Spencer just shook his head as I handed him thirty-five cents for the gelding's keep. I could detect the amusement behind his look of skepticism.

Late that evening I paced the boardwalk, looking at the town. The opera house was advertising a play, with a cast out of New Orleans. I read the boards that showed the top billing, and the supporting cast of eleven. But it was the third name on the list that caught my eye — a Katrina Thornton.

I'd recalled a Thornton family had lived on the plantation just east of Mosswood. Then, thinking of Mosswood, I was reminded of the affidavit I still needed to sign and send to Dumont in New Orleans. I determined to send it the next day.

I also remembered that the Thorntons had a daughter named Katrina. I figured she'd be around sixteen by that time, and so I dismissed it, as I thought she'd be yet too young to travel the country alone with a troupe of actors. As I pondered further, I recalled as well that Malone had told me Mr. Thornton had been murdered, and his widow forced to sell the plantation after someone had set fire to the crops. It came back to me that it was none other than the Champlains who had then bought the Thornton place.

It wouldn't take much to figure that my infamous relations were the probable culprits behind both the murder and fire.

I heard applause coming from inside the opera house, as I started back to the hotel.

Seven

THE SUN WAS peeking over rimrock country when I turned in the saddle to check my back a mile west of Junction City. I rode the Smoky Hill Trail that would take me to Abilene. Genius had wanted to run, and I'd given him rein, but by this time he'd settled down into what locals called a space-eating walk

It had rained overnight, and the countryside lay fresh and green. It was a golden day of sunlight picking gleaming pearls of dewdrops off the bluestem grass. Except for meeting an occasional lonesome soul driving a horse and buckboard, or a wagon, I rode down an empty path. From the landscape around me, I concluded it must have taken a hearty and brave individual to homestead there, in the middle of nowhere; and yet, after the War Between the States, they seemed to come by the thousands to settle in the West.

This was a vast and lonely land, untouched by plow, except for small areas of broken earth close to homesteads; but it was a country that tugged at my heartstrings.

Left of the wagon trail the Smoky Hill River meandered, with low sandy banks and islands of sandbars. Willow trees edged the eastward-flowing water, with delicate, slender leaves on hanging limbs sweeping the current. An occasional patch of timber, mostly young cottonwood, covered the inside horseshoe bends. I hadn't been in Kansas long, but I could tell by its effect on me that the land grew on a person. Beyond the river south lay the ravine-slashed hills that followed my movement west.

Sunset glowed golden red across the undulating prairie grass when I rode into Abilene. I stopped at the Twin Livery, just north of the Kansas Pacific tracks, to stable Genius. Jeff Olson, the owner, was a tall gangly man with handlebar whiskers at his upper lip. He was standing by the double doors when I rode up and dismounted.

He looked my horse over, and thinking a while announced, "That's a good-lookin' blue roan your ridin'. I don't think I've seen more than a half dozen in my lifetime — and most were mean and hard to handle. You had any problems?"

I told him I hadn't, ". . . But then it depends on the rider. I doubt anyone else could get very close to him. He's kind of particular who sits on his back."

The hostler seemed not much believing nor impressed, then pointed. "Pick a stall; the hay's in the loft."

After giving the gelding a drink from the tank, I pitched him some hay and gave him a bait of corn and a good rubdown. Satisfied he was content, I walked out the double doors and crossed the railroad tracks to Texas Street.

Tom Smith was the Marshal of Abilene those days, and he'd ruled the town with his fists. There were those at first that thought he couldn't control the rowdy Texas drovers without a six-gun in his hand, but after seeing him in a few fights, no one wanted to tackle the feisty New Yorker.

I'd checked in at the Merchants Hotel near six o'clock, and after cleaning up a bit was soon eating a hearty supper in the dining room. Having thus satisfied my own needs, I strolled the boardwalk. My boots made a hollow sound as I crossed three blocks of Texas Street. I'd stayed out of the saloons, for I'd figured it could be another week before Malone reached town and I didn't need an unpleasant confrontation with a drunken drover. I knew I was not infallible, unlike some young punks that carried a six-gun and looked for fights. I was willing to use my weapon if need be, for I was aware, being new in town, that trouble could boil over at a moment's notice.

The Kansas evening was pleasant and cool, with nature's familiar night rhythms. The only other sounds along the street fell out of the open saloon doors in desultory talk, with an occasional loud curse, along with a piano's tinny music.

Strangely, I felt comfortable in Abilene, a town fast becoming known across the country for its gunfights. I hesitated to believe I was born for a life that carried death on its shoulders, yet I felt no fear as I walked the streets.

I went back to my hotel room, laid my six-gun at my side, and in minutes was asleep.

Monday marked a week, and I still hadn't seen anything of Malone. That afternoon, as I walked by the Novelty Theater, I noticed the billboard advertising a Shakespeare play, with the same cast that had been listed in Junction City, and Katrina Thornton on the boards.

The hands of the clock in the lobby pointed to half past seven when I stepped outside the hotel and walked the short way to the theater. I bought a ticket and found a good seat three rows back from the stage.

Before long, a tall gangly man with garters on his sleeves walked out, stepped down the six steps to the side of the platform, and began to play the upright piano — familiar tunes like "Yankee Doodle," "Dixie," and "Oh, Susannah." He was an accomplished musician, and it took no effort to enjoy his music.

At eight o'clock sharp, the curtain rose, revealing the drama of the Shakespearean scene. When the stage darkened and the light focused, it became obvious that the part was being played by the skinny little neighbor girl I'd remembered from Louisiana. She had indeed grown up.

Katrina had become a stunningly beautiful young lady with dark ringlet hair, long lashes, and large blue eyes. After the close of the fifth act and three curtain calls, I made my way backstage. I didn't have to introduce myself; Katrina knew who I was the minute she laid eyes on me.

"Sean Sinclair!" she called, and rushed over to give me a hug, holding me like we'd known each other intimately for years. Then taking my hand, she turned to a woman in the back room, whom I also recognized.

"Mother, it's Sean! . . . You remember Sean Sinclair!"

"Of course I remember — the son of Robert and Elizabeth Sinclair. My goodness, lad, it was a long time ago when you disappeared from sight. We never knew what happened to you. "How are you, Sean? . . . You must tell us what you've been doing these past ten years!"

I spent much of my time during the next five days with the Thorntons. They described how they had been forced to sell the plantation to pay off debts after Mr. Thornton's murder. And it was then that they had moved to New Orleans. But a year earlier they had run low on funds and were unable to find suitable work. Because Katrina's mother had been an actress before she'd married, they both signed on with a group that traveled the West, playing from town to town. I learned that their next scheduled stop was Denver, and they were leaving by stage in two days.

Twelve chimes were ringing on the entryway clock when Katrina walked into the Merchant's Hotel dining room. Her mother, the group's manager, was meeting with the producer at the theater, and it offered Katrina and I our first chance to be alone. After we had ordered our meal, she looked at me with those beautiful blue eyes and smiled.

"You've made my life happy again, Sean. It's the first I've felt any gaiety since we lost my father and our beautiful home on the delta. It was a home I loved so dearly. . . so many precious memories . . . but our meeting has returned a joy to my life I've not felt for a long time."

Katrina peered into my eyes and blushingly confessed, "The first time I laid eyes on you, Sean, I felt love in my heart . . . and now again I have those same feelings."

I was somewhat unsettled at her confession and didn't quite know how to reply, but I simply went with my senses. ". . . I'm taken with you, too, Katrina."

I told Katrina about Malone, what he'd done for me, and that I had to find him before making any decision about my future. Then after our meal, we went for a walk and talked the hours away. By the time the sun was into afternoon, I felt an understanding . . . that at some time we would talk seriously again. I walked Katrina to her room at the hotel, and when we'd parted she gave me a kiss.

"Don't forget me, Sean; I want no one else." Then she walked into her room and closed the door.

Suddenly I felt a loneliness as I walked down the darkened way, as if

I'd lost someone special. I had just turned nineteen — that would make Katrina sixteen. I'd hoped it would turn out that we would someday share our lives together . . . but only time would tell.

That evening the bartender at the Alamo let me know he'd heard Malone was in Council Grove. And early the next morning the stage for Denver rushed into the Abilene Wells Fargo station at half past five, in a cloud of dust. I helped Katrina and her mother onto the coach, followed by other cast members, then without wasting a minute, the driver called out, "All *aboard!*"

From Wells Fargo I walked to the stables. I'd soon be on my way to Council Grove. The barn was still dark, but I could make out Genius in the far stall. Yet something wasn't right; I could sense it. I looked around, but nothing stirred.

As I reached Genius's stall, gunfire racketed beneath the rafters, red bursts from a dark stall not twenty feet away. My six-gun was in my hands, firing at a figure I could barely make out.

The barn filled with gunsmoke as I watched the shadow slump to the floor. I still stood on my feet, but I'd been hit.

Olson came running into the stables and caught me as I staggered toward the door. He had the local doctor there in minutes, who looked me over and shrugged.

"Son, it's nothin' serious. The bullet went clean through your arm and the splinter I took from your shoulder come from the post next to the stall. But your assailant's not doin' near so well," he added, pointing at the gunman that had tried to kill me.

The bushwhacker was moved into the light, where the doctor could look at his wounds. My heart seemed to stop for a moment. I recognized Daniel Champlain.

The Champlains were still after me. I had hoped they'd given up, but they seemed worse than a pack of wolves on the hunt.

Two days later, with the clock of the sun at eight in the morning, Abilene lay behind me as I took a trail south, heading for Council Grove. I rode the prairie grass with my mind wandering off other places.

Champlain had lost a lot of blood and would be laid up for a couple weeks, but word was he'd live. I wondered if after this he would finally quit the family's quest to kill me, but I doubted it. I was realizing that the Champlains wouldn't be happy until they had finished me off and owned all of Mosswood.

Malone had told me there was no way to shake hands with a rattlesnake, so you shouldn't try, and I was slowly coming to the understanding that the Champlains were nothing but a nest of the vipers.

Yet I wondered about Terrill. He hadn't shown up in Abilene. . . .What had happened to him?

There was something I liked about Terrill, even though he surely was riding as close to an outlaw's trail as a man could get. I'd seen times when I think he liked me and genuinely wanted to be friends, but the trouble was that I still wasn't comfortable in trusting him.

The far western sun was painting a golden light on ashen clouds and gleaming an intense red glow across the prairie grass when I hit the Santa Fe Trail leading into Council Grove. An hour later, my shadow led me down the street to the hostler's, where I stabled Genius. It was seven o'clock when I checked in at the Hays House, and half past seven when I sat down to eat supper.

The next morning, as I entered the dining room, a local rancher walked in behind me. When I was seated along the far wall, the man walked up and introduced himself. With hand out, he'd announced, "I'm Chancy Sharp."

I likewise introduced myself, and invited him to join me. Chancy was thirty years old and a bachelor. He'd said he'd never had time to marry — too busy putting together his future. He was raised on the river at Hannibal, Missouri, grew up poor, and left home when he was fourteen with a hunger in his belly. And he'd promised himself as he worked his way West that there'd come a day he would not ever again be poor.

As I got to know Chancy, it wasn't hard to see that his early days were the driving force behind his fierce ambition to succeed. He was always striving for more, yet in reality it seemed he'd already reached a level of success. Chancy owned a six hundred forty acre spread north of town on the Neosho River, and he not only ranched, but he drove and traded cattle from Texas, taking them to Abilene and selling them for a good profit.

In those days, Texas still had a lot of wild-roaming unbranded cattle left over from the Mexican disruptions and our own Civil War, and Chancy had a network of wranglers hunting the bovines, cutting them out of the brush, and slapping their brand on the critters. He'd buy the longhorns from the brush-poppers anywhere from six to ten dollars apiece, then hire his wranglers, make a drive, and sell them in Abilene for eighteen to twenty. On his last drive a year earlier, Chancy'd confided, he'd profited nearly six thousand dollars on the thousand head — a tidy sum for a half year's work. Chancy was for certain a man on the move.

Eight

IT WAS AROUND eight that night when I walked into Council Grove's Blue Duck Saloon and Dance Hall. Two cowboys stood at the bar and the gambling tables were full of players. On the west side of the building three couples were dancing as "Oh, Susannah" was played by two fiddlers and a man on the piano.

As I looked into the friendly blue eyes of the bartender, he reached across to shake hands.

"Ye're new in these parts, strang'r. What's ye're name?"

I nodded. "I am new . . . and I'm Sean."

"No last name, laddie?"

I'd thought a moment, then answered, "Malone . . . Sean Malone, out of Louisiana." Like everyone else who heard the name Malone, the bartender was startled for a second, then his face began to relax a bit and he smiled.

"Nice to meet ye, Sean. I'm Tom MacArthur from the braes of Scotland, by way of Canada . . . but lat'ly from the rimrock country southeast of Junction City. What'll ye hav' to drink, me boy?"

I ordered a beer and paid MacArthur the price he'd asked — a nickel. When he walked away toward another customer, I turned to look around the smoke-filled place.

I could see three busy poker tables . . . and Terrill. He was farthest away, with his back to the wall. I didn't know if he'd seen me enter, but I would guess he had. Terrill never missed a thing. And from the chips stacked before him, it looked like he'd been winning.

After surveying the room, it appeared Malone was not in the place, so I'd turned back around to talk to MacArthur who was busy getting drinks, and when he finished I asked if he'd seen James.

"Nay," he replied, "he left here two days back — and none too soon to suit me this time."

I asked him to let me know if Malone showed his face. "I'd appreciate it if you'd get word to me; I'll be at Chancy's ranch, north of town, for a few days."

"Ah, ye know Chancy, do ye?"

"Yes, I met him at the Hays House, and he invited me out to his place."

MacArthur laughed. "Aye, Chancy's a prince of a guy; but hang onto ye're mon'y belt. He's a real business man!"

As we spoke, Terrill walked up to the bar and cashed in two hundred dollars worth of chips. He slipped the bills into his pocket and spoke.

"Evenin', Sean . . . any luck finding Malone?"

I told him he'd apparently left there two days earlier. And with a goodly share of irritation, I told Terrill, "I was late arriving, thanks to your brother Daniel. . . . He'd tried to kill me in Abilene, and I had to put a couple bullets in his hide. But the doctor said he'd live."

Terrill nodded. "I heard. . . . I'm glad you didn't kill him, Sean, for I'd have been forced into something I'd not want to do."

I was surprised by his response and caustically asked what that would be.

Terrill looked through me with cold, expressionless black eyes. "I'd have to kill ya, Sean."

I was amazed. "Why, you can't mean that! . . . Daniel's the one who needs killing! He murdered my mother and father, and the good Lord only knows who else down there in Louisiana."

"Maybe so . . . but Daniel is full-blood kin; I'd have no choice."

I started to get my dander up, when in a flash Terrill drew his left-hand six-gun, pointed it toward me, and fired two shots. It happened so fast it took me a second to realize he hadn't killed me, and that the bullets had whizzed past my right arm. I turned, and a man at the end of the bar dropped to the floor with a six-gun in his hand.

I looked at Terrill — my eyes must have asked the question, "What happened?"

Terrill nodded his head in the direction of the dead man. "He'd pulled his gun to shoot you. . . . Seems you have more than one enemy, Sean."

Terrill walked over to where the man lay in a pool of blood, then added, almost annoyed, "Well, maybe not. . . . It could be the same source. This man's name is Louis Gauthier, a friend of Daniel's, from Louisiana."

The Council Grove Marshal showed up, asked a few questions, then called the incident self-defense as the man was carted off to the morgue. I thanked Terrill for saving my life, and he just shrugged and smiled. "We are related you know, even if it's only by marriage."

When I walked out the swinging doors, he said good-bye, with what sounded like a hint of disappointment in his voice. "See you around, Sean."

I knew Daniel must have sent the man to kill me, and the thought made me shudder. When I mounted Genius I wondered how many others were waiting to finish the task. . . . And what about Terrill? Would he have shot the bushwhacker had he known he was sent by Daniel? . . . Or maybe his sister Lucia had sent the assassin.

Terrill had indeed saved my life, but I still didn't know where our limits lay.

An hour later I was at the hotel, fast asleep.

On Saturday, a week after the shooting at the Blue Duck, I was still at Chancy's ranch. It had been a busy time, and I'd helped around the place, riding herd and fixing fence. That Thursday we drove a hundred head of cows and heifers to the north pasture where there was better graze. Evenings Chancy and I would sit up late talking about our own experiences, and I was enjoying myself. But I figured I'd better soon be heading back to town.

Chancy had taken a liking to me and didn't want me to leave; I think he had few friends, and was often lonely. He even offered me a foreman's job at the ranch if I'd stay. But I knew that wasn't where I needed to be in life right then. Nevertheless, Chancy and I had become good friends, and I knew that in the future I would return.

I loved the peace and clean country air, and about then had decided that someday I'd have a cattle ranch of my own.

It was noon when I entered the Hays House dining room that day. The place was full, so I shared a table with a wrangler from Texas. He was on his way to Montana, and from what he'd told me, with the Sioux and Cheyenne on the warpath, it could be a dangerous place. But I still envied his adventure.

It was two o'clock when I returned to the Blue Duck. MacArthur had sent word that Malone was in Manhattan — he'd heard it from a cowboy passing through. It looked like I'd have found Malone sooner had I stayed put at McClusky's two months before.

It was coming onto August of 1870 when I rode beneath a blazing sun, so large it seemed to fill the sky with brass. I was trailing in grasses with the aroma of earth and wildflowers as I came to the river. The Kansas was running low, and the gelding splashed easily across the shallows, but along the north bank it channeled deep for about a hundred feet. I felt Genius's feet go out as he dipped down and began to swim. In moments, he waded out on the north shore with water rushing off his back. I was wet clear through, but it felt good.

When I dismounted, the afternoon sun was in the west, just above the trees. I tied the blue-roan to the hitching rail in front of McClusky's saloon, then walked through the double doors and up to the bar. As usual, the darkness caused me to take a minute to acquaint to the room and its customers.

When I shook hands with McClusky he was nodding his head toward the poker table in the far corner. I could make out five players.

My heart hit a double beat. The one with his back to the wall was Malone. I noticed, as well, three thirsty men at a table near the back stairway sharing a bottle of whisky. I ordered a beer and walked over to Malone's table, then stood there watching the game for several minutes before he peered up from his cards.

"Sean! . . . What're you doing here? It's good to see you, boy! . . ." Then a confused expression furrowed his brow and he looked around the room like he had just realized where he was. He looked at his cards, slowly folded, and picked up his chips. The other four players said nothing, but watched as Malone walked to the bar and cashed in, for a hundred twenty-five dollars.

"Come on," he told me, "we got a lot of catching up to do!"

I had the feeling the other four wanted to say something about his leaving the game early, but I think they were too fearful to speak out.

Malone thanked McClusky after receiving his cash, then told him we would be in his room if needed.

"Aye, James," McClusky replied.

Malone led the way up the dimly lit steps and down the hall to his room overlooking the Kansas Pacific depot. The room was next to the one I had stayed in when I had been there in June.

Suddenly he was almost beside himself with excitement, and he couldn't quit talking. Apparently the shock or surprise at seeing me had triggered something and had brought his past back into the present. The years of his life that for a time seemed to have been erased quickly returned.

He'd asked about Sarah first, and I filled him in on everything I knew. That evening, Malone telegraphed her in St. Louis.

> *Sarah,*
> *Sean found me. Must have had amnesia.*
> *Am okay now. Be home soon.*
> *Love, James*

Malone and I dined at the Adams House Hotel and I hardly had time to eat, answering all of his questions. Then he left to ready his horse stabled near the saloon, and I followed soon after to see Platt, the hostler. I arranged for him to stall my horse, and have him ready to travel by seven the next morning, in plenty of time to catch the eastbound train at eight.

When Malone caught up with me, we returned together to McClusky's. But the minute we walked in the door, the barkeep waved us to the back.

"Marshal Emmons was here lookin' for ya, Malone. He's got a warrant for your arrest . . . something about a murder out in Georgetown, Colorado.

"I told him you'd been here earlier, but you'd left the bar around four."

Malone was obviously concerned. "That shooting was self-defense, Travis, and it's nothing but a trumped-up charge to get me out of the way. The problem is, I can't be taking the time now to be sitting in some jail.

". . . Sean, we've got to leave now! Run over to Platt's and get your horse . . . bring it back here, and put it out back by the door. While you're gone, I'll get our gear together."

I was back with Genius in a little over half an hour, outfitted and ready to ride. Dismounting, I tied the gelding to a clothesline post near the back of McClusky's.

It was nine o'clock whcn Malone grabbed a kerosene lantern and we stepped out of McClusky's into the night. I heard the match snap, then flash into a bright flame as Malone lit the wick. He led the way, in a halo of light around our feet, down a pathway encroached with weeds lifting into the atmosphere the pungent odor of goldenrod. After a hundred yards or so, we came to a dilapidated shed of a barn in a grove of walnut trees.

Malone lifted the latch, stepped inside, and walked over to a stall. He raised the lantern and I could plainly see the saddled chestnut gelding, rope tied, munching hay. But the lantern light had outlined Malone like a target in the darkness.

It must have been the first time ever that James Malone had let his guard down, and whatever the reason, he had exposed himself and he never had a chance. A shotgun blast and gunfire from near the doorway roared and echoed off the interior walls. In an instant I was back out of the light, firing my six-gun as fast as I could.

There were three of them. One wasn't moving, and the other two were clearing brush, running away from my following shots as fast as their feet could take them.

The one in the barn was dead, lying by the door. He'd tried, but he never made it to the opening. Blood was on the ground outside, and down the path, so I knew I had hit at least one other bushwhacker.

I went back inside to check on Malone, almost hesitating to look, for fear he was dead. Hardly anyone could survive a close-range shotgun blast, along with .44 slugs. But when I turned to check on him, the barn was blazing fire. The lantern had landed in a pile of hay on the dirt floor, and flames were leaping onto the plank stalls.

I rushed over and picked up Malone, carrying him to safety. Then I went back in and led out his horse. The barn was fast filling with smoke, but I hastened back again for a bridle and found one in the store room. Safely out, I checked Malone. His heartbeat was weak, but he was breathing. At least he was alive.

I closed my eyes for but a second, trying to gather my own strength from deep within. I could not allow my mind to even consider the thought of losing him. Then I went to the outlaw, at the edge of the doorway, and ransacked through his clothes. I found a billfold, and took a ring off his finger. In moments, I'd put Malone's things on the dead man, and pulled him farther into the barn.

Ten minutes later I was riding north out of town, leading the chestnut with Malone lying over the saddle. I could hear the clanging of the fire wagon, and when I looked back, the purple sky was painted with a glow of red.

Up the wagon road, along the Big Blue River, we traveled the night. When I finally stopped to make camp, it was nearly morning.

Malone was still alive, and I prayed to God for guidance. I made a bed of willow, and when I'd laid him down on it he took on a peaceful look in the soft morning light.

I knew Malone was in God's hands now.

Nine

THE FOLLOWING DAY I'd found the caves north of Garrison along the east side of the Blue River. McClusky had told me about them earlier, and they were known by only a few locals, so I figured they'd be a good place to hide out. The spot I'd picked was a shallow opening facing south, in a canyon of mostly oak. You couldn't see the grotto until you were within thirty feet of it, and it was close to the river, where I could fish for our food.

We had been there ever since Malone was gunned down, and he was still hanging onto life. It was nothing short of a miracle that he'd made it that far, but he was a strong man. He had in recent days just begun to show improvement, eagerly accepting his food and water. And shortly after, declaring his mettle, he was wanting to feed himself.

"They thought they had me this time, Sean . . . but we fooled their murdering hides, didn't we, lad?"

The relief from the pressure I had been under got the better of me, and tears welled in my eyes. I turned away as I affirmed, "Yes, Malone, you showed them."

He looked around and asked how long we had been at the cave.

"Two weeks," I replied.

"Two weeks!. . . My God, I thought it was yesterday! You cared for me all that time?"

I nodded, smiling. "Fed you, bathed you, and prayed over you night and day. I wasn't about to let you die, Malone." After pausing a moment, I continued with what I had to say. "Malone you've got to quit living on the edge . . . you need to settle down. It's not fair for Sarah to have to be worrying about you all the time. She loves you." I wanted to include myself in the love and worrying, but it wasn't the manly thing to say.

Malone peered over at me, and I was surprised by his nod of affirmation. "You're right, Sean. I love the lass. I'll be going home as soon as I can sit a saddle. I've got my memory back, and can recall all that happened in Georgetown. I want to tell you about it, so that if I don't make it, or if I'm killed, the mining stock will be yours. I'd told Sarah before I left that if I didn't return, you were to have the shares. They're in my safe at White Oaks."

"You'll make it, Malone . . . and Sarah told me about your winning the stock."

Malone then explained what had occurred on his trip to Colorado. "After that game, I held fifty percent of the stock in the Aetna Mine. I soon took off for Georgetown and spent a day there before I rode up to the mine. I walked in the office and introduced myself to Julius Tyson and Jake Moody as half owner. They also had fifty percent — and they were speechless, until I showed them my ownership affidavit.

"When the shock wore off a bit, Julius tried to convince me the stock was worthless, that the mine was making no money.

"'It's barely breaking even,'" he'd said, "'and the only reason we haven't shut down is the hardship it'd cause the miners.'"

Malone continued. "I'd asked to see the mine, but they refused, claiming it was too dangerous. I could tell they weren't going to be cooperative, and after letting the two thieves know I'd be back, I retreated to the hotel to figure out what action to take.

"But the next day, when I left the hotel, I was followed. When I went to pass the alleyway by the cafe, I'd noticed the shadow of a man and I could see the outline of his gun. I quickly stepped into the passage as I drew my gun, saw his ready weapon, and fired. The bloke never got off a shot, and the other man who'd been following me had disappeared.

"It seemed my mining partners had wasted no time in their attempt to have me salted away.

"But with some snooping on my own, and after visiting with some of the miners, I found a talkative sapper, a Darrell McCook, who took a liking to me. From him I soon learned the mine was indeed producing high-grade ore, and the two owners were taking most of it and loading it out at night on pack mules. . . . But where they took the gold, he didn't know.

"Apparently the vein they were working had only recently been discovered, but it was even richer than their previous drift. 'Jewelry-type ore,' McCook called it. On some pieces of the crumbly ore, you could separate the gold with your fingers.

"McCook also confided that many of the miners themselves were high-grading — stealing some of the richest ore — but their thefts soon became known to Tyson and Moody, and the miners were being searched when they left each day.

"About a week after talking to McCook, I broke into the mine office. After closing the window coverings, I lit a kerosene lamp and went over their books. What the two had told me seemed to check, but I figured there had to be a second set of records somewhere, with what they were actually running through the place. I'd searched the office, but found nothing.

"I was on my way to leave, and as I passed behind the desk, I heard a squeak in the board below my feet. Under there I found the second set of accounts.

"I went back a year in the listings, and it looked like they had been stealing around ten thousand dollars a month for themselves. What they'd taken over the past ten years could be close to a million dollars."

"That's a lot of gold, Malone . . . .Why didn't you go to the authorities when you had the evidence?" I asked.

"I don't know, Sean; I should have, but I thought I could handle it alone, the way I've always handled things — trust no one but yourself. It *was* a lot of gold stolen, with no one to stop them.

"When I confronted them, they denied it at first, but when I told them I'd found the second set of books, they confessed.

"I demanded as my half-owner rights an accounting and restitution.

"Moody, the surly one, looked at my holstered six-gun and I believe was figuring on drawing his weapon. I looked him in the eye and told him he should go ahead, pull his gun. He refused."

I interjected, "He probably got to thinking about the man you'd killed in town, and figured, likewise, he'd never have a chance."

"I suppose so . . . " Malone said, then added, "They told me it would take some time to figure out what they owed me. I told them I'd give them a week, then after restitution they'd need to retire. I'd hire someone to run the mine."

Tyson got upset, insisting they had some say on what was to be done there. But I straightened out his thinking.

"'I don't think you do,'" I told him, "'unless you want to answer to the law and spend the rest of your life in jail.'

"The thought of jail changed their minds."

Malone said he'd left the office and mounted his gelding for the five-mile ride into town.

"On the trail, I considered the circumstances and realized I'd need to be especially wary. They were no strangers to having someone eliminated; but I was confident I could handle the situation. However, the one thing I hadn't considered was their going into action so fast.

"My mind was elsewhere when I rounded a bend in the narrow mountain trail two miles from town. Suddenly from out of a nest of boulders came a swarm of six or seven men. They'd grabbed the reins of my horse and pulled me from the saddle. Before I could reach my six-gun, they threw me to the ground and beat me with clubs.

"An eternity passed as they battered me, before everything finally turned black. Yet in my far-away unconscious state I could hear their voices.

"'He's dead; load 'im in the wagon and dump 'im out of sight. But make sure you get 'im at least thirty or forty miles from here!'"

I was amazed.

"Yes, . . . it was just like a bad dream," Malone explained. "Then sometime later, near daylight, they threw me in a ravine along the South Platte River. Luckily for me an old miner was panning for gold upstream and saw the thugs. Through a patch of aspen, he'd watched them dump me into the chasm and cover me over with brush.

"Several weeks later, the placer man had almost nursed me back to health, but I remembered nothing of the past before the beating. It put a frustrating ten-year gap in my life.

"I knew that something was wrong — something missing. But I had no recollection of Sarah or Henry, or you, Sean, until I saw you at McClusky's. Then suddenly it all came back.

Malone grew even more serious. "The mine in Colorado is a bonanza, but all the gold in the world isn't worth my losing Sarah. I doubt I'll ever go back to Georgetown, even though the cutthroats are stealing what's rightfully mine — and that does stick in my craw."

"But why did the Manhattan Marshal have a warrant for your arrest?" I asked him.

"Well . . . the only explanation I can fathom would be Tyson and Moody. They'd thought I was dead and so had done nothing about my shooting the man they'd sent to kill me. Somehow, recently, they must have discovered I was alive, and had that warrant issued.

"That makes sense," I agreed. "Knowing you were alive, they hoped the warrant would get you bottled up in jail and hopefully hanged. For insurance, they must have hired the three thugs that tried to kill you there in Manhattan.

"But, Malone," I smiled, "your partners don't know they didn't get the job done . . . and even now probably believe that you're dead!"

"How's that?" Malone asked.

I explained to him about switching his identification with the gunman in the barn and he laughed — the first time I had heard him laugh since the shooting.

Malone added, "For all they know, I could be *legally* dead!"

"It's something to think about," I said. "It might keep your enemies off your back, so that you can live in peace, without looking over your shoulder all the time."

Two weeks later, Malone was well enough to ride and we were taking the wagon road into Manhattan. The Blue River flowed sparkling over my left shoulder; it was among the prettiest streams I'd ever seen. It meandered throughout the wide valley guarded by lush, steep hills and promontories, and canyons that chaperoned the clear running creeks from out of the broken landscape, making their way below.

Malone and I talked little, and as we rode along the river I listened to the long pools of deep water gushing into the shallows of intermittent rocky riffles, singing to the countryside. Stretches of high, meandering clay banks and ledge rock channeled south the clear running water. Its fresh coolness rising off the blue liquid gave a feeling of peace. Then, downstream at Manhattan, the Big Blue rushed to a stop where it flowed into the Kansas River.

Rain had fallen twice in the past four weeks while we were camped at the cave. One was a gully-washer, but the Blue River never once had muddied up like the streams would do in the East. The valleys here were grass, not at all like the broken land along the Mississippi, that turned the waterways a dismal muddy brown after each rain.

Some two miles north of Manhattan we splashed across the Blue River at a wide riffle, reined our mounts to the southeast, and took the Military Road to Wamego. We figured we had better stay out of Manhattan, not knowing what Malone's situation might be in the town. And if the authorities thought Malone was dead, we didn't want them knowing otherwise.

I'd thought about riding into Manhattan by myself, to get what news I could on Malone's status, but we figured I would raise too many questions that might be hard to answer. As it was, it looked like I had moved on and left the country after Malone's death.

Wamego's main street was nearly empty at six o'clock when we reached the depot. Jacob Brown, the station clerk, told us a train would be pulling in at eight fifty, its destination St. Louis. We bought our tickets and made arrangements for our horses to travel with us.

We'd recognized no one at the depot, or on the boardwalks. And we stayed out of the saloons, where Malone might be known. A few minutes before nine that night, in the glow of the station's lamplight, we boarded the eastbound train.

The final boarding call came, and we took our seats. We looked around at a quiet dimly lit car nearly empty of passengers. One lone man and an elderly couple appeared to be sleeping.

The train wheels jerked, picked up speed, then moved down the tracks into a clicking roll. Relaxing, I leaned my head back and felt the relief from strain as the train flashed by the countryside. I peered over at Malone, and I could tell the long day had put a burden as well on his healing body. His eyes were shut and he appeared peaceful, resting on the upholstered seat.

I couldn't help but notice, though, how helpless he appeared as he lay back, totally different from the tough, hard-as-a-nail *hombre* that gave pause to even the most fearless of men.

I leaned into my seat, listening to the steady beat of the wheels and the chug of the train plunging through the black night. A sense of joy suddenly came upon me, lifting a heavy weight of fear from my heart.

Malone was safe, and tomorrow we'd be home.

Ten

SUNLIGHT COMING THROUGH the window woke me from a sound night's sleep. It took me a minute to figure out I was in my own room at White Oaks. It soon would be two months that I had spent just relaxing and being lazy.

Malone was his old self by that fall of 1870, and I had never seen a happier couple than he and Sarah. Their being together again had made worthwhile my trip West to find him. But despite my joy at their happiness, I missed Katrina, thinking of her often. I was anxious to head West again.

It was late October and the autumn had painted harvest colors across the countryside. I loved the beautiful golds and reds in the trees, but the fallen dead leaves skittering across the land reminded me that wintery days and nights were getting closer.

I had written to McClusky to tell him I was in St. Louis, thanking him for the help he had given me. But I suggested he tell no one of my whereabouts, and I never mentioned anything about Malone. Even though McClusky was a friend, I thought the fewer who knew Malone was alive and well the better. Sometime in the future I would tell McClusky the story of our escape, but when I could do so face to face.

I received a return note from McClusky two weeks later. His

well-written prose surprised me, as it differed from the way he often spoke. Yet I shouldn't have been amazed. Almost everyone in the West at that time over the age of twenty had been born in the East, and many were indeed well-educated men. McClusky wrote his condolences on Malone's death; he told of the firemen finding Malone's body in the burnt debris of the barn, and how the Marshal had notified the Colorado authorities of the death.

When I showed Malone, he laughed until tears came to his eyes. For some reason he thought the whole thing was funny. His contagious laughter caused me to join in, but I never did view the circumstance of his feigned death as truly humorous; I saw it more as a practical way to keep at bay the jackals that were after his hide. If Tyson and Moody thought Malone was dead, they'd surely quit looking for him with hired assassins.

The fall months passed, and with the holidays upon us. Christmas Day was an especially festive occasion, for Malone and Sarah were married. Then at the end of the month, I received a letter from Katrina. She was in San Francisco; her mother was well, and their trip had been a success. Their plays were bringing in crowds, and in January they would be in Los Angeles for several months. Through the summer they planned to travel the mining towns of California and Nevada. In September, she'd added, they would be back again in Denver.

Katrina wrote that she'd missed me and hoped I could get to Colorado in the fall. I knew that I missed her too, and it came to mind that she would be seventeen the next summer. A lot of girls married at that age, or even younger. I was certain she was the lass I wanted to share my life with. Nothing was going to keep me from meeting her in Colorado.

The next day I wrote Katrina — mostly about my adventures the previous summer. But in the last paragraph I shared my feelings of love for her and my hopes that we could have a life together in the future.

The cold St. Louis winds of February 1871 brought another letter from Katrina, from Los Angeles. Circumstances had suddenly changed. Her mother had gotten married and, from reading between the lines, I don't think she liked her new stepfather very well. She missed me, and looked forward to seeing me that fall. She added, as well, that if I so wished, she would quit the tour and join me in St. Louis — though truthfully she felt obligated to her mother to finish their two-year contract that would end in the spring of '72.

"*Can you wait?*" she asked.

I wrote her the next day, confirming that I felt as she did about commitments and that by all means she should not break her contract. My love could wait, even though I would anxiously count the days until I saw her again.

While both Malone and I were reveling in the joys of love, Lucia Champlain was sitting in her dismal parlor in Louisiana, looking through a list of poisons. Her evil source was part of an infamous collection that the voodoo practitioners of the Champlain family had passed down for generations, a book of different potions, their composition, and the plants they'd come from.

Lucia had decided on spurlock for her next venture. She intended to gather some from the swamps and make a brew. But she would have to handle the liquid carefully, for only a drop in a small cut could mean a horrible, agonizing death.

When her brother Daniel walked in the dark room that day, she ignored him. He sat down across from her, and noticed she was dressed as if she were in mourning.

"What do you want me to do, Lucia?"

"Nothing!" she sternly declared. "I'll take care of it myself. All you've done the past eleven years is blunder. First you couldn't find him; then after an ungodly eight years, when you finally located him back East, you still couldn't catch up to him.

"You botched things in Abilene, Daniel, when you had him under your sights. Then you hired that Gauthier fool to kill him, and he failed to get the job done and got *himself* killed in the process! You've been in St. Louis the past four months and apparently have never even got close to him! . . . You've done nothing but fail!"

Daniel was both embarrassed and angry. "I know full well, Lucia, but Sean's grown now, and he's hell to meet with a gun. He knows what I look like, after Abilene, and I can't get near him anymore.

"Louis was a good friend — I'd known him a long time — and he would've gotten the job done in Council Grove if Terrill hadn't stepped in and killed him."

". . .That's another thing! Why was Terrill, our own brother, protecting Sean? He has to know I want that boy dead."

Daniel shrugged. "I don't know. . . . I wasn't there. All I got was hearsay. I was so upset I'd have killed Terrill myself if he wasn't kin.

"And as for St. Louis, White Oaks might as well be a fortress. It's owned by James Malone, but a lady named Sarah Jones lives there as well, with some long-time family servant who doesn't let her out of his sight. He's a Creole by the name of Henry Ducette. . . . He prowls the place day and night, and he's deadly.

"I tried to get close to Sean several times and narrowly escaped there with my life. That Creole handles a bowie knife like it's a part of his hand."

Daniel continued, trying in vain to gain Lucia's sympathy. "When I lay abed in Abilene, Lucia, Terrill came to see me. I told him he shouldn't have killed Louis, but he just shrugged his shoulders and scolded me. . . . Told me Louis was no good. Said I knew it, too. He thinks he did me a favor, claiming that Louis wasn't right in the head, and that sooner or later he'd have killed *me*, friends or not!"

Daniel glanced at Lucia out of the corner of an eye, trying to gauge her response, then rambled on. "Anyway, Terrill said I ought to be forgetting about Sean. . . . I think he really likes the boy. Says he doesn't want to be forced into killing him. . . And told me Sean's too good with a six-gun for me or anyone else, and likely could end up killing one of us Champlains.

"He said outright . . . 'You tell Lucia to *forget it*!'"

Lucia cursed Terrill. "That's too bad. I'm the eldest and I make the decisions on what we do. By summertime I'll see to it that the boy's gone. From what you told me, he might marry that Thornton girl, and if they have kids, there'll be no end to the number we'd have to eliminate.

"No, Daniel . . . we got to figure out a way to kill the lad without any more mistakes. Once we get control of the property, we'll find the treasure, even if we have to dig up the whole place.

"But from now on, I'll take charge of the search and you can tag along; but let's make it clear . . . you'll do what I tell you!. . . And it'll have to be sometime when he leaves the protection of White Oaks.

"Now get out of my sight! I've got some planning to do."

Daniel was muttering to himself when he walked out of the room. ". . . *She'll find out. That boy's gonna be harder to kill than she thinks. If it was left to me, I'd forget it. Except for his putting a bullet hole in me, I almost like the kid. . . . Anyway, he's tougher than any Champlain I ever knew . . . except maybe for Terrill.*"

It came to Daniel, then, that my talents, indeed, reminded him of Terrill.

Lucia was obsessed with having me killed before I took a wife or had children, who would then become my rightful heirs. There was no way she could know that earlier I had made Sarah my beneficiary, and now was changing it to Katrina.

Malone and I had determined my travels for the next few months, before I would meet Katrina. I had places I wanted to visit, and tasks for Malone that needed to be done. And so it was that on April 10th, 1871, the train wheels squeaked and the steam billowed from under the railcar as it rolled to a stop at the Junction City depot. I unloaded Genius from the stock car and rode up the slope to the main street of the sleepy town. As usual, Spencer Jones was sitting in his favorite chair in front of the livery, leaning back, eyes shut, taking in the early morning quiet when I spoke.

With his eyes still closed, he barked, "I knowed ya was there, but I was hopin' you'd not disturb me this time a day!"

"Sure," I answered back. "I'll just go ahead and pick out a stall. You sleep." Spencer never answered, nor opened his eyes. I watered the gelding, picked out a stall, and pitched him some hay from the loft. Then I walked to the opened double doors and stood in the golden sunlight as it started pushing purple shadows from the street to the underside of the walkway canopies farther down the way. I looked at my pocket watch; it was half past seven. I peered up the boardwalk and saw people were starting to stir on the street. A spring wagon pulled to a stop in front of the General Store; a lady walked the boards, stopped at a shop, then unlocked the door and stepped inside.

High above the street a soaring hawk circled, and with dark wings spread wide, he screamed to the world. I thought maybe he had wanted me to know that all was well as he looked down from his royal throne in the sky.

Across the way, a gust of wind picked up dust from off the street and carried it a good block before an unseen hand dropped it back to earth. I felt good when I stepped past Spencer into that fine morning.

"Where ya goin'?" he asked.

I stopped and turned around. "To the cafe . . . for breakfast."

"Figured as much," he replied as he jumped up and asked, "Mind if I join ya?"

"No," I smiled. "I'd be honored with your presence, Spencer."

When we passed the butcher shop, a frazzled-looking dog lay on the boardwalk with eyes shut and its head on its paws. It never looked up, just wagged its tail as we passed.

We sat at a table along the wall of the cafe, and noticed only a few people in the place; but by the time we had ordered, it was starting to fill. A drunk across the room — obviously out all night — was causing a bit of a disturbance, so Spencer got up and escorted the man outside. In a few minutes he was back, just as breakfast was brought to our table. As we ate, a large man wearing an apron walked out from the kitchen and thanked Spencer for removing the offender.

"It's all right," Spencer said. "I took him to the livery; he'll sleep it off and not remember a thing."

Apparently Spencer's role in the town was somewhat that of a peace-keeper.

"Who was the man?" I asked.

"Oh, that's Reginald Kempthorne," Spencer replied, ". . . from out East, in Baltimore. He'd been raised in a proper and well-to-do family, and graduated with a college degree, but he came West some time ago with a bad drinkin' habit. . . . Sober, he's a good man; but liquor's got him in its clutches. Most of the time he sleeps in the loft at the livery."

I glanced at Spencer as I took a bite of bacon. He had a lot of people buffaloed; many believed he was a disagreeable grump. But underneath it all, I could see he had a heart of gold.

After a night in Junction City, Genius and I loaded onto the next train for Council Grove. I had decided to travel the rails, rather than the longer route on horseback, for I had many stops to make on this trip. The engineer pulled in for water just southeast of Junction City, at a place called Skiddy. Trains those days still had to stop every ten to twelve miles to fill up with water, and sometimes wood, if they were getting low.

I was heading to see Chancy. I'd taken to him, and to ranching, when I had last been out there, and was wanting to spend a few days with him, riding in the country air and camping out along the Neosho River.

Ahead, on my right, I could see the railroaders filling the boiler from a water tank set on a framework of wooden posts. As the steam engine slowly puffed its energy, I surveyed the countryside, noting a panorama of pastel greens amidst the dark skeletal branches of trees and scrub brush. Alongside the chartreuse sprouting willow leaves were clustered patches of wild plum covered with white flowers, and an abundance of redbud trees racemed in magenta blossoms across their dark branches.

In my pocket was a power of attorney from Malone, for his fifty percent ownership of the Aetna mine in Colorado. He had wanted to put the shares in my name, but I'd refused. Instead, we agreed on the notarized paper, showing my authority to act in his behalf with the stock.

Malone had warned me to go to the authorities and not try to take control of the company on my own, as he had done. "And if you do nothing, that's okay, too," he added. "I'd have gone back myself, not for the gold as much as to see justice done."

Malone wanted to see the two murdering thugs — his partners in the mine — hanging from a tree; he had wanted to go himself, but Sarah had asked him not to. Malone also had warned me that my identity was no longer a secret to the Champlains, so I might as well use my proper name. He thought it might even be safer, particularly in the West, for he'd left a number of folks there eager to shoot him on sight.

I agreed it would probably be best, but I had been proud to be called Malone. And anyone in the West that I'd considered a friend already knew my real name anyway.

The day before I'd left St. Louis, I had ridden Genius across the vast acres of White Oaks. It was a beautiful place in the spring, with all the growth being born again of new, untainted seed. I had stopped to rest at my favorite spot along the Mississippi. The magnificent wide waters never failed to remind me of Louisiana.

I thought of Ma and Pa, and our home, as I lay back in the grass, the sunlight warm on my shoulders. The earthy smell of the river water and the fragrant grasses in the warm sun reminded me of a place Ma used to take me when Pa was away at sea. I promised myself that there would come a day when I would return to Mosswood.

By the time I unloaded Genius at Council Grove, the noonday sun was high in the Kansas sky. I walked across the street, the renowned Santa Fe Trail, and ate at the Saddlerock cafe and hotel.

Eleven

MORNING SUNLIGHT broke golden across the eastern emerald hills, and when I awoke it had already chased the long purple shadows into the creek bottom. I'd been at Chancy's for going on a week, and I had relished every minute of my time, checking on the cattle and riding fence line.

That coming Monday Chancy was heading for Texas to buy as many as two thousand longhorns and make a drive to Abilene. He had asked me to go along, and if I wanted to make an investment, he'd take me in as a partner. Chancy figured three months for the drive, which would put us in Abilene around the first of August.

I'd had no plans until September, and so agreed to the trip. I had close to twelve thousand dollars; Malone had added the four thousand to my deposit at Wells Fargo, for what he called the work I had done while he was gone.

I told Chancy I'd put up as much as ten thousand, and he seemed pleased. "That much?" he questioned, then adding, "That'll be about half. I'll put up ten, and we'll be equal partners. Twenty thousand should be enough for the cattle and expenses."

I surely thought his partnership offer was generous, but said,

"I'm not sure it should be equal. You're the one with the connections and know-how."

"No," he came back. "We'll split any profit. I must warn ya though, it's a risky venture. Think it over before ya decide."

I asked what cattle were selling for in Abilene, and he told me around twenty to twenty-one dollars a head. I reasoned we surely could double our money at those prices.

Chancy shook his head. "Hardly, Sean. . . . If we start out with two thousand head we'll be lucky to hit Abilene with sixteen hundred. Besides the cattle, we'll have expenses — a sixty-horse remuda and a chuck wagon — though we can recover most of that outlay by selling it when we hit Abilene.

"And we'll need to buy food . . . and then there's the nine wranglers and cook's wages, though we won't need to hire a trail boss; I can take care of that, and you can be my *segundo*.

"We'll be meeting renegade Indians and hostile ranchers wanting to cut our herd for crossing their land. And it could happen that we'll have outlaws trying to take our cattle from us. We might lose the whole herd, or the outlaws might get away with part of the stock. . . . Hopefully, if we're hit by rustlers, they won't be successful.

"It can be a hard business, Sean. There'll be times of drought, then maybe storms and flash floods down the draws as we travel, or lightning causing stampedes. I've known drives that made it to Abilene with less than half the cattle they'd started with, and some ventures lost everything. If that happens, your money's gone.

"But most drives finish with a profit. This will be my third trip out of Texas. I broke even on my first, but my last one turned a profit when I sold the stock in Abilene, even with my expenses above the cost of the herd."

"I guess I just wasn't thinking clear," I told Chancy. "I know it could be a risky undertaking, but I want to give it a try."

Chancy had contracted with wranglers in Texas — the brush-poppers — and they were to have a herd of close to two thousand head gathered up by the first of May. He explained that ten years earlier, in 1861, when the Texans had gone off to war, there was no one to care for the cattle herds, and the longhorns ranged free. They'd ended up scattered across the state, from the wilds of the Cross Timbers woods in the east to the brush-covered arroyos of the Brazos in the west. It was anybody's guess who these cattle belonged to, and as a result, anyone brave enough to go in and slap a brand on the critters considered themselves the owner.

The longhorns, called mavericks, were tall and rangy with horns eight to ten feet, point to point; they were the lean, rugged descendants of the fighting bulls of Mexico that over time had also been left to roam the sparsely populated Mexican land. But the breed would never have survived indefinitely without human intervention, Chancy affirmed, despite the fact that they had lived through droughts by eating prickly pear and mesquite brush, and going days on end without water.

Chancy'd described how during the War Between the States the rugged longhorns had increased in numbers, due to their confrontational nature as well. They easily protected their calves from the predatory panthers, bears, and wolves.

But they were a difficult animal to gather, particularly when a cowboy had to pull them out of the brush to a holding area. Mostly it was one animal at a time with a lasso, and many a cowboy had lost fingers and arms, some even killed, when caught in a rope between two of the beasts, nearly two thousand pounds each, pulling in opposite directions.

It was the 20th of April when Chancy and I rode into Council Grove. He was on his favorite black and I was riding Genius. The morning countryside around us was a huge colorful basin that spring had painted in chartreuse, opal, and magenta — a panorama that glowed brightly beneath the weathered gray rimrock above the town. We rode down the slope together, straight in our saddles and bent on success, along the blue waters of the Neosho, with the sunlight gathering sparkles from off the surface. Intermittent riffles of white water splashed among the gravel and boulders, rushing by clay banks in a swift current.

The Missouri, Kansas & Texas Railroad depot — the "Katy" they called the line — was crowded with mostly townsfolk, there to watch the train unload supplies and to quench their curiosity as to who was coming to town and who was leaving. By eight we had boarded the train for Emporia. It was close to ten that morning when we unloaded our horses and rode off southwest toward Wichita.

Uvalde was a tough town, in the southwest part of Texas, some fifty miles from the Mexican border, and still plagued with lawlessness and Mexican bandits. Chancy and I pushed open the swinging doors of the Corral Saloon like we owned the place. As we walked up to the bar, every eye in the dingy room looked us over. I'd already dusted off my clothes with my hat after tying Genius to the hitching rail, but the cowhands inside could still see we had ridden a rough trail, and figuring we were kindred souls, they went back to their own private world.

When the bartender looked at Chancy, a gleam of recognition lit up his face. "*Buenas tardes*, Chancy! . . .What brings ya to these parts? Another batch of angry Texas longhorns?"

Chancy nodded, smiling. "*Buenas . . .!* Tex Dobson was to have a herd gathered and branded for me by the first of May."

"Well, ya won't have to wait long; it's already the 28th. Are ya needin' any wranglers?" he asked.

Chancy didn't have to think long. "I sure do! I could use nine good ones and a cook."

The bartender, an Irishman named Butch Calhoun, assured Chancy that he knew of at least six to eight cowhands lazying around, and thought they'd jump at the chance for some work.

Calhoun had been over the hills and up the creek, so to speak — a tough-looking *hombre*. As we visited, another hard-worn cowboy came through the doors, apparently looking for someone, and when he spotted Chancy and I at the bar, he'd pulled his six-gun. But before he could get his finger at the trigger, my own gun was spitting bullets of red flame.

The man fell to the dirt-encrusted floor. Chancy holstered his half-drawn Colt and peered over at me. "Why, thanks, Sean. I think he might've had me! He'd cleared leather and was still raisin' his pistol when you hit him. . . . I've never seen a faster draw! How'd you get into action so fast?" Chancy asked, obviously amazed.

I shrugged. "It just comes natural, Chancy." Calhoun meanwhile had sent for the town Marshal, and in minutes he was looking down at the dead gunman. He questioned the cowhands sitting around the room, and all agreed that the man they identified as Joe Jenkins, a local rancher, had been the first to draw his weapon.

The Marshal peered over at me. "Did you know him?" he asked.

"No," I explained. "He walked in glaring at us, and when he went for his six-gun I drew and fired."

The Marshal started to say something else, when Chancy interrupted.

"He was after me," Chancy affirmed. "Sean just happened to be standing nearby. Jenkins and I'd had an argument a year back, and I'd thought I'd convinced him the cattle I'd bought were free range . . . but apparently he still carried a grudge."

"Well," the Marshal said, "it was a fair fight, and I'll make no arrests. But you'd best walk wary, for Jenkins was liked by a few of the other ranchers — though I'd say some will be relieved, for he was a hothead and liked to run over people. . . . Still, they don't like outsiders comin' in and buyin' cattle from anyone but them."

"We'll walk careful, Marshal," Chancy replied, "and if anyone wants to check my herd, they'll be showin' the Rocking C brand."

The Marshal nodded. "No more shoot-outs." Then he motioned to a cowboy in the room. "Clyde, clean up here, and take Jenkins to the undertaker."

That evening we met with Tex Dobson. He was a tall, rangy Texan with a heavy drawl. Chancy and I had already sat down at a table along the far wall when Dobson walked into the hotel dining room. After we'd been formally introduced, I caught him peering at me a little longer than normal. I think he was trying to figure out who I might be, when I broke the ice.

"Tex," I said. "You wouldn't be from Georgia, would you?" I told him I had been to Savannah with my Ma and Pa when I was just eight. "We were there for two months, and I remember the local accent."

Tex acknowledged that his folks had left Georgia when he was twelve, some twenty years ago, and they'd settled in West Texas along the Pecos River. He added, "When I came back from the war, my folks were dead. Killed by Comanches. I found their scattered remains and buried what I could of 'em on some high ground overlookin' the river. I've been roamin' ever since.

"A year after that I was breakin' my back for Joe Jenkins at thirty dollars a month. He soon had me rangin' out and roustin' longhorns from the brush. I was good at it, and Jenkins knew it. I was bringin' him a hundred longhorns a month and he was sellin' 'em for eight dollars a head — eight hundred dollars a month.

"After three months of ropin' and pullin' mavericks from anywhere I could find 'em, I went to Jenkins and told him I was goin' longhorn huntin' on my own. He got angry and told me he'd have me arrested. . . . I told 'im to go ahead. They weren't his cattle any more than they were mine, and I was tired of doin' all the work for thirty dollars.

"He could see I was determined to go it alone and offered to pay me four dollars a head on everything I brought him. We shook hands on the arrangement, and Jenkins told me to bring him all I could. It didn't matter to him where I got 'em, and if they didn't have a brand, I was to slap his on 'em.

"I strayed afar in the wilds gatherin' cattle for the man, and by the next spring I'd pulled five hundred forty head out of the brush and branded 'em. He never paid me the four dollars a head I had comin', and I tore into him. We had a ferocious knock-down fight, and I had the honor of winning. But that was all; I walked away with nothin'."

Tex continued his story. "After that I was determined to work for myself, not some four-flushin' rancher." He looked over at me and nodded. "I'm glad you killed 'im. I was going to have to do it myself sooner or later. He's had his henchman try to get rid of me twice in the past two years, but you can see they didn't get the job done.

"I never took the time to track him down, and the few times I did see him he wasn't alone."

I looked at Chancy and asked, "How'd you and Tex get together?"

Before Chancy could reply, Tex intervened. "It was the year after I'd left Jenkins. I managed to hire four other wranglers willin' to take a gamble on makin' some money. I had little cash, but I'd keep 'em in food, along with a promise of a fifty percent share of the profits, and they agreed.

"Chancy and I met here the next spring, at the Corral. He was lookin' for cattle and I was huntin' a buyer. I had nearly two thousand head, with no one to take 'em off my hands. Chancy bought 'em all, and he and I have had a good partnership since. He takes my cattle, and I give him a better-than-goin' price."

Chancy smiled. "It's worked out for both of us."

"But this'll be my last year for poppin' longhorns," Tex hastened to add. "It's gettin' harder and harder to find the critters, and the ranchers are gettin' more and more hostile. I try to stay on open range, but they claim the mavericks wherever they're found. I'm tired of arguing with 'em. This batch of critters I've got now has been a test. We've had to beat the brush harder than ever this year. We've worked three thousand square miles along the Rio Grande, up to forty miles north of the river, from the Nueces to the Concho. And I'm plain wore out.

"I believe I'm headin' for West Texas, or New Mexico. With the money from this sale I'll have plenty of cash to buy me a ranch."

Tex gave us his contact in Uvalde, in case we needed help for another cattle drive. And he agreed to sell us the two thousand head for nine dollars each. The going rate most ranchers were charging the drovers that year was ten.

It took us a week to round up ten wranglers, a cook, a chuck wagon, and the supplies we needed. We managed to buy the sixty-horse remuda for fourteen dollars and fifty cents a head; the chuck wagon and supplies ran nearly two hundred. The thousand sixty dollars we spent altogether would leave us nine hundred forty for the trip to Abilene, and we figured it should be more than sufficient.

The next day, Chancy and I rode to where the wranglers were gathering the herd for the drive, and I was shocked at the scene. I looked over at him and expressed my surprise. "Gosh, Chancy, there must be several hundred calves, and yearlings and heifers."

"Yeah," he replied, "Maybe even more. They're not included in the count. Some won't survive the trip, but if we're lucky, many will. I'll tell you somethin' else, Sean. We've well over two thousand head of longhorns. Tex always gives me a generous count. It wouldn't surprise me, counting the yearlings, if we'd at least twenty-five hundred head to harass along the way to Abilene."

As I watched amazed, and wondered how we'd get them all to our destination, across from us, riding around the cattle, I could hear Tex's soothing, rhythmic song —

Git down little dogie, git down . . .
With a rope in my hand
And a longhorn to brand
Git down little dogie, git down.
Git up little dogie, git up . . .
A horse 'tween my knees
In a West Texas breeze
Git up little doggie, git up.
Git 'long little dogie, git 'long . . .
A bawlin' sortie forth

On a trail headin' north
Git 'long little dogie, git 'long.

Twelve

THE SUN ROSE like a bright golden flower above the brush and prickly pear along the Nueces River on the morning of May the 4th, the day we started for Kansas. From the arroyos, brush, and bunch grass west of Uvalde, we turned the cattle northeast. It was a mixed herd of steers and cows, as wild as a flock of prairie chicken. We pushed them hard, but they didn't move worth a darn until an old mossy-horned steer, weighing at least two thousand pounds, with one bad eye and a dozen scars from many a fight, shouldered into the lead and took the herd north. That hard, independent old critter was tougher than a bucket of nails, and so we called him Nails.

One wrangler on the left rear was herding the remuda. Three were riding drag, two at flank, two at swing, and two at point. The chuck wagon to the left of the herd traveled in front of the point. Chancy, as trail boss, rode ahead of the herd to scout for water and pasture come evening

That first day I went with Chancy to learn his tasks. I wanted to be a part of all there was to do on a drive, and spent at least two days at each of the wranglers' different positions around the herd.

To hold down the grumbling, and to show no favoritism, we rotated the wranglers each day to the next clockwise cowboy, so that everyone shared duty at the rear. Drag riding was the wranglers' worst position because of the dust raised by the cattle. It meant riding three days of breathing through a bandanna. It was also the toughest riding post, for it required the continual badgering of the injured and feeble or young calves, an endless effort of man and horse to keep them up. In no time the rider's horse would be worn out and needing to be replaced.

We were a week and some sixty miles northeast of Uvalde when we crossed the Medina River, thirty miles west of San Antonio. It'd been rough going, but we made ten miles that day, and each succeeding day seemed a little better, with the longhorns getting accustomed to the drive. We lost a few yearlings and a couple lame steers that couldn't keep up; we'd shot one of the limping steers and butchered him. Hopefully, in another six days, we would make it to Austin and continue north on the Chisholm Trail. I'd learned that the Indian trader Jesse Chisholm had first marked the crossing, in 1864, from Wichita, Kansas, to the northern Texas Red River country. The trail now went north from Wichita, to Abilene, and far south through Texas, to Austin and San Antonio, from the Red River.

The weather had been good for our drive, and with the wet spring, grass was plentiful. The herd seemed particularly spooky, however, and we each took shifts gingerly riding around them at night, singing soft lullabies to them. Sometimes, close to midnight, the herd would get up for a short stretch and then lay back down. Old Nails seemed to always know when we were ready to move the herd out, and he'd be there in front leading the way. None of the others would argue with him, and obediently followed along. That old cut bull was worth a dozen hands.

Chancy was particularly worried about thunderstorms, so whenever I rode out to pick a campsite, I'd find a place with a natural barrier to the south; in case of a stampede, the herd would head north and no back-tracking would occur.

Five days north of San Antonio we'd had a gentle rain, and the drag riders could breathe easier throughout the day. North of us the rains looked heavy, and the next day we crossed the flooding Concho River. We lost several of the weaker cows and yearlings in the crossing. The Chisholm Trail was a wide swath of hoof-beaten earth through there, and we'd had to swing wide at times to find enough grass and water.

In late May, we were stopped by a party of some fifteen Comanche warriors. They'd wanted to talk, and gave us the peace sign. When Chancy and I, along with two wranglers, rode up to the Chief, Chancy told me to show no weakness in our bargaining or the renegades would for sure hit the herd. I was surprised when the Chief demanded a hundred head of cattle for crossing his land. But after much haggling, we ended up giving him eight steers, two cows, two yearlings, an old .44 Winchester rifle, and a Starr six-gun, along with a hundred rounds of ammunition. Knowing Indians desired weapons, Chancy had brought several along, just for such purposes.

Our negotiations finished, we pushed on north, thankfully without firing a shot. We were lucky to have come across a sub-Chief willing to negotiate and keep his word.

We were making good progress, then early one morning, north of Waco, we ran into a driving rainstorm. The day turned dark, and a lightning bolt lit up the sky, its thunder cracking like a shot through the prickly atmosphere. The already spooked longhorns panicked and bolted into a rampaging stampede. We did our best to keep them together when they took off charging to the north, but many managed to scatter out and away from us to the west. We lost a wrangler in the melee, thrown from his horse and trampled to death.

Just before noon, the sky cleared and we spent the rest of the long, tired day rounding up strays. By evening Chancy figured we'd lost some four hundred head that we couldn't find or gather out of the gullies and ravines choked with scrub oak and brush. That night we buried the young cowboy on the high ground above the Chisholm Trail. I realized then that we couldn't afford another disaster.

On my twentieth birthday, 1871, at around noon, we could see the Red River twisting through the countryside like a winding sash of blue where it was free of the willow trees that elsewhere edged along the water. We crossed the river, into Oklahoma, without a hitch and without losing a critter.

Two weeks later, north of Oklahoma City, I was off northwest hunting for a camp site when I heard rifle fire. I figured I should check, to see if someone was in trouble. The shot had come from farther off than I thought, for after a good trot from my gelding, and four miles later, I slowed him down and dismounted before topping a rise. At first I could see nothing; then again I heard a rifle blast, close and nearby. A cloud of gunsmoke rose from among a nest of boulders at the base of the hill. In front of them native grass flourished in the remote narrow valley for at least a hundred yards to a bank of willow and cottonwood trees, along what appeared to be a small stream, probably branch water from a spring. The boulders, hiding the rifleman, had broken from off the ledge rock along the rim of the hill.

I didn't move, for fear of being discovered, then I saw the warriors camouflaged in the grass. Slowly they crawled their way toward the victim, and as near as I could tell, there were twelve of them — a small Kiowa war party on the hunt. The poor fellow in the boulders didn't have a chance; they had him cornered. But I couldn't leave him there to die alone; he needed help. He had no way to escape; his horse lay out in the open and was dead.

I caught the warriors off guard, and with my rifle hailing fire, I got three of them before they reached cover. I had hoped those left would ride off, but they didn't. I'd not ridden Genius that day as he'd been worn to near exhaustion, and I had picked out a black from the remuda. I knew I had to move, or the Kiowa would circle behind me.

Before they knew what was happening, I had spurred the gelding downhill. By the time I was within fifty feet of the boulders, bullets were slicing all around me. I hit the ground running and dove into the boulders with rifle in hand.

A youngster, not quite seventeen, looked me straight in the eye and said, "You should've rode on; we're trapped here and time's on their side. . . . My ridin' buddies rode off and left us here."

I peered out toward the warriors to locate my horse. He was down, not moving, and surely dead. The youth had said "us." I looked around. Back in the shade of a rock was another man, who'd lost his weapons in the attack, and I could see he was in bad shape. He was moaning, and when I looked over I discovered he'd been shot in the stomach, and in terrible pain. The trouble with his kind of wound was it might take all day to die.

He'd asked for water, but I had none. My canteen was on my saddle, with no way to get to it.

The lad and I watched our front, but the warriors were careful. We knew they were working toward us, and once close enough, they'd rush us. A half hour later, I saw a blade of grass move slightly. It wasn't the wind, and I fired. The redskin raised up and fell back. That left eight more to worry about.

By noon it was blazing hot, and I was thirsty, but said nothing. There was no breeze, and I was wringing wet with sweat. It had to be well over a hundred degrees, with the sunlight radiating heat off the rocks.

I learned that the boy's name was Dan Robertson; he was out of Tulsa. Then he'd added, "They call me Danny."

I questioned him. "You said your buddies rode off?"

"Well, . . ." he hesitated. "I hope I can trust ya, mister. It was like this. . . . For the past year we'd been rustlin' cattle and we were plannin' on hittin' the herd east of here this evening, the ten of us, besides Rex Crumpton, our boss. We were lazyin' around when he sent Jeff Rose and I off to the south, to a clump of trees. Crumpton was wantin' to know if it was a good camp site, with water.

"After 'bout a three-mile ride, we got into this valley, and all hell broke loose. We fell into a beehive of Kiowa. My horse was down, and we'd both been hit, though my wound is just at the flesh along my arm. But Jeff'd been hit hard. His horse kept on runnin' south; I expect the Indians caught him. From where we fell off our horses, we'd managed to crawl into these boulders. That was eight this morning.

"A few minutes later we could see our partners sitting their mounts on the hill to the north. I figured they'd heard our rifle fire and had come to our rescue. But after watchin' for five minutes or so, Crumpton rode off. I guess he'd figured the cost to save us was too high."

"Probably so," I replied. "You called them partners . . . but I'd say they sure weren't your friends. Anyone who'd ride off to let a man die is a snake in the grass."

The boy nodded. ". . . And if I get out of here alive, I'm done with 'em."

"How old are you?" I asked.

"Goin' on seventeen . . . Jeff's twenty-eight."

Jeff had been moaning off and on for some time, then suddenly he let out a horrible scream, and begged for Danny to kill him. "Please, Danny . . . I can't take the pain . . . please . . . kill me."

"I can't do that, Jeff," Danny told him. "Just hang on . . . we'll make it out of here!"

Jeff knew he wouldn't make it. "No, not where I'm hit. I'm dyin'. Please help me [illegible]"

His cry of agony was almost too much for Danny and I to bear. But before we could dwell on it any further, all at once the Kiowa appeared out of nowhere and rushed us with lance and gun. I was shooting as fast as I could with my six-gun. I jumped out of the boulders into the open to face them. I killed two, then it was hand-to-hand, and before I could ward it away, a sturdy looking young warrior had plunged his lance into my left shoulder. I grabbed his arm, and he tried to pull back, but my grip was too strong; his face cringed with horror when I lunged forward and slit open his belly with my bowie knife.

He lay helpless on top of me. After pushing him off, I looked around and saw I was alone. No Kiowa remained in sight; they had retreated back into the bush, except for those I'd killed and my last victim, who was crawling off. I let him go; it didn't matter. I knew he'd soon be among the dead.

I stumbled back into the boulders, hanging onto the lance in my shoulder. I looked back and counted four dead or dying warriors. But Danny also lay there, with a bullet to the head.

It looked like he had killed one Kiowa. At least he'd gone down fighting, unlike his cowardly friends that'd left him there to die. I figured there must then still be at least four able-bodied redskins in the brush, and reloaded my handgun for another charge.

But first, the lance point in my shoulder had to be removed. I put a stick between my teeth to bite onto, then grabbed the shaft of the lance and, with a strength I hadn't known possible, pulled it out. Despite a momentary spinning of the earth beneath me, I somehow managed to stuff the gaping wound with my kerchief.

I peered again toward the trees. The warriors were all out of sight, and they had managed to carry off their dead. I'd hoped they had decided to leave, for surely there had been enough bloodshed. I quickly ran low along the ground to my horse, pulled off my canteen and saddlebag, then rushed back to the boulders, relieved that I had not been fired upon.

I took a long brackish drink from my canteen and sat back for a minute to rest. I was worn out. I took a small flask from my saddlebag, poured the stinging alcohol into my wound, and wrapped it with a piece torn from my shirt.

I was caught off guard when I'd heard Jeff scream again, begging for someone to kill him. I took Danny's six-gun and put a shell in the chamber. I took it back to Jeff, and handed him the pistol.

He forced a shallow smile. "You got 'em didn't ya? I wish I could've helped," he said, almost breathless.

"They're gone," I told him, though not knowing for sure.

He asked where Danny was, as his brow pinched with pain.

"He's resting," I lied, except maybe it wasn't a lie.

He moaned what sounded like "Good . . . Danny's a good boy." Then he quietly added, "If ya make it out alive, see to it he goes straight. He's too good a kid to end up hangin'. . . . I might deserve to die . . . but he don't."

Exhausted from the pain, he lay back and closed his eyes.

"I"ll see to it," I answered, and as I walked back to my post I heard a "Thanks," and then his moans from where I had left him there in the shade.

I went back to my nest in the boulders and looked out into the now-quiet emptiness of the rolling Oklahoma prairie. I heard a pistol shot racketing behind me, and I didn't have to look to know that Jeff was dead. Soon after the shot, I heard horses riding off to the southwest. The Kiowa had had enough and were finally leaving.

An hour later, with the sun going down, I was walking east, carrying my saddle over my good shoulder. With my shadow leading the way, I plodded what seemed like several miles before stopping. In the distance I could see two riders coming my direction, and when they got closer I could tell that one of them was Chancy.

After hearing my story, Chancy sent a wrangler back to camp for a shovel. We buried Jeff and Danny on the brow of the hill, just above the boulders where they had fallen before the overwhelming odds. I found my Bible in my saddlebags, and by lamplight I read the *Twenty-third Psalm*. Chancy read from the book of *John*, the first four verses of the fourteenth chapter.

> *Let not your heart be troubled. . . . In my Father's house are many mansions: if it were not so, I would have told you. I go to prepare a place for you . . . that where I am, there ye may be also.*

From Danny's description of the outlaw Rex Crumpton, I would have known the coward anywhere. I'd hoped they would try to take the herd, for if there was ever a man I despised to the core, it was Crumpton, and I'd prayed that God would forgive me.

Danny had said that Crumpton liked to hit at dusk, when things were dim. But he probably wouldn't go after the herd until he'd picked up another two men — replacements for Danny and Jeff. And that would give Chancy and I at least a day to make our plans.

The following evening a contented red sun dropped slowly behind a hazy horizon, and in the dimness swept a purple dusk across the rippling plains. Six of our wranglers, along with Chancy and I, were waiting in ambush for the expected cattle rustlers. We hid along each side of the higher ground west of our camp, in some buckbrush, the most likely place for the outlaws to approach. Three wranglers were crouched with me in the brush on the north, and Chancy with his men were to the south.

It wasn't long before the outlaws cautiously rode up to the eminence and stopped to look things over. From there they could make out our camp in the trees by our glowing fire. To the north, the longhorns were lying in a pasture of native grass. Crumpton's heart must have raced to see such an easy prize. Through the almost silent night air I heard the rustler whispering to his men: *"It's perfect, boys. Circle around and hit the herd from the east. Those dumb cowboys have left us a flawless alleyway to the west."*

Then Chancy shouted our signal to open fire. "*Let 'em have it boys!*"

Rifle fire lit up the night, and gunsmoke filled the air with its acrid smell. Horses were rearing and whinnying, and others ran off in all directions. Four rustlers fell from their horses, as others spurred their mounts, charging off as fast as they could to escape the hail of gunfire that followed them west.

We buried the four along the Chisholm Trail, and carved in the wooden marker:

Four unknown rustlers.
They tried to take our herd.

Rex Crumpton was not among the four killed; he was one of those able to ride off. But I knew that by morning he could be dead. I'd had him spotted when we opened fire. I didn't have a clear shot, yet I knew he was hit hard, by the way he shouldered over in his saddle.

Thirteen

WE NEVER KNEW when we actually had crossed the border, but on July 20th, the morning we hit Caldwell, Kansas, it felt like home. That night we camped on the north side of the Chikaskia River. We had a lot of herding cattle to do yet, but everyone's spirits were lifted now that the drive was soon coming to an end, and after supper we sat around the campfire swapping yarns.

The wranglers were mostly all young men, from my age to twenty-eight, but the cook, David Monroe, was going on forty. We called him Dave, and he'd been a wrangler in the Lone Star state since the age of twenty-two. He'd been on many cattle drives, from Texas to the Mississippi River, before the railroads changed things when they reached west to Abilene.

Dave was from Albany, New York, and educated at a respected Eastern college. In 1853, he'd graduated. He was twenty-one when his father died in a fire at home — a story that brought back some sad recollections of my own Pa's death in similar circumstance. Dave's mother, shortly after his father's death, likewise died, of consuming grief the doctor had said. A few months later, Dave decided to go West, for he had no job and but a hundred dollars in his pocket after paying off his father's debts. Dave decided the frontier was where he would make his fortune in life, and stories he'd heard of Texas made it seem a likely destination.

When Dave had reached the Cross Timbers area of East Texas, no jobs were available for a college graduate — with a specialty in Literature, no less — and so he applied for ranch work. It took him a while to become a wrangler, but he'd had a patient foreman, and Dave stayed with it. After a year of hard riding, being thrown, and climbing back in the saddle dozens of times, the neophyte from the East had become a fair to middling cowhand.

When Dave was thirty, on a cattle drive to the Mississippi, the camp cook was killed in a stampede during a rainstorm. Dave liked to cook, and he never did much care for day-to-day wrangling, so he'd asked the trail boss if he could have the job. Apparently, it was an easy decision, for no one else had wanted it.

Dave was a master at making the barest of food palatable, and he'd never failed to put out a decent meal. The wranglers loved his cooking; he was always coming up with something new, often using an area's local plants and berries.

Dave finished telling his story, and the night turned quiet for a spell as we lay back before the fire. Those times we shared around the camp I mostly listened to the tales told by others. It seemed like a good way to learn. But I broke the silence that night to tell of my own early days on the delta, my year at sea, and the wonderful times at home, with Ma and Pa, when I was youthful and sinless.

After finishing my stories, I rubbed my chin covered with a week's growth of whiskers and reminisced, "I miss those days of innocence, before reality set in; at times they seem still almost reachable, but like my dreams they quickly move away. . . . And soon this cattle drive we share will also fade into nothing but a memory."

Dave agreed, then spoke.

I remember, I remember
The fir-trees dark and high;
I used to think their slender tops
Were close against the sky;
It was a childish ignorance,
But now 'tis little joy
To know I'm further off from Heaven
Than when I was a boy.

I smiled and asked Dave who'd written those words.

"The English poet Thomas Hood," he acknowledged.

"Ah," I responded. "I don't know why, but most of the bards I've read and liked are English."

"Well, that's because there are more of them," Dave replied. "There are some good American poets, and there'll be many more in the future, because our Americans are an intelligent, hard-working, and caring people. And they're a passionate lot, always striving to become the best in what they do."

I thought Dave certainly had that pegged right.

The days plodded by as each river and creek crossing became another milestone: the South Fork of the Ninnescah River, Slate Creek, the Arkansas River at Wichita, Gooseberry Creek, Jester Creek, Sand Creek north of Newton, Antelope Creek, the south branch of the Cottonwood River, French Creek, Silver Creek, the north branch of the Cottonwood, the west branch of Turkey Creek, and many other minor branch-water crossings.

It was the 4th of August when we saw Abilene in the morning sunlight, gleaming off the distant buildings. From the moving cloud of dust raised by the cattle came a chorus of nearly fifteen hundred bawling longhorns and two hundred calves and yearlings as we slowly trailed toward the town. I could feel the excitement in the air and see it on the faces of our wranglers.

Earlier in the day, Chancy had ridden ahead to make arrangements for selling the cattle. After crossing the Smoky Hill River, and upon his return, we pastured the cattle near the water, some two miles from town.

Leaving the wranglers to tend the animals, Chancy and I then rode into Abilene, to the Drovers Cottage on Texas Street, just east of Buckeye. We tied our mounts to the hitching rail. I was covered with dirt from head to toe and beat the dust off my clothing with my hat before walking through the door.

Cattle were bringing nineteen dollars and fifty cents a head in Abilene, if they were in good shape. The buyer rode out with us to look over the herd, and after moving around the longhorns a couple of times, he seemed pleased enough and thought we could probably bring the cattle into the yards some time the next day. One herd was ahead of us that needed to be processed and loaded for shipping.

By the time we'd returned to camp, the wranglers were anxious to hit Abilene and blow off some steam. To keep the herd under control, Chancy had let only three cowhands go into town at a time. To make it fair, we had them draw lots for who would get time off, first to last, but they'd need to be wary, for James Butler Hickok — Wild Bill they called him — was now Marshal in Abilene.

We had a count of fourteen hundred and eighty-two longhorns. That Friday, at the sale barn, we sold a hundred eighty calves and heifers, a remuda of fifty-two horses, and the chuck wagon. Three days after hitting Abilene, Chancy paid the wranglers each one hundred fifty dollars, plus a fifty-dollar bonus. We sent four hundred dollars back to Texas to the dead cowhand's family.

Chancy and I ended up with around twenty-eight thousand dollars in pocket — a handsome profit of four thousand each.

On August the 6th, after shaking hands, with a promise to come see him in the future, Chancy rode out of Abilene bright and early, headed for his ranch on the Neosho River. He traveled with Dave, whom he hired to work for him. He liked the Texan, and he liked his cooking.

It was still early, around half past six that morning, when I returned to the Merchant's Hotel to find Henry Ducette sitting in the lobby, waiting for me. I was more than surprised, but pleased to see the old man, though I instantly worried if everything was all right back at White Oaks.

"Henry!" I greeted the Creole. "What are you doing in these parts?"

"I'm a-lookin' for ya, Mr. Sean. Missy Sarah don't want me to go . . . but she need me no more. Malone can care for Missy now. An' I wanna ride with ya if y'll have me."

I was taken aback; I couldn't imagine him ever leaving Sarah's side, but I couldn't say no to that grand old man.

". . . Sure, you can ride with me, Henry. I'd be honored to have you along — though where I'm going could end up being dangerous, especially if I check in on Malone's gold mine."

Henry's eyes lit up with excitement. "Suits me good," he replied. "I'm needin' to be roused; it keep me young."

I laughed. "I know it does, but what about me? Maybe I'll end up not so young!"

"Ahh, phooey," he replied. "No one be as good as you with gun or knife, Sean Sinclair, and you knows it."

"Maybe . . . except for you or Malone," I replied. "Come on, Henry, let's go to breakfast."

I learned that Henry had arrived in Abilene by train the night before, and slept under the stars in a patch of willows along Mud Creek. Daylight was climbing over the hills in the east when he'd gone to the hotel looking for me. I wondered, though, whether it had been Malone who in truth had sent old Henry to watch over me.

Some time around the 1st of September, I was to meet Katrina. The Kansas Pacific had completed its line into Denver the previous August, and I'd decided that Henry and I would leave in a couple weeks for the Rocky Mountains by train. I figured I had at least a week to show him the Kansas countryside, so I bought him a four-year-old black gelding from Olson the hostler. Henry was totally taken with the mount.

At daylight the next morning we rode east out of Abilene along the Smoky Hill River. The golden sunlight dappled the earth beneath us and the underbrush below the cottonwood limbs that moved against sailing ships of clouds in the sky. Only the sounds of our horses' hoof falls, the clinking of their bridles, and the squeak of saddle leather broke the silence as we rode in God's country. I could tell that Henry loved the nurturing land as much as I did, and though I hated to, I broke the silence to ask about Malone.

"Malone — he's good!" Henry exclaimed. "Malone and Missy spent the winter in Savannah, but they were back at White Oaks when I leave to find you. Missy not wanted me to go, but Malone told Missy it be okay.

"Malone health better now, but at times I see a wanderin' look, like m'be he want to ride a gamblin' trail again. Then next time I glance at him, it be gone. He fight the battle, but I think he know he have to settle down."

"I hope so," I said. "And I just hope nobody crosses him, for I'd pity the poor soul that ever did."

Henry nodded. "Aye. . . . He ride the waves of danger, that be one sure thing."

"Henry," I asked, "your choice of words reminds me of my father's own first mate, the year I sailed the seas. Were you ever a sailor?"

"Aye, I sailed," Henry acknowledged. "On th' hurricane deck of many a ship . . . m'be ten years before I work for the Joneses."

"Ahh, I thought so," I said, as we continued on to a special little sanctuary I had found earlier along the river. Henry and I spent the day there, catching catfish and resting under the Kansas sky.

Two days after our time along the Smoky, in the darkness before dawn, Henry woke me from a deep sleep and cautioned me we must quickly leave Abilene.

"Two people hunt for you, Sean . . . a very beautiful woman, that Lucia Champlain, be dressed in black and accompanied by a brother they call Dan'l. Not but five minutes past they were here, askin' fer ya. An' now they know yer room, Sean."

Henry was agitated. "These're bad people . . . I can tell ya, v'ry bad. . . .We must now go!"

I looked at my pocket watch. It was four in the morning, and I wondered whenever did Henry sleep. He was always on the alert it seemed. But I gratefully agreed that we should leave, and in minutes I was dressed, put together my bed roll, and slipped down the back stairway with Henry close behind.

In moments we were at the livery, picking up our horses. Darkness still ruled over the countryside when we left behind us the dim horizon of lamplight in Abilene. Our plans had suddenly changed, of necessity, but we would catch the train farther west, at Ellsworth.

As we rode, I told Henry all I knew of the Champlains, and when I'd finished he nodded.

"Missy and Malone had already told me some," he said. "And I've heard others tell of 'em, for they bad people, 'tis known — especially that Lucia. She be into voodoo . . . and poisons.

"I think we mus' be rid o' her, Sean."

Henry surprised me. "No . . . no, " I replied. "There must be another way to convince her she'll never get Mosswood."

Henry shook his head. "No, Sean, death the only way for someone that evil."

I tried to reassure Henry and change his mind. "We'll think of something, Henry. There has to be a way other than bloodshed."

Henry shook his head but said nothing.

We rode a land of rolling hills, where the grass had turned from prairie to what the locals called short-grass plains — a beautiful rolling country, almost treeless except for the willow and cottonwood along the creeks and rivers. It was an open, endless, deceiving land that to a distance looked level, but in truth rose up and down through draws and small valleys.

We rode wary, never skylining ourselves, before topping the crest of each rise to see what lay beyond, for in addition to the Champlains, we had no desire to come upon a horde of angry Indian warriors hidden in the next coulee.

The following day, near the Smoky Hill River, we boarded the train at Ellsworth and took the rails into the gleaming red of a huge setting sun. No one I knew was among the other eight passengers on the car. Henry and I sat across from each other, figuring we could stretch out and sleep.

I had my head back, ready to nap, when the door opened from the adjacent car. Striding through the passageway was a figure in black, sporting two tied-down six-guns. When I saw the man's outline, I recognized Terrill before I even saw his face, and he sat down across the aisle.

He greeted me with that disarming smile. "I figured you'd get on at Ellsworth."

"What do you mean?" I asked. "How'd you know that?"

"I know you, Sean . . . maybe better than you know yourself."

I peered over at Henry who was taking it all in, and unless I was wrong in my guess, the old man hadn't missed a thing either. He had a puzzled look on his face, so I introduced him to Terrill.

In the back of my mind, I pondered how it happened that Terrill always showed up about the same time as the other Champlains.

Denver was a booming town in 1871. Gold had been discovered back in 1859 at the confluence of Cherry Creek and the South Platte River. The site was at the crossroads, and the party of prospectors had named it for James W. Denver, Governor of Kansas Territory, which at that time had extended out to that area. Some hundred thousand miners flooded the nearby slopes, and in 1861, the federal government established the Colorado Territory. The once peaceful setting, a meadow of Rocky Mountain wildflowers, was by '71 booming with businessmen, miners, women of the night, gamblers, and thieves, each looking for their fortune in life.

Our train pulled to a stop with the scraping sounds of iron wheels sliding on rails of track, and throwing bright sparks in front of the depot. When I stepped down from the parlor car stopped near the station, I'd checked to make sure my six-gun was in place. As Henry and I walked to the stock car to pick up our horses, I peered around to the west to look at the mountains.

I'd heard of the great Rockies, but for some reason I wasn't prepared for their majesty. The air I breathed was far lighter, crisper, and cooler than anywhere else I'd ever been, and the only thing I could think of to compare each breath I took was a drink of cold, fresh branch water.

Henry and I unloaded our horses, mounted up, and rode the few blocks to the livery. Terrill had unloaded his horse when we did, and as he rode off, he called out, "They're gonna be followin', Sean . . . keep a guard. See ya later!"

Henry's eyes followed the gunman until he was out of sight. "He be no good, I d'not trust 'im."

The sky was clear, but an afternoon downpour had left the streets in a quagmire of mud. Yet multitudes of people, nevertheless, sloshed from boardwalk to boardwalk. The city was beginning to hue down into the purple shadows of evening when we walked into the Statler Hotel.

A day past us by as we loafed around the city and rode the area thereabouts. Something in the brassy and hot August sky warned a body that summer was past its prime and aging fast.

That night, Henry and I made plans to ride to Georgetown.

Fourteen

THE MORNING SUNLIGHT gleamed brilliant, probing into the purple shadows along the Platte River. Henry and I rode a lonely pathway among the whispering aspen on a trail of buff-colored gravel leading into the foothills. West of Denver a few miles we hit Clear Creek and the wagon road to the mining towns.

It would be at least eighteen days before Katrina would arrive in Denver. Henry and I had plenty of time for the trip to Georgetown to check on the village and the Aetna Mine. I had told him he could stay in Denver and rest, as he looked around the growing city, but he'd have none of it. He had become protective as a mother grizzly as far as I was concerned, and if danger was to show, he wanted to be there to cut off its head.

That night we stayed in Central City at a small hotel on Eureka Street. We'd heard plans for the prestigious Teller House to open the following year. The Central City-Black Hawk region lay in a narrow canyon overshadowed by steep talus slopes and escarpments. Most of the placer miners had run out of gold, though a few were still working along the streams, living in shallow caves or canvas huts. The rich gold in the area was now coming from lode mines owned and managed by large companies.

At the hotel that evening I talked to a miner named Joe Woodman, another of the educated from the East, a Harvard University graduate. He had seemed a lonely sort, and wanted to visit. He was a placer man and preferred to work above ground — at least that was what he'd told me. He had peered at me, stroking his whiskers, and admitted, "I'm comfortable where the air is fresh and the view to my liking." Then he told me his story.

Earlier in his travels he'd found some rough, jagged nuggets. Panning upstream on Clear Creek, he soon ran out of the metal. Backtracking, he found more of the ore in a dry runoff branch that headed toward an escarpment of incoherent rock. Moving up the talus slope, he found even more.

At the top of the gravel, in a water-eroded rift, the rock glowed with gold. Woodman had found the source of the rough nuggets — the mother lode, seamed with a rich strata of ore.

By summer's end he had picked his way some fifteen feet into the rock face, the hole drifting downward into the mountain. The vein had widened out from where he'd started at the face of the opening, the ore not as concentrated, but still rich with golden webs. It was obvious to him that he would soon have the need for another drift and the hiring of men. But for weeks, he'd been having nightmares about the massive pinnacle of rock, from the darkness above, caving in and entombing him.

Inside the widening tunnel, Woodman began hearing noises where there were none, and the slightest fall of a pebble or the least groan of the mountain were wearing at his nerves. He began forcing himself into the mine each morning.

But the mine was not his only problem, he'd told me. He'd been wounded twice by claim jumpers, though luckily he'd been able to defend himself with his Sharps rifle from certain death, as he hid behind a barricade of timbers.

Then in late September of the past year he'd stood outside the drift. As Woodman described it, sweat poured from his brow when he visualized the coffin-like quarters inside the mine. It was then that he walked away from the drift and two days later he sold out to a mining cartel for fifteen thousand dollars.

Along with the ore he'd already mined, he'd grossed nearly twenty-five thousand. Woodman laughed when he told me, "The last I heard, the company had successfully mined nearly a million dollars in gold."

It seemed strange that Woodman wasn't bothered about having let a massive fortune escape from his grasp; and it was an end to a miner's venture not uncommon. Before the evening had drawn its final curtain,

Woodman explained to me how to get to the Aetna Mine, northeast of Georgetown.

At eleven the following morning, Henry and I rode into Georgetown, located along Clear Creek. It was a thriving hive of people when we dismounted and tied our horses to the hitching rail in front of a local store. I noticed the boardwalk was some two feet higher than the hard-packed street, no doubt anticipating the often rapid-melting winter mountain snows.

Georgetown had been settled in '59, but was not incorporated into a town until 1868. Now three years old, it was a typical mining town, overrun with miners and gamblers.

I hitched my six-gun holster into place as I stepped up onto the boardwalk. There were so many people milling about that no one paid us any mind as we walked along the store fronts, melting in with the crowd.

At noon, the saloons and eateries were starting to fill when we walked into the Timberline Cafe. Henry and I sat at a table along the far wall, and after ordering dinner, I asked our pretty red-haired waitress if she knew of a Darrell McCook.

She nodded, "I know him," looking down at me with a question in her blue eyes. "What d'ya want with Darrell?"

"Nothing in particular," I told her. "I just wanted to talk to him. We have a mutual friend — a James Malone."

"Malone. . . " she said. "The name's familiar, but I can't put a face to him. You're not connected with the Aetna people, are you?"

I could tell she was trying to protect Darrell for some reason or another, and I took a chance when I answered her question. "Connected, yes, but not friendly with the management.

"My name's Sean Sinclair, and this is Henry Ducette," I told her, as Henry nodded. "If you see Darrell, tell him we're friends of Malone. . . . We'll be at the hotel next door. I'd like to talk to him."

The waitress had seemed to relax when I'd said I was not friendly with the management, enough to introduce herself to us. "I'm Helen Dobson. And Darrell's my boyfriend.

"I'll see him sometime later this evening and pass it on that you want to get together with him."

Around eight that evening, past dark, Darrell came by the room. I soon learned he had been keeping a low profile, especially after two efforts had been made on his life. He'd thought the culprits were Tyson and Moody from the Aetna, figuring they'd learned of his friendship with Malone, though for the past year, he'd had no unpleasant incidents.

I told Darrell that was probably because Malone was dead. I figured it still best for no one to know otherwise.

I showed Darrell my power of attorney for Malone's half of the Aetna stock, and Darrell acknowledged he still had friends there and would see what he could learn about the operation.

Two days later, Henry and I rode the winding wagon road of brick-red and buff-colored gravel up to the Aetna Mine. Before us stood a weathered, frame, nondescript small building with "Office" painted in black above the door frame. In the area behind the structure were several barns and sheds. To the right of the buildings, some hundred yards at the top of a slope, was the heavy beamed structure of the mine shaft. To the right of the shaft, waste rock had been dumped into a ravine. Looking back down the trail, we could see the beautiful forests of aspen and pine guarding the way back to town.

We dismounted and tied our horses to the hitching rail, next to three others. We walked into the office, and I asked for Tyson and Moody.

"They're not in," was the reply from a bald middle-aged man sitting at a well-worn desk. He peered at us over his silver-rimmed glasses.

The one-room building was large enough for three desks behind a makeshift rough wood counter. When I walked up to the man, Henry stayed by the door to make sure we would not be interrupted with a surprise.

The man rose from his desk and held out his hand. "I'm Joshua Kline, the bookkeeper. What can I do for you?"

Shaking his hand, I introduced myself. "I hold authority, via power of attorney, for the James Malone half of the Aetna Mine."

Kline became obviously nervous, his hands shaking as he looked over my papers of ownership.

"I'd like to talk to Tyson and Moody. . . .Where are they?" I asked.

". . . They're in the mine, checking on a new drift with the foreman. I look for them back any time now." Kline continued to peer at me over his spectacles, then at Henry.

I thanked him for the information, adding, "We'll wait."

The clerk nervously shuffled the papers on his desk as we stood by. Ten minutes ticked off the wall clock behind him, then finally two rough-looking characters walked in the back door. Before the clerk or I could say anything, the heavier of the two, who turned out to be Moody, looked at me and growled, "We're not hirin' any help!"

". . . Not looking for work," I replied. "I'm looking for Tyson and Moody."

The scowl and threatening look grew deeper. "I'm Moody," he answered. "What d'ya want?"

I peered over at Henry; now tense as a cat. He was ready for action if necessary. I handed Moody my documents and in a calm voice identified myself. "My name's Sean Sinclair, representing via power of attorney the James Malone half of the Aetna Mine."

While Moody looked over my credentials, his carved facial features quickly became enraged. Red-faced, he threw the papers back to me and shouted, "You'll play hell gettin' any of this mine!"

In a split second, he drew his six-gun. I beat him to the draw, but before I could fire, I heard Moody's weapon hit the floor and saw Henry's bowie knife penetrate to the hilt in Moody's chest. Moody dropped, moaned, then lay dead. Tyson never moved, but I could tell by the hate in his eyes that he had the potential to be the more evil of the two.

Henry walked over to Moody and removed the knife, cleaning the bloody blade on the man's shirt. When Tyson finally spoke, Henry was watching his every move.

"Gentleman," Tyson said, fast regaining his composure. "Let's settle this peacefully. My partner was a hothead and shouldn't have forced a fight. . . . It appears that you and I are now each fifty percent owners," he coyly explained, peering at me.

"I'll gladly run the mine, and we'll share in the profits."

It seemed Moody's death hadn't displeased Tyson a bit.

I suggested the authorities be notified, and Tyson had the clerk go for the Marshal. While Kline was gone, I asked to see the books. Later that day, after a prolonged investigation with us at the mine office, the Marshal returned to Georgetown, satisfied the killing was in self-defense. But before he'd departed, I showed the lawman my papers verifying my representation for the fifty percent ownership in the mine.

The sun was in the western sky that evening when I handed the accounting books back to Tyson, books that showed hardly no profit, barely breaking even. Closing the covers slowly, I looked him in the eye.

"Now show me the second set of books," I sternly ordered. Tyson was shocked, figuring I would accept what he'd first given me. He glared back, and if looks had the power to destroy, I would have been a dead man.

Tyson recovered from his surprise at my demand, and masking his untruth calmly replied, "There are no other books."

"That's a lie, Tyson. There *are* other records," I told him, "and I want to see them now!"

Tyson peered at Kline, who nervously looked away; then, desperately trying to think of a way out of the dilemma, he apparently conceded to himself that I knew of the second set of books and he replied, "Sure, . . . but they're not here. Come back tomorrow, and I'll have 'em for ya."

I looked at Henry. He was ready to strike, but I shook my head and spoke. "Okay, tomorrow morning. But you be here with the records, or the authorities will be following behind."

The sun was hanging lazy above the western peaks when we left the Aetna. I was looking at the picturesque mountain view when Henry interrupted my thoughts.

"You too trusting, Sean. I should've killed 'im. You see his eyes? It's the one place evil can no hide. An' he make the Champlains look like children."

"Yes, Henry," I acknowledged, peering back at the faithful Creole. "I know the man is evil. I could see it too; but even when I called him a liar, he made no move for his gun. How could I justify killing him?"

"I know, Sean, ya be wantin' to be fair, but he will no be; wait and see. . . . I could've killed 'im, and I hope I no regret it.

"Malone would've killed him!" Henry added, peering at me with a challenging yet acquiescing look.

When we pulled into the stables at Georgetown, purple shadows lay long across the street. A stunning black gelding was stalled next to mine. It came to me that I'd seen that horse before somewhere, but I passed it from my mind. Henry and I left our echoing boot steps to the passing of day when we walked into the hotel lobby.

There was no way to describe the shock both the Creole and I experienced in that instant. Sitting before us was Malone. The moment he saw us he jumped up from his chair, rushed over, and had us both in a bear hug. With that engaging smile of his, he looked at me and inquired, "Where've you been, Sean? I've been waiting around most of the day!"

It was nearly six by the time we'd eaten supper and Henry and I had filled Malone in on the day's happenings. Then Henry asked about Sarah.

"She's at White Oaks," Malone replied, "and doing fine, Henry. I had business in San Francisco and decided to check on you boys, and maybe stay over a couple days."

After supper, Henry and I stood in the lobby talking, and decided we would leave for the mine in the morning, after an early breakfast. When I turned around to tell Malone it might be safer for him to lie low, not knowing for sure if he was still wanted by the authorities, he was gone. Not only was he nowhere to be found, the black gelding I had seen earlier at the stables was missing as well.

But Henry told me not to worry; Malone could take care of himself.

It was past seven that evening when Malone saw the lantern light coming from the Aetna Mine office. He'd dismounted and loose-tied his gelding to a pine tree some hundred yards away. He softly patted the two horses tied to the office hitching rail, as he crept to the lone window that was partly open.

Inside, Tyson and a tough-looking companion, named Luke Jensen, were in conversation. Malone listened to the plan outlayed between the two lawbreakers, a scheme of twenty thugs who were to storm the hotel, kill me and Henry, then set fire to us all. Malone heard Tyson order the scoundrel to hit us around eleven and have the job completed before midnight.

"I want to see the flames when I ride into town," he told the outlaw.

In an instant Malone had kicked in the door. The thug grabbed at his six-gun, but he never had a chance; he took two bullets and slumped to the floor. Tyson rushed out the back door, with Malone fast behind.

I was in the lobby later that evening when Malone walked in the door.

He had that half-smile of his lighting up his face as he greeted me. I could tell that mischief had been afoot.

"Let's hit the hay, Sean."

The three of us were eating breakfast the next morning when the Marshal entered the dining room and walked over to our table. Looking down at us, he said, "We found Luke Jensen outside of town along the road . . . shot twice, through the head and the heart. His horse had wandered into the stables sometime during the night. . . ."

The Marshal seemed to pause long and hard. ". . . Doin' some backtrackin', we found him at daylight. Did you men happen to hear or see anything suspicious goin' on?"

Malone answered. "Not a thing, Marshal. We were here at the hotel."

The Marshal looked away, then back at Malone. "Well, someone sure done me a favor. . . .That renegade's been nothin' but trouble." He said no more, then walked away.

I glanced over at Henry. "I guess we'd better be heading for the Aetna. . . . Let's hope we don't run into trouble."

Malone spoke up. "No, Sean, . . . let's relax today. There's time enough tomorrow."

Fifteen

THE AETNA MINERS found Tyson's body at the bottom of the mine shaft. He was covered with lacerations, and had a broken neck. The local authorities investigating found no bullet wounds, and determined the death an accident. They concluded he had slipped in the dark and had fallen down the shaft.

We were there at the mine that day, and Henry tried to hide his grin at the Marshal's opinion, whispering to me, ". . . He fell by the grace of God, . . .or m'be someone give a little push. . . ."

Malone had come with us to the mine office, and after he had introduced himself, the lawman seemed to study him. Malone had said nothing regarding the official's version of Tyson's demise.

As it turned out, the Marshal knew more about Malone than he had first let on. When he turned to leave, he said, "By the way, I don't know if it's of interest to you, Malone, but the charges of murder filed against one James Malone were dropped some time ago." Malone's trademark smile returned.

A heavy burden had been lifted in that instant. Malone immediately spoke with Joshua Kline, the Aetna clerk, who acknowledged that he had been a very reluctant keeper of the two sets of books. But with Tyson's and Moody's deaths, his burden, as well, had been resolved, and he made arrangements with Malone to go over with him every detail of the accounting.

Malone also hired Darrell McCook to manage the mine for a percentage of the profits, and McCook was given instructions to find the heirs of Moody and Tyson. I learned later that Moody had no heirs, but Tyson had an eighteen-year-old daughter in New York. It seems Tyson had abandoned the lass when she was two, the child being raised by her mother.

She was paid her part of the stashed gold, soon found, that was hidden in an abandoned mine shaft some two miles north of the Aetna. Her twenty-five percent amounted to some one hundred fifty thousand dollars. The daughter was also to receive a monthly check for her share, as long as the mine operated profitably.

Joshua Kline, who Malone felt was at heart an honest man, was continued on to keep the books.

Meanwhile, Henry had left for St. Louis nine days earlier. He worried about Sarah, for with Malone gone, he felt he should be at White Oaks.

On the 28th of August, Malone left for San Francisco by rail, which now connected both coasts. I bid him farewell at the Union Pacific depot.

The next day, I relaxed. Katrina would be in Denver in two days, and things were surely looking up. I praised a merciful God for all His blessings. I'd felt that things couldn't be better when I walked into the dining room for supper that night, as six chimes greeted me from the wall clock when I sat down at a table along the west wall.

Then suddenly an unexplained feeling of doom came over me, and I felt for my six-gun resting in its holster along my leg. I was reassured as I touched the cold metal. I canvassed the tables in the room, and found across the way, the most beautiful black-haired woman I'd ever seen. I at first took her to be my age, but at second glance I thought she was probably in her early thirties. As it turned out, she was nearly forty.

She smiled, and I looked away. When I looked back, she smiled again and stood up. As she approached my table, she said, "You don't know me, do you, Sean?"

She was right. I didn't know her, but from the feeling I had in the pit of my stomach, I should have guessed.

"I'm Lucia Champlain, your aunt," she said, holding out her hand. "May I sit with you? For years I've wanted us to spend some time together."

"Please . . . sit down." I gestured to the chair across from me. After I'd said it, I'd wished I hadn't, for I knew in my heart that the beauty of the woman was but a mirage. A dark ringlet of hair fell down along her soft face when she purred, “Finally we’re together. You don’t know how much I’ve looked forward to our meeting.

“Sean, dear, I knew you at once from what Terrill and Daniel had told me; but they failed to note how handsome you were. I should have known you’d take after your father and mother. They too were a handsome pair, envied by everyone.”

I tried to smile, but never answered Lucia. My mind was traveling faster than I could contemplate. I knew I had to stay alert to everything she said, every move she made.

We ordered our meal and engaged in pleasant small talk. After finishing, I was looking for an opening to excuse myself when, to my amazement, Terrill appeared and sat down at the table.

“Hello, Sean — and you, Lucia, what are you doing in Denver?”

I could tell by the look on Lucia’s face that she was not happy to see her brother; but they did embrace. A half hour later I excused myself and went to my room. I put a chair beneath the doorknob to keep out any unwanted intruders. I quickly undressed and lay in bed with my hands behind my head.

Lucia had never fooled me for a minute. I knew she’d wanted me dead. Her expertise was poisons, and I was sure it would be her way. Guns would be out of the question, unless she could find me helpless and in some isolated place with no one around . . . . No, I was certain, her way would be poison, and I would have to be especially wary.

Downstairs in the dining room, Terrill looked over at an obviously angry Lucia. “Lay off the boy, Lucia; you don’t need the treasure. And you don’t need the land. Haven’t I provided enough for you and Daniel and Julia to live respectfully at Blackstone? If you need more money, I’ll see to it.

“The lad is family. Doesn’t that mean anything to you? And besides, sister dear . . . I like him!”

“No!” she spat out. “I’ll not lay off. He must die. He’s not family. I’m the eldest Champlain and you should be following my orders. Instead, Terrill, you stand in my way.

“You be careful you don’t go too far for your own well-being.”

Terrill already knew he had no control over his sister, nor could he reason with her. He stood up and looked at Lucia without saying a word, then turned and walked out of the room, his black frock coat covering his two tied down six-guns. Walking the steps to the second floor and his room, he felt a helplessness for the first time in his life.

He lay in bed, his thoughts rambling. He liked me, but could do nothing to prevent the inevitable. As for the treasure, he was sure Daniel and Julia didn't care about it, as long as they lived well.

Terrill feared no man, but Lucia had him cornered. He thought he should have stayed at the saloon, where he was having a string of good luck with the cards — or maybe it was that the players were simply stupid, as usual.

His thoughts jumped back to me. He knew he must warn me again about Lucia, but he believed I was a smart lad. What worried Terrill as much as anything would be if I ended up killing Lucia in self-defense, forcing him to keep the family honor and thus kill me.

Perplexed by it all, he rolled over and went to sleep.

Safe upstairs in my room, I blew out the kerosene lamp, crawled under the covers, and beseeched the Almighty for guidance in this earthly turmoil. For some reason, I thought of Ma, who had always waited for me as I said my nightly prayers.

A slight noise at the door woke me in the night, and I listened for it again from out of the darkness. It sounded like someone was trying to turn the knob and push open the door. Then it all stopped, followed by long, light footsteps sweeping down the hall, until I could hear nothing more, only silence.

I awoke at daylight and smelled perfume. I knew it was Lucia's. The chair was still under the doorknob, so no one had been in the room. The aroma was stronger where I had hung my clothes. Then I remembered it was probably from my shirt, for Lucia had laid her hands on my arm the night before at supper. I wondered why hadn't I noticed it when I went to bed, and then I figured it was because I'd grown accustomed to it during the evening.

A knock at the door brought me back to the moment. It was the maid with a pitcher of fresh water. I poured some in the porcelain bowl to shave. Then I filled the glass on the dresser to take a drink . . . but some inner warning told me to pour it back. I put a portion of the water in a small dish and set it beneath the dresser.

I shaved, then went downstairs for breakfast. But I walked past the doorway of the dining room, out the door, and to the cafe down the street. Lucia was a resourceful person, and I didn't know whether or not she had yet found a way to poison my food or drink at the hotel. I was determined not to set a pattern as to where I took my meals.

After a large platter of ham and eggs, I went for a walk. I had to put some distance between myself and the voodoo priestess, as Henry liked to call her, for I might slip and end up dead.

I knew I couldn't just kill the woman, simply because I thought she might try to poison me. They'd hang me from the nearest tree. And besides, I couldn't do it anyway. I knew I had to get out of Denver, and away from Lucia.

Katrina was to be in town the next day, and I had decided we would marry and leave Denver as quickly as possible. Her life would be in danger as well, if Lucia was to learn Katrina was to inherit Mosswood.

I walked down the boardwalk to the theater to look at the billboard. Even to see Katrina's name would make me feel better. *The Taming of the Shrew* was to start the following day, but as I scanned the list of characters I could not find Katrina. I recognized none of the names, and realized it was not the same company of actors managed by Katrina's mother.

I found the manager of the theater in his office, and upon questioning, he told me he'd received a telegraph from Cheyenne a week earlier, that the theater troupe had canceled its run. Mrs. Thornton had unexpectedly died, and the group had broken up. The manager told me he'd been lucky to find another company of traveling actors to take their place. He knew nothing else.

I was stunned and started to walk away when he asked, "By the way, you wouldn't be Sean Sinclair?"

I stopped in my tracks. "Yes," I replied. "I am."

"Well, I have a letter for you. It came in the mail yesterday."

He shuffled through some papers on his desk and handed me the envelope. I immediately recognized Katrina's handwriting. I put the letter in my pocket and returned to the hotel.

As I entered my room, I could see under the dresser, next to the dish of water that I had put there earlier, lay a dead mouse. I began to sweat thinking of how close I had come to drinking that water, and then wondered what would have happened if I had cut myself shaving.

I looked around the room, surveying everything in sight. I noticed nothing out of place. Once again I put the chair under the doorknob. I removed the chimney from the kerosene lamp on the small table, and struck a match. It lit up the dark room as it flashed into a glowing golden flame between my fingers. After lighting the wick, I replaced the chimney and sat down to open Katrina's letter.

August 25, 1871

Dear Sean,

Mother has died and the troupe has broken up. I write this letter secretly, and it has taken me several days to do so for I am watched continually by my stepfather, Floyd Shane.

The past months have been a nightmare. Mother was treated horribly, and then last week she unexpectedly died. The doctor here in Cheyenne could find no reason for her death, and I suspicion my stepfather killed her. Over the past few months they'd had several caustic fights. Mother had put away nearly a thousand dollars since Abilene, and Shane had wanted the money. She refused, knowing he would lose it drinking and gambling.

I am frightened of the man in more ways than one, for recently he has made advances toward me. Yesterday he suggested that we marry, and I vehemently refused. He has taken mother's money, and the four hundred I had saved, and refuses to give me the cash to get to Denver. I am nothing more than a prisoner and never out of his sight.

If I can, I will sneak away to the authorities. Once away from Shane, I will try to get to Denver by the first of September. But if you are reading this letter, you will know I was not successful.

I have noticed a kindly lady here in town, and hope I can slip her this letter, to mail for me, without my being discovered.

Whatever you do, Sean, do not come to Cheyenne, for it is too dangerous.

With Love, Katrina

I laid the letter on the table. I was stunned. What was I to do? She'd said not to come to Cheyenne, but I couldn't just do nothing. My only choice was to head there in the morning. I would find Katrina some way. She was to be my wife, my prayer, and God's promise.

That evening when I left my room, the maid was in the hallway dusting. I almost walked by her, but I slowed and asked the young lady about the pitcher of water.

"Miss," I said, "I'd like to ask you a question.

"When you filled the pitcher with fresh water this morning, had the vessel been washed?"

"Oh, yes, sir. I washed the pitcher myself in hot boiling soapy water. The clerk would fire me if I didn't."

"Did you leave it somewhere away from your sight after it had been washed?"

"No, sir. I filled it with water and brought it directly to your room."

The maid had a worried look upon her brow and asked, "Sir, was there anything wrong with the water? If there was I'll be fired; the clerk wouldn't stand for it."

"Oh, no," I told her. "It's nothing for you to worry about; the water was fine."

I didn't want her to feel she had done anything wrong, but continued, "I thought the vessel had the aroma of a strange perfume."

"Oh, it don't seem possible," she said.

I was puzzled as to how the poison got in the water, but when I started to walk away, the maid called to me. "Please, sir, wait a minute. . . . As I recollect, there was a strange thing that had happened to me when I was partway up the stairs to the second floor.

"A lady staying here at the hotel bumped into me, and I almost dropped the pitcher. I would have, but she grabbed hold of it and handed it back to me."

"Was it a beautful tan-skinned lady with black hair?" I asked.

"Why, yes, that was the woman. I think her name is Champlain. She seemed so nice."

Later that evening I went to the General Store for my repast. I bought canned meat and crackers. From the barrel I took a pickle. For dessert I bought a can of peaches, opening it with my knife and then using it to stab the halves. The peaches were a treat, and I finished them all.

Near half past nine I walked back to the hotel. I paid for the night, then told the clerk I was tired and planned to sleep in the next morning. But before I had spoken, I'd seen Lucia out of the corner of my eye, coming out of the dining room, and I knew she had overheard my conversation. She walked up to me, once again putting her arm on mine.

"Now, Sean, it's too early for bed. Come up to my room and we can share some wine together. We're family, you know."

"Not tonight, Lucia, maybe tomorrow. I'm just too tired."

Lucia accepted my explanation insisting, "But don't you disappoint me tomorrow."

"Sure, Lucia," I said and walked to the stairway. I could feel her eyes on my back as I walked up the steps, and a chill went through me.

Again I braced the door. I felt like I had just avoided doom, and wondered how many times one could look death in the eye.

It was two o'clock when I went out the window and dropped to the ground with my bed roll. At the stable, I mounted my horse and reined him north.

By the time the sun rose in the east, I was ten miles out of Denver. A rooster crowed in the distance, and I felt in charge of things again. I turned over my worries to the Almighty, as His Word had told me to do.

Sixteen

CHEYENNE lay in the Territory of Wyoming in 1871, encircled by a country of blue sky and golden horizons. It had been a peaceful site of settlers' tents in 1867, as the town was born. Lonely and dust-blown, it soon became a wild, gun-fighting village of wooden false-fronted structures. Half of Cheyenne, when I arrived, was made up of saloons. The growing community, in the middle of nowhere, was some ninety miles and not quite two days north of Denver by stagecoach.

It took me a little longer to make the ride on Genius; I didn't want to run him to death, so I took my time and soaked in the scenery. Passing along my left shoulder was an unforgettable vista of wildflower meadows, infringed with aspen and emerald pine trees climbing up the canyons and steep slopes to the bare-faced escarpments of the Rockies.

I thought about Katrina's letter. She had pleaded that I not go to Cheyenne. I wondered why. Was there something more about her stepfather than might be a threat to me as well? I didn't believe her feelings had changed; I was sure she loved me.

The sun was busy painting red hues across the brush and short grass when I rode into town. I checked into a two-story frame hotel that looked like it'd been constructed in a hurry, but it appeared to be the best on the boardwalk. I'd no sooner signed the register when I heard gunfire coming from down the street. The clerk didn't seemed concerned, so I figured it must be a fairly common occurrence and walked up the steps to my room.

It was late when I left the hotel and walked to the cafe down the street. The boardwalk supported a swarm of people that seemed to be going from one saloon to another. I felt uneasy with all the riff-raff about, and dropped my hand to my six-gun resting quietly in my holster. The cold steel felt comforting to my touch, and I continued on, reassured that I had checked to be certain it was loaded before I'd left the room.

When I entered the packed cafe, a drunken cowhand bumped into me, as he tried to get out the door.

"Watch where yer goin'," he'd growled.

I apologized, cautiously, as one does to a drunk.

"Ya better be sorry," he slurred. He stared at me with eyes that I doubted could focus well, his right hand resting on his holstered six-gun. He paused a moment, then stumbled on down the street.

My eyes followed him into the next saloon and then I relaxed, thinking to myself that this was a tough town where a body had better stay alert. Cheyenne had three variety theaters at that time, but no Opera House. It wouldn't be until '82 that the first one would be built and entertain the locals with outstanding talents like Lillie Langtry.

After checking out the theaters I soon learned that two of the shows were nothing more than lines of scantily dressed dancing women. But I was sure that Katrina's mother's troupe would have played at the other theater, and so I stopped to talk with the manager. He remembered the actors, and thinking back he recalled they had played there about a week before Mrs. Shane, Katrina's mother, had died.

"It was a surprise to everyone," he said. "She seemed to me a picture of health. . . . That was around the 20th of August, and I was closed the rest of the month, but luckily had another company booked to play the 1st of September."

Katrina's mother's troupe broke up, and the actors left town. Where? He didn't know.

After several more questions, things I needed to know, he had no answers. I thanked the man for his information and turned to walk out of the theater. He could tell I was discouraged and apologetically hastened to add, "Sorry I couldn't give you more help . . . and maybe this won't be anything useful either . . . but I did overhear Floyd — Mrs. Shane's husband — tell one of his poker buddies that he was leaving town and heading west with his daughter. I never heard him say where they were going."

I paused at the doorway and expressed my gratitude. "Much obliged; it does help. At least I know the direction they took."

West could mean any number of towns, and figured I needed more information. I knew, as I paced the boardwalk, that if I was to learn any more, it would be in the pits of dim lights and bawdy music at the saloons. The taverns of Cheyenne were the places I had hesitated to go into, for circumstance beyond one's control could involve a person in a lot of trouble, especially after dark.

It was going onto nine when I walked through the swinging doors of the Plains Saloon, the third place I'd been in, with no luck at finding the whereabouts of Mr. Shane or Katrina. I walked up to the bar and ordered a rye whisky. The bartender seemed talkative, and after a few minutes I asked if he knew Floyd Shane. He looked me in the eye somewhat askance.

"He a friend of yours?" The big Irishman asked.

"No . . . not a friend . . . for when I catch up with him, he'd better have some good answers to the questions I'm going to ask him."

The barman nodded. "I'm glad, 'cause he's about as low-down a skunk as I ever met. He teamed up with a no-account that hung around over at the Jezebel, and I threw him out of here the first time he hit my place. I was wary of him, and soon caught him, along with his buddy Slick Crawford, cheatin' at cards."

I told the barkeep enough of my story that he understood I had no love for Shane; yet he had no idea as to his whereabouts.

"All I know is what I heard bruited around town . . . that Shane and the daughter had left about a week after his wife died."

"She was his stepdaughter," I clarified.

"Oh, I hadn't heard. . . . But the one who might know where he was headed would be Slick, his buddy. He still hangs at the Jezebel . . . on the south side the tracks. But if ya go there, best be wary. It's a tough place. I'm doubtin' ya can get any information out of Slick, but I could be wrong."

It was late when I walked into the Jezebel and shouldered my way up to the bar. I ordered a whisky, and after the bartender had filled my shot glass, I turned, leaning back to put my elbows on the bar. The smoke-filled room was busy.

From the description I had of Slick, I figured he was the character with a gold vest, playing cards at the table along the west wall. I scanned the rest of the room and could see more than a few drunks at the scattered tables were sharing bottles of whisky and doing all they could to vex the ladies of the night.

A cowboy sitting at one of the tables had his eyes glued to mine when I peered his way. It was the drunk that had bumped into me hours earlier. He looked like maybe he'd sobered up a bit and was beginning to feel like a grizzly with a sore tooth.

I faintly smiled at the malcontent and turned back to watch the poker game, but to play it safe, I unlatched the thong holding my six-gun. Before another hand had been dealt, I felt a tap on my shoulder. It was the drunk.

"You makin' fun o' me?" the cowpoke challenged.

"No," I told him. "Just trying to be sociable."

"You the one that bumped me earlier?" he asked.

"No," I replied. "That was you who bumped. But it's all right; no damage done."

". . .Ya think you're pretty smart don'cha?" I tried to miss the whiskey-tinged spray from his mouth.

"Not really," I shrugged.

"What're ya doin' here anyway?" he asked.

I was weighing my words . . . hoping not to say the wrong thing.

"I came in to talk to Slick. He's playing cards over there." I gestured to the table.

"So you're a friend of that thievin' card shark! . . . *Well, draw, damn you!*"

I drew my six-gun and slammed the barrel down on the drunk's head, before he had his gun out of his holster. He dropped to the floor with a thud, and lay there unmoving.

The cowboy standing next to me looked down and asked, "Is he dead?"

I was getting tired of dealing with drunks, but told the man, "No, he'll wake up in an hour or two; but he'll have a sore head."

The cowboy nodded and returned to his drink. I could see the men that had been sitting with the drunk giving me a threatening look. They came over, ignoring me, without a word, and carried the man outside.

Things hardly slowed down at the Jezebel — it seemed to be only a minor excitement for the patrons — except every so often the customers were checking me out with a suspicious eye.

The card game broke up, and Slick walked up to the bar and spoke.

"Nice shot, cowboy; only you should've killed him. He's been after me for some time. I'd have killed him by now, but he always has his buddies with him."

"What's he after you for?" I asked.

"He thinks I cheated him out of some money," Slick replied and laughed.

"Mind if I ask you a couple questions?" I queried.

He looked at me with the hint of a frown and a bit of irritation. "No . . . I guess not."

"Do you know where your friend Shane was going when he left Cheyenne a couple weeks ago?"

Slick hesitated, raised his eyebrows, then looked over at me. "Well, the way I see it, I don't owe him any favors. . . . He was headin' for Utah Territory. The man's one of them Mormans. But if you're lookin' for him, you'll never find him. . . . In case ya didn't know, those people're thicker'n molasses."

"How is it you're willing to be telling me where he was headed, you being friends and all?" I asked with a goodly amount of suspicion.

"We *were* friends. But he skipped town owin' me a lot of money."

I turned to leave, then looked at him. "Much obliged for the information."

"*De nada*," he replied. "And by the way — kill the bastard for me!"

I never answered Slick, and walked out of the Jezebel into the darkness along the boardwalk. Ten minutes later I was in bed asleep.

About that time, Lucia left Denver on the train to St. Louis. From there she was to take the steamboat to New Orleans and then to Blackstone. It had been a week since I had disappeared, and after several days of sleuthing in Denver she couldn't figure out where I'd gone. It galled her no end that she had failed in her attempt to eliminate me. She was sure she'd had me when she'd slipped the potion into my water pitcher; she had waited patiently for someone to find me and spread the news of my untimely death. I could only imagine her disappointment when she saw me later that morning.

But Lucia determined she could be patient for my eventual and — as she thought — certain demise. She believed it was just a matter of time before she would bag her quarry. And she'd finally admitted to herself that she could understand why Terrill was so accepting of me. She'd grudgingly conceded to herself that I did have some redeeming traits; but no matter — she was determined I had to die. Mosswood and Pa's treasure it hid were too important to let slip away.

Lucia watched out of the train window, racing by the grassy plains of Kansas, and noticed a patch of nightshade with its pink blossoms and dark green leaves. A hint of a smile lit her face. She would have liked to stop the train to pick some of the toxic plant, to add it to her collection. Yet, no matter, for she really preferred using hemlock; it took but the smallest drop to eliminate an unsuspecting victim, and she had an unending supply of the deadly plant, since it grew profusely in the Louisana swamps and within only a mile of Blackstone.

Lucia thought about me . . . she'd considered me to be an attractive youth, and for a fleeting moment her corrupt soul vanished as she wished she might have had a son of her own — perhaps much like me. But when reality set in again, she realized that I was no fool to trifle with, and apparently well experienced with weapons. Yet, again, losing herself in what might have been, she considered how useful I might have been to her, another day, another time, to teach and share her knowledge of voodoo and potions.

No one else in the Champlain family was up to the task, she was certain, except for Terrill, and he had no interest. All Terrill sought to do, she'd mused, was to wander the earth and play cards. Indeed, she knew he was truly a merciless gunman, but he had turned soft in practical family matters. And concerning the necessity for killing me, Terrill had become a big disappointment.

Lucia lay back in her seat as the train rolled the tracks, closed her eyes, and remembered back when she was sixteen. It was 1848, and she had gone to New Orleans to learn the art of voodoo, and the making of elixirs and potions, with the amazing renowned Queen of voodoo, Marie Laveau. The grand monarch of New Orleans voodoo was fifty-four at the time, and both revered and feared by blacks and whites alike.

Lucia's time with Laveau had changed her forever. She gloried in her new-found powers and her ability to master others through fear. Added to that, Lucia was beautiful . . . and she knew it. She was well aware that she turned the heads of all red-blooded men.

Yet she rarely looked back at those wishful eyes that were cast upon her every movement. For her, love was out of the question — a human weakness to be kept under lock and key. Not that she wouldn't use her wiles if it was to her advantage, to accomplish what she wanted. Lucia had seen many a lover in her time, but those few who thought they were successful in their conquest were soon relieved of any assets — and were not around to talk about it.

Lucia thought of her sister Julia who would soon be thirty. Dear Julia was a problem . . . for she apparently relished her secondary role to men, as Lucia viewed it — engaged to marry twice. But again, interestingly, one of those suitors had disappeared, and the other had died before the wedding.

Nevertheless, undaunted, when given the chance, Julia continued to sneak out to meet each new beau. Yet she'd never fooled Lucia, who knew well Julia's mission.

Lucia's thoughts returned to me, and she smiled, thinking it too bad that I wasn't blood; this might never have had to go so far. But she would wait. "*Sooner or later I'll succeed*," she whispered to herself, and drifted off to sleep to the soothing rhythm of the rails.

The day after talking with Slick, I'd learned a few more details about Shane and Katrina's departure from Cheyenne. I'd found a man who had seen them get on the train heading west. Katrina, he'd said, looked quite unhappy, and certainly not a willing traveling companion. The man had walked up to Katrina and had asked her, beneath the scowl of Shane, if she needed any assistance.

"Oh, no," she'd said, stammering, "I'm fine."

The man wasn't sure she'd meant it, but there was nothing more he could do. He watched Shane hustle her onto the railcar.

I was nearly beside myself with anguish and worry for Katrina's well-being. "When was this? . . .What day was it that they left?" I'd asked the gentleman.

He paused a moment, thinking back. "It was four days ago — that would have been the 30th of August."

My heart sank. I was four days behind. I prepared to leave Cheyenne, and the next morning I loaded Genius onto the train and walked to the passenger car. The Wyoming sky was predictably clear and vast that morning when I settled into my seat.

I glanced over at the depot as I heard the "All *aboard!*" followed by the engine's repeated *chug . . . chug*. The railcars jolted forward, and then the jolts decreased as the train increased its speed down the iron rails.

It would be a couple days before I reached the Salt Lake City area. . . . I wondered then what was I to do? . . . Where would I look?

I prayed that God would lead me to Katrina.

Seventeen

AFTER DEPARTING the train, Shane and Katrina had stepped down onto the rocky plateau of Promontory, Utah Territory. The location had become famed two years earlier when the Central Pacific's president drove the last spike connecting the Union Pacific and Central Pacific railroads, making it the first rail bridge between the East and West Coasts of America. The town of canvas and log structures sat on a desolate landscape of rock against a backdrop of sheer isolation.

From the train they went to the livery, where Shane kept a buckboard. Katrina was restrained in the back, with a rope, and partially covered by a blanket. It was useless to struggle, so she complied with his demands, and wisely so, for as a result, he relaxed his restraints, as she'd figured he would. But the thought never left her that she had to find a way to escape — and when that time came, she knew she must not fail.

Katrina could only see portions of the rough countryside as they moved in what she believed was mostly an easterly direction. After several miles, they traveled an open road of rock and sagebrush. By evening, they rode on a well-traveled wagon trail higher into the Wasatch mountain range, covered with scattered woods of aspen, fir, and spruce. Early the next morning they left the hard-packed way, and turned onto a narrow lane encroached by a forest of aspen. As the light from the woods lifted and the purple of night began its invasion, they stopped at a small cabin. After two days of travel, Katrina had no clue where the shelter was located.

Darkness owned the small room without any windows. Katrina lay on a cot, trying to figure a way out of her predicament. It was the same day I had boarded the train in Cheyenne.

The two-room cabin where Shane had taken her was occupied by a rough-looking pair known to Shane, and from what Katrina had overheard in their conversations, and names bandied around, it was a place frequented by area outlaws. One of the thugs, a tall, gangly man, mostly arms and legs, had made her very nervous and uncomfortable, for he couldn't keep his eyes from her.

She'd listened to their hushed voices, however, and soon learned that, as she had suspected, Shane had indeed killed her mother — by lacing her food with arsenic. The two other outlaws had said nothing to Shane's confession, but by their silence she'd had the idea that even they were surprised and perhaps didn't approve. Most brigands those days treated women with a deference, and to purposely harm a female was surely rare.

The next morning, the two bandits were gone. Later, however, another thug appeared at the cabin, someone Shane didn't know. From what Katrina could learn, he too was another outlaw, and he and Shane had talked by lamplight until late in the evening.

Katrina knew the time was probably close to midnight, as she'd heard no voices for a while. She quietly checked the door, but found it was locked. She had no way to escape.

Six days had passed, as near as she could tell, since they had left Cheyenne. She lay on her crude cot, wishing her mother had never married Shane, but Mrs. Thornton had been lonely, had believed his lies, and fell in love with what she thought he was. Her mother was just forty-three, and much too young to die.

Katrina hadn't liked Shane from the beginning, and soon realized he hadn't a decent bone in his body. But why was it she'd been able to see through the man's facade of evil, and yet her mother had not? Perhaps it was really true that love was blind.

Katrina said she'd thought of her own love for me, but she knew in her heart that it was not a sham. And she'd wished that her mother had never told Shane of the money left from the sale of their land in Louisiana, and what she had gained on the tour. With no resources to delve into, an opportunist like Shane would have moved on to greener pastures.

But wishful thinking wouldn't free Katrina from the bondage she faced, and she'd realized she would have to do something soon. She had fought off Shane's advances to that point, but he had given her an ultimatum. It was all right, he told her, that they not marry; but he'd not wait.

On their third day at the cabin, early in the evening and after eating supper, Shane took hold of Katrina's arm and motioned to her room. Whispering, he threatened, "I'll come to your bed tonight, and if you fight me I'll slit your throat!"

Katrina had no doubt Shane would kill her when it suited him, whether she gave in to him willingly or not; and she'd concluded rightly that her malefactor would wait until his outlaw acquaintance lay asleep before he came to the room. Katrina knew she had to find a way to escape before that, and somehow make her way to Denver. Though frightened and anxious, she made up her mind. Shane would not touch her.

Earlier that day, she had managed to sneak a carving knife beneath her dress, when she was forced to cook their dinner. Yet, as her mind worked over her plan, she wondered that even if she did escape, where would she go?

Katrina heard Shane unlock the bedroom door. Unclothed, his figure was outlined by the dying embers of the hearth as he walked into the room. Katrina lay on the bed, fully dressed, the knife tight in her fist beneath the folds of the fabric.

"Don't do this," Katrina firmly stated. She wished she could tell the evil creature that it was his life that would be taken from him if he insisted on his plan.

Shane was taken aback by her tone. He had figured she would be crying and begging for mercy. He smirked in anticipation. "No . . . it's payoff time, Katrina."

Shane hovered over her, and when he finally lowered himself onto the cot, Katrina plunged the knife, with all her force, into the soft part of his belly, slicing upward. He began a scream, but his words had no voice, and he fell to the bed, his stinking breath gasping for air. In minutes he lay dead.

Katrina, shaking from the encounter, rolled off the bed, away from the wicked and disgusting person before her. She wanted to run out the door, but quickly decided she must slow down and collect her thoughts.

She'd found Shane's Colt six-gun in the other room, and with much trepidation began to hastily tie the other drunk and sleeping outlaw to the metal iron of the headboard. She was quick with her hands, made strong from tying the knots of many a backstage scene.

She rustled around the cabin and found some warmer clothing that came close to fitting, and quickly she made up a bed roll, packing some leftover food, the dreaded carving knife, the six-gun, and a belt full of cartridges.

She had found only a few dollars in Shane's clothing, and a quick search unearthed no more. But wasting no more time, she started south down the narrow road as the moon was high. She had taken a roan, one of the two horses tied in the shed behind the cabin.

As the horse paced along, suddenly, and without warning, Katrina's breath seemed to be taken from her. She broke down into sobs that she tried hard to smother in the silence of the night. The realization that she had just killed a man had settled in.

She stopped riding long enough to be ill along the side of the road, and then, composing herself, realizing she must get hold of her fears and emotions, she quickly rode on into the darkness.

Six hours and twenty miles later, the bare hint of coming daylight began to filter down through the forest of trees. By that time, Katrina felt able to accept the reality of the killing — the realization that it had to be Shane's life or her own — and she was able to concentrate on finding some way to return to Denver.

Doubts, and then brief panic, began to creep into her thinking as she blindly rode into the leftover shadows of night, with only a thin sliver of gray coming from the gravel trail to light her way down the mountain. She'd said she wondered what she would do if I didn't want her now. What if I wouldn't want someone who was capable of killing a man?

But Katrina brought herself back to the reality of the present. "Sean *loves* me!" she almost shouted aloud, and the sound echoed back at her — "*. . . loves me! . . . 'oves me! . . . 'ves me!*"

Katrina had described to me the narrow, winding trail and the mountain stream gurgling as she rode in the mist of the foggy morning. And then immediately behind her, up the trail, she could hear the beat of hooves racing in her direction. She quickly reined her gelding back of some boulders and brush just west of the stream, and had no sooner found her hiding place when the drunken outlaw she had tied up in the cabin galloped by. She'd thought he was probably going for the law, or to find his outlaw friends, but she was wrong; all the thug had wanted to do was get miles and miles away from that cabin, for he had figured he was a doomed man if Shane's other friends found him. They would never believe a young girl had been the killer.

Thoughts of Katrina filled my mind as I got off the train at Wasatch and spent the next three days hitting the towns of Echo, Devils Gate, Ogden, Corinne, and Promontory. It was in Promontory where I'd questioned the rail clerk who had seen Shane and Katrina the week before, and where I'd learned they had picked up a buckboard and team at the stables, taking the wagon road east. It worried me that the hostler remembered that Katrina had been so obviously frightened.

That day, when I had stepped down from the train at Promontory, Katrina was two days south of the cabin she had fled.

In those early morning hours, Katrina came to a crossroads. From a break in the forest, looking down to the south, she could see the Union Pacific tracks far and away in the distance, and smoke lifting invitingly from a small village near the tracks. She didn't know it at the time, but it was the town of Corinne.

She'd reasoned she should stay clear of places where Shane's outlaw friends might be looking for her, and she was certain they would be watching the railroad towns. For all she knew, the law might be looking as well.

And so she took the mountain trail east, that was by far the least traveled path. She'd gone the day without meeting another soul on a narrow road that took her north and into even higher elevations. She'd begun to wonder if maybe she should have chanced the town she had seen earlier from the eminence, but she continued on her way.

With her thoughts conflicting as to what she should do, she rode on, listening to the roar of a rushing river coming from the deep purple canyon below the trail. She camped that night in a nest of boulders by a clear pool of fresh spring water, and after building a small fire, she ate part of the food she had packed. Then she lay beneath a blanket, with the Colt six-gun close at hand.

Before she could sleep, the night sounds came walking in on silent feet.

Katrina was frightened and on edge by the unseen resonating in the timbers, but her confidence returned when she remembered the six-gun.

At daylight, relieved she had indeed made it through the night, she finished the few scraps left over from her supper, saddled her mount, and continued her way northeast. She was on the mountain trail when the sun rose golden above the peaks, and in less than two miles her horse breasted rimrock, near a summit covered with a forest of pine and aspen. She pulled the horse to a stop, pausing there. She felt perched on a soaring cliff, as she peered far down at a grand basin that she would later learn was near eight thousand feet above sea level. Below, throughout the undulating high country, twisted a mountain stream through lush and colorful green meadows for miles. To the far summits north, bare peaks were creviced with snow.

The timberline, where she sat her horse, was a good thousand feet above the pass. Katrina was amazed at the view, and spoke to her mount.

"Well, fella, it looks like we've found paradise."

Surprisingly, the horse shook his head as she patted his shoulder and reined him down the trail. She rode on with an unexplained new confidence.

At a switchback clearing framed by aspen, she looked down at a small village nestled in on a flat bench. Miles of grassland to the west stopped at a purple mesa gracing the sky. South of the town, a wagon bridge crossed the deep blue stream, bordered with long grass and patches of willow. Moving on, the steep, declining, switchback trail she rode bottomed out a good mile before it crossed the shallow waters and led into an empty street of false-fronted buildings — what appeared to be a ghost town. But in an instant Katrina saw a lone figure along the boardwalk; she wondered what waited below, as she peered down through the blue haze of the sunlit morning. Would this be her safe destination?

When she reined her horse down the trail, she'd had a premonition that this place indeed might be a haven. Smoke lifted from a chimney at the west end of three blocks, and the ring of an anvil echoed from the blacksmith shop. "*It looks peaceful*," she'd thought, as she rode down the trail.

Like a beautiful young princess from nowhere, Katrina rode across the rumbling bridge into Carson Butte. Those there claim that when she arrived, the town was born again from certain death. What few people remained in the village had said the place was down to ten families — not counting those in the mountainous country surrounding — and two of those Carson Butte residents stopped what they were doing to watch her quiet entry into town.

Katrina reined her horse up to the hitching rail at the General Store, dismounted, then went in and immediately asked for a job. The owner was so taken with the lovely young woman he hired her on the spot. And it paid off, for it wasn't long before every male up and down the miles of basin had heard about the beautiful angel working for Pete Landry and his wife Mary. Miners and cowboys rode from afar just to see Katrina, and they always bought something, whether they needed to or not.

Carson Butte had set down its roots back in 1864 when Jake Carson, a placer miner hit it big in the nearby streams. The gold rush lasted for three years, and then the metal petered out. Back then, the street held as many as two thousand people crowding into a town of roustabouts, claim jumpers, and lawlessness. But besides the no-accounts, a number of good people came with the rush. At its brisk peak of sixty businesses along the main street those days, twenty had been saloons — that is until James Clayborne rode into the rowdy village and its council hired him as Marshal.

Clayborne was a couple inches shorter than the five-foot-nine average at the time, but he weighed two hundred pounds, all muscle. Fists alone wouldn't have tamed the troublemakers, but he was as fast as high mountain lightning with a six-gun — and needless to say the cheaters, roughnecks, and killers were soon run out of town.

By the end of 1870, only fourteen families remained in Carson Butte. They realized they were in one of the most scenic spots along Utah's northern border, and that without a railroad the hamlet would probably not grow; but they didn't care.

The town council had been made up of four no-nonsense pioneers, who were its anchors. Pete Landry, sixty years old at the time, was the mayor. He and Mrs. Landry ran the General Store with compassion for their neighbors, but they'd never let it become a weakness. Grace Shore, in her fifties, was a widowed, graceful woman who owned and operated the dress and yarn shop. Five-foot-seven in her bare feet, Grace was taller than the average.

Julius McBride, then forty, was the blacksmith, a copper-haired, portly and heavy-shouldered man, who never really understood how much stronger he was than others. And Slim — George Bentley — was thirty-eight tough years, orphaned at ten. He'd grown to the age of sixteen on the streets of New York City, when he'd grabbed a freight and rolled off the train in Kansas City. He carried some hundred seventy pounds on his six-foot frame, mostly skin and bone and muscle. He was a tough man to tangle with, for he knew what it took to win a fight. He'd holstered a well-worn Army Remington six-gun, and knew how to use it. At first glance most thought Slim to be cantankerous, but under his rough exterior beat a heart of gold. It was Slim who owned the stables.

Katrina joined this mix of determined settlers, and was given a room where she could stay, with a door that could be locked, in the back of the Landrys' store. Her pay was thirty cents a day, and fair wages at that, considering she was furnished room and board.

When Katrina had arrived and had gone to work for the Landry's, Mary had taken a dress and shoes for her to wear; but after a week in the same set of clothes, Katrina spent her first pay at the dress shop. She'd actually spent a bit more than she had in hand when Mrs Shore kindly told her she could charge whatever she wanted. And with her dresses in tow, Katrina said she'd felt on top of the world.

The following Monday, Katrina's security at Carson Butte would unexpectedly be challenged. She had caught Mr. Landry glancing over at her several times that morning, and when she'd looked back, he had turned away. Finally, he'd walked over to where she'd been working.

Landry acknowledged that he'd hesitated to pry in her matters, but he had to have a word with her.

"Well . . . it's more of a question, Katrina," he added. ". . . That horse you rode into town, stabled over at the barn. . . it carries a Diamond S mark on its hip . . . a known outlaw brand . . . and it's causin' some talk hereabouts. Can you tell me how you came by the gelding?"

Katrina had never thought about the horse's brand, and panic almost took hold. She thought all her good fortune would be lost, and tears filled her eyes. Pete's wife, Mary, had overheard the conversation, and took Katrina in her arms.

"It's all right, child . . . we just need to stop the conjecture."

Katrina told the Landrys her story — everything . . . even the killing.

Mrs. Landry was beside herself. "You poor child! . . . But don't you worry a whit, we'll take care of what's necessary . . . don't you worry about a thing!"

Katrina had never known such kindness. The next morning, the roan was gone, along with its saddle and bridle. In its place stood a steel-dust mare — a swap Pete Landry had made with Washakie, the chief of the Shoshone camped over by the mesa.

Eighteen

I FOUND THE CABIN where Katrina had been held captive. Her bloody dress lay crumpled in the corner. The log shelter was left in a mess, like there had been a desperate struggle. Someone had half-heartedly tried to clean up the blood, and at the sight of the hardened fluid my heart sank, thinking it might be Katrina's.

Outside the cabin the tracks of at least six horses had chewed up the ground. In a grove of aspen, possibly a hundred yards west, near the mountain stream, I found a fresh grave. I had to know who was buried there, so after locating a shovel in the horse shed, it took me but minutes in the loose soil to find the body some three feet deep.

It wasn't Katrina. It was a stone-faced man with dark hair, and from the description I'd had of Pete Shane, I thought it might be him, but I couldn't be sure.

From the grove I'd walked back to the cabin with my thoughts on Katrina and wondered what I should do next. I knew I'd need to head back to the railroad towns, for where else would she go? . . . But then, had she escaped?

I worried that maybe it wasn't Shane's body in the grave, and that he was alive and had taken Katrina elsewhere. And I wondered who it was that had buried the body? Too many unanswered questions clouded my thinking.

While my attention had been elsewhere, I had let my guard down and never noticed the four men standing in front of the cabin, watching my every move. These were no choir boys that waited beneath the canopy of a lodgepole pine; they were tough-looking characters, each armed. I marveled at how they had ridden up without me hearing them. Then I remembered the roar of the stream not fifty feet west of the grave site, and figured it probably had masked any sound made by their horses.

I broke stride to a stop some fifty feet from them, and spoke. "What can I do for you?" The biggest of the four roared back. "I want information! But first I wanta know what *you're* doin' here? . . . Who are ya?" he demanded.

As he talked, the other three spread out to where there was a space of four to five feet between them. My mind was racing, trying to figure some way to escape the inevitable, for I could see by their attitude that things were going to boil down to bloodshed. But what gave me a fighting chance was that the big man, their spokesman, was inquisitive. He'd wanted to talk, and I figured he'd start no shooting until he had some answers, or until he knew he'd get none.

There was no way out of this scrap I was facing without taking lead, unless I got lucky. I knew I had to find some way to give them a hard target, and so I stalled for time. I could see the closest cover was the trees to my right, ten feet away.

I finally answered the man. "I'm Sean Sinclair. . . what's it to ya?"

I stood my ground, unmoving, for I'd wanted to go for my six-gun when they least expected it. My response seemed to confuse the outlaws. I could tell it wasn't what they'd anticipated from someone facing four armed men.

He shouted again. "Was it you that killed Shane? . . You might as well tell me! I'll find out one way or 'nother!"

A deafening silence hushed the air, only to be broken by the false promise the gunman offered.

"I tell ya what I'm gonna do. You tell me what happened to Shane, and I'll let ya ride out of here!"

At least I'd found out it was Shane buried back in the trees. But I also knew the thug was lying, and before he had gotten the last word spoken, I went for my gun. It caught them all off guard, and red flashes raced twice from my handgun before they'd got off a shot.

For a split second they were in shock . . . completely surprised that I would start a gun battle with the four of them looking down my throat — and it probably saved my life.

Continuing to fire, I turned my body to the right and crouched down to make a smaller target. I jumped toward the trees, thumbing the hammer of my Remington as fast as my targets came on line. But I'd felt the jolt of a bullet hit my left shoulder, just as I moved into the cover of the trees.

I could see the loud-mouthed outlaw was down. I'd not have to look close to know he was not a part of the living, for I had aimed two shots that carried certain death. Two others lay unmoving. But I thought one was still out there, though he might not be among the living either, for I was certain I had given him a hot bullet.

I refilled the cylinder of my six-gun and readied myself for more action. I checked my wound, and luckily the bullet had gone clear through my shoulder. But blood was flowing fast, and so I stuffed my handkerchief into the torn flesh. I was surprised to find another bullet wound some six inches lower, in the thick part of my arm — taken aback that I had no recollection of when I'd received that second round.

I needed my saddlebags for the bandages I carried, but was wary of the missing outlaw and shouted at him. "Hey! . . . How about a truce so we can clean up this mess!"

There was a long silence. Maybe the rogue *was* dead. . . . Then came the call of a man in pain.

"You sure raised hob!" he told me. "I'm hit bad. . . . Just come on in and finish me off; I'm in no condition to stop ya."

I wasn't about to go running in there and meet a hail of bullets. The man could be lying. "Where are you?" I called.

He said he was lying north of the cabin some fifty feet. Cautiously, I inched up to the shack and canvassed the ground to the north. He was there all right, and I went to him and took his weapons. When I'd lifted him up, sharp pains went through my shoulder, but somehow I managed to carry him to the cabin and lay him on a cot.

I knew his wound was serious, for he'd been hit high in the stomach. He was hardly more than a boy, and reminded me of the youngsters I'd run across on Chancy's cattle drive from Texas.

I asked the boy how old he was.

"Eighteen," came his weak reply.

I asked his name as I examined his wound.

"Jefferson Clark . . . and a descendent of William Clark, the explorer," he tacked on with pride before he'd flinched with pain. "But Ma and most of my friends call me Jeff."

"Well, I'd say those are mighty fine credentials, Jeff," I replied, and then hastened to add, "I'm Sean Sinclair, originally from Louisiana; but I haven't been back for eleven years, and right now home is where I hang my hat."

I needed to care for my own wounds, as they were continuing to bleed, but the lad's belly was needing attention. I'd remembered seeing some watercress earlier by the brook, and rushed down to find it again. Malone had long ago told me the plant could be used to treat wounds and bleeding. I picked a hatful, then quickly returned to the cabin.

After crushing the leaves in a bit of water to make a paste, I put the poultice on Jeff's wound and applied a bandage. Then I washed my own, and applied the dressing and bandage. I felt weak from the loss of blood, and lay down in the lower section of the bed. I closed my eyes, holding my six-gun across my chest, and stayed there for a time, listening to the boy's hard breathing. Most men never recovered from his kind of injury, and only the Good Lord could tell if he would live.

I felt sanguine about my wounds, thinking they were probably not serious, but I knew enough about the tearing of flesh to know that any injury can become a danger if not cleaned.

I awoke some time later with a start, and wondered how long had I been asleep. Outside the cabin, purple shadows were working their way eastward beneath the trees. Jeff's breathing seemed heavier, and he was sleeping fitfully. His forehead was hot, and I knew the lad had the beginning of a high fever.

I quickly went to the mountain stream where the willow edged there boled up to the riffling water. I cut and stripped the bark from several of the trees and rushed back to the shack. I put the bark into a pot of boiling water in the fireplace, then lifted the lad up and spoon-fed the broth between his fevered lips.

After getting down all the liquid I could, I laid him back down on the cot. Then I drank some of the willow broth myself, figuring it might ward off my own infection and fever.

I prayed — for us both — and I figured I'd done all I could for the boy. God was the master now.

As I'd pondered our circumstance I knew it was dangerous for me to stay there in the cabin with the boy, yet I also knew I could not leave him behind, by himself. If he did recover, I thought it could be a good week before he could travel, and so I decided I had to find us a sanctuary, some place of protection where we would be safe from any other of Shane's friends or outlaws that might appear, until young Jeff was well.

It was dark when I came upon the cave downstream. The opening was covered with manzanita growth, a handsome shrub of dark-green leaves and deep red berries — survival berries they were called. They were edible, though a bit tart, and I knew they hung on the branches throughout the winter.

I never would have found the cavern, but I'd slipped on a rock and near the ground was a tunnel-like game trail that ran up to the face of the canyon's escarpment. Some ten feet farther south was an opening through the cover, up to the rock face. At the granite, I could see that larger animals had moved along the cliff a few feet to the hidden cave.

Once inside, I lit a match, revealing the large cavern and belying the low six-foot opening. There would be plenty of room for us, and our horses.

Darkness had enclosed the mountainside when I returned, and Jeff seemed to be breathing a little easier. I'd hoped he would be on the way to recovery. I managed to sleep a few hours that night before waking, then couldn't go back to sleep, so got up. It was daylight by the time I'd settled Jeff and the horses at the cave. As a golden sunlight began painting scribbly dapples on the forest floor, I rode back to the shack and erased all tell-tale signs of our movements to the cavern.

Near the cave I stopped at the brook, where I drank long from the ice-cold stream. I filled my canteen, and went back to Jeff. He craved the water, gulping it down and wanting more. I'd found some staples in the shack, so opened a can of beans and spoon-fed Jeff. Between the two of us, the can was soon empty.

By then, I was worn out — my eyes heavy — and I lay down for a minute of rest. The last thing I remember was looking over at Jeff who was peering back at me. When I awoke, he was sleeping and his breathing again seemed better. I stepped outside the cave and found the sun high in the cloudless sky, glaring a shimmering light down through breeze-blown aspen leaves. I figured the time was close to noon.

It was late that afternoon before I finished digging the grave for the three outlaws, and the work had started my wounds to seep blood again. I'd dug a four-foot-wide shallow grave next to the one already there, big enough to take the three outlaws. I'd wrapped each gunman in a blanket from the cabin, then covered them with the dirt. I felt obligated to read over them from the Holy Bible, yet thinking to myself that maybe I might have already done that deed one too many times in my young life.

I returned to the cave, and put a fresh poultice and bandage on my wounds. By that time it was late afternoon. Jeff lay there awake, watching me, and when I looked his way, I could tell he was in pain. He'd closed his eyes and I heard him murmur, "God, please forgive me. . . ."

Then after a moment's pause, he continued in a weak voice, "Sean ya needn't try to save me. I'm no good, and those I've traveled with were sinful men. I thought ridin' with Red Logan was somethin' special; he was supposed to be the fastest man with a gun in the West. But you made him look like a fool . . . made us all look like fools. And that's what we were!

". . . But it's too late now for me."

"Why do you think that?" I asked. "You'll make it, Jeff. I knew this morning that you'd past the worst, and you'll be riding that gelding of yours before the week's out."

I was trying to give the lad some hope, and added, "God will see to it."

But Jeff obviously had thought a lot about his situation. He shook his head.

"No, even if I do get through this, you'll have to turn me over to the law . . . but it doesn't matter now, Sean, 'cause I know I'm dyin'."

I didn't want to hear that. "No, Jeff, you can make it; and I'll not turn you over to anyone. It seems to me if you've asked God's forgiveness, He's always true to offer it."

Jeff acknowledged he knew that was right, for his Ma had taught him so.

"Forget about the law, Jeff. I know, and God knows. And He's forgiven you; it's in His Word."

Jeff seemed amazed that I wouldn't turn him over to the authorities.

"I've not been around anyone decent as you, Sean. I only wish we'd met a year sooner, before I'd picked up with that crowd. I'd give anything to ride the trails again . . . without any worries. . ."

"Put it aside now, Jeff," I replied, and I could see the tears welling in his eyes. I stood up and went outside so that he could have his privacy.

We were needing meat for our sparse diet, and so at daylight the next morning I was able to kill a small doe. We enjoyed a filling meal of venison and greens, and afterward, as we spoke, I'd handed Jeff the money I had taken from the pockets of the outlaws, some two hundred dollars in bills and change.

"It's yours," I told him. He looked down at the money and shook his head.

"No, Sean, you should keep it. I'll not need it where I'm goin'."

I tried again to give the lad some hope in the midst of his doubting. "I think it's fitting, Jeff, that you be the one to take it, for it can give you a fresh start in life. Their horses are yours, too, but if I were you I'd sell them, and turn them into cash."

Later, when I felt that Jeff was feeling more positive about his plight, I questioned him, wondering if he'd ever seen a young woman at the cabin. He hadn't, and was surprised that even someone like Shane would stoop to kidnaping a woman.

I realized I was losing time in looking for Katrina, and the trail to her whereabouts was getting colder. Yet I knew she was a smart lass, and I hoped she could find her way back to Denver, or even to White Oaks in St. Louis. I reasoned I'd have to stay with Jeff until he could ride again. And then, as soon as I could, I would head for the railroad towns to the south. I didn't know exactly where I was, and knew I would have to almost feel my way through the wilderness to the nearest town.

But that night, Jeff had a turn for the worse, and his fever once again raged. I made another broth of willow bark, and he thought he felt some better, but in an hour his pain had increased. I knew then that he was for certain dying. I stayed by his side that night as his breathing became more labored. Just before sun-up, he passed on.

I'd thought I could will the lad to live, but I couldn't come against his own words, for I believe that God will honor what you want, not what another wants for you. If only the boy hadn't insisted he was dying, for it seemed to set into motion his words. It came to me then that you eventually get what you believe to be in store for you. I just wished he hadn't kept repeating he was going to die.

By daylight, I was heading south leading four saddled horses, with Jeff across one of them. I didn't want to bury him with the others; I thought he'd deserved better.

The next afternoon I breasted the rimrock overlooking a vast slope of forest down to the valley below. I could hear a train whistle in the distance and searched the landscape. Off to the southeast I could see smoke billowing from the engine's smokestack as it labored up the grade of the mountain.

I buried Jeff there along the rim, beneath a ponderosa pine, where before him lay God's perfection of grandeur. I would have liked it there myself, were I not able to carry on in this world, and I figured he would too.

When I once again mounted my blue-roan, two chipmunks scurried across the graveled ways beneath the trees.

Two hours later I rode into Corinne.

Nineteen

THE 10TH OF JANUARY 1872 in San Francisco was damp and cold, but the Western Pacific trade-winds kept the temperature above freezing. Still, it reminded me of a chilling April day in Kansas, when I had ridden into a wet western wind blowing across the prairie grass.

In 1780, American colonists had arrived in the Pacific Coast area first peopled by native Indians, then the Spanish, and then the Mexicans. The place, named *Yerba Buena* — Good Herb — by Mexico, would be called San Francisco by 1847. It was a busy seaport town located at the tip of a peninsula surrounded by water on three sides — the Pacific Ocean to the south, and San Francisco Bay to the north and east. The horse-traveled way into the city was up the peninsula, from the south, on the *El Camino Real*, tying into the Butterfield Trail that crossed the southern part of America.

The city had been built on a sequence of abrupt hills, the highest just under four hundred feet. Close to the hub of the town's activity and wharf were the prestigious Nob Hill and Russian Hill, where since Gold Rush days the rich and privileged had built their elaborate mansions.

I had been there a week, staying at a small hotel on Montgomery Street. For the previous three months I'd been riding the rails and searching the towns from Cheyenne to Sacramento, looking for Katrina. I'd found no trace of her; it was as if she'd dropped off the face of the earth. But it was a big country, and I couldn't cover it all. I had almost come to the conclusion that she must still be in the Utah Territory somewhere, except I believed her every instinct would be to work her way east. I'd only hoped she wasn't yet a hostage.

I had come to San Francisco from Sacramento looking for Malone, who was supposed to be out there. He was reliably canny, and I thought that maybe he'd have some ideas on what had happened to Katrina. I had telegraphed Sarah, inquiring whether Katrina had contacted me in St. Louis, but there'd been no word from her, nor at the Statler Hotel in Denver. It had me buffaloed, but I wasn't giving up; I was determined to find her if I had to turn the West upside-down.

It was back in Denver that Malone had told me he would likely be in San Francisco until January. The shipmaster he awaited would dock, he figured, sometime that month. But I had not run into him anywhere, and had about decided he must have finished his business and headed back to St. Louis.

I had thought about going back to Utah, earlier in December, but the state was deep in snow and I wasn't about to try crossing the Sierra Nevadas that time of year. I figured I'd wait in California until April. And so, with nothing but time on my hands, I decided I might look for work — not that I needed to, for I still had nearly fifteen thousand dollars in my Wells Fargo account. But I just couldn't sit around and do nothing. God had made man to keep busy and surely contribute something to this world.

Around six o'clock I went to a cafe near the wharf on Bay Street and ate my evening meal. It brought back lingering recollections of the sea fare of Louisiana. I took a walk along the quays, and it was then that I noticed among the three-masted ships in the bay a newly arrived clipper setting anchor. I stopped to watch the crew scurry about the deck, preparing to dock. But the hour was nearing the time of mischief along the waterfront, and so I decided to return to the hotel.

I passed by many of the waterfront saloons and dance halls — dens large to small, clean to filthy. You could take your pick of what kind of entertainment suited your fancy.

The Gold Coast saloon, farther into the town, had its swinging doors wide open as I approached, and when I stepped into its golden lamplight squared on the boardwalk, I was met with a blast of raucous piano music and boisterous laughter. I moved past the husky doorman who looked me over with predictable suspicion, but said nothing. Had he searched me, he would have found a six-gun tucked behind my belt that was covered by my jacket, and the bowie knife sheathed at my back. From what I'd seen along the waterfront, I wasn't going anywhere unarmed.

The place was packed with customers that night. To the left of the bar a roulette wheel whirred around to a musical clinking stop, and three card games were nearby in progress, with each table full, along with two craps tables.

Just then, from the west end of the room came an excited shout, as a player threw his dice across the green of the table. Farther back I could see five poker tables, all involved in serious play. And from a large area to the right and rear of the bar came the piano and banjo music, where eight scantily dressed ladies were dancing in line on a stage framed with rich, red velvet draping.

I shouldered up to the bar and ordered a shot of whisky from the burly barkeep. Most barman like to talk, but this hulk of a man, with his sleeves rolled up, was all business. When I put a nickel down to pay for my drink, he coolly announced, "A dime more!"

"Fifteen cents?" I queried. "I paid five when I was in here two days earlier."

"Not when the girls are dancin'," he blurted, and picked up the fifteen cents.

I hated the taste of liquor, but if I went into a saloon I usually bought a shot to sip until I left. That night I took my drink and sauntered to the back where the poker games were in progress. I had looked over the players earlier, and could quickly see Malone was not among them. Yet now, once farther into the room, I could see another game in progress, hidden from easy view and behind a small partition. From the look of the chips, it was a high stakes game.

I wasn't surprised to see Malone, back to the wall, dealing out the cards.

"Five card stud," he announced, as the cards whirled around the table, almost in a blur.

He happened that moment to look up and saw me smiling at him.

"Sean!" he grinned, and acted as though he had been expecting me. "Don't leave . . . I want to talk to you."

I nodded an acknowledgment.

Half an hour later Malone cashed in his chips. From the saloon we walked to my hotel, where I picked up my gear and checked out. We went to a house he owned on the lower slope of Russian Hill — a place high enough up the steep incline to have a panoramic view of the bay and the ships in the harbor.

I put my things in the guest bedroom, and by that time it was near midnight. I turned in, leaving Malone reading the papers laid out on the parlor table.

When I awoke, my pocket watch showed seven o'clock. I jumped up with a start. I hadn't slept that late for a long time. It took me a minute to recall that I was at Malone's house, and not far from the wharf.

I wanted to see the bay, so I raised the curtain in my room. But I couldn't see a thing. Fog had rolled in from the sea and had obscured everything outside my window. I walked into the kitchen, and saw Malone, and a strange man at the stove cooking breakfast, a man apparently of Chinese descent.

"Meet Chi Lin," Malone said. "He cares for the house and does the cooking."

"Nice to know you, Chi Lin," I nodded as the man bowed.

After a hearty breakfast, and when the table had been cleared, Chi Lin disappeared and Malone and I sat there, just the two of us. It seemed like old times. He peered over at me.

"The *Dolphin* docked yesterday, with my cargo from China and India, and I'm here to sack the master, Ring Jeffries. He's been one of the best seamen in Sarah's fleet of clipper ships — but I have it by good authority that he's been smuggling opium, peddling it to someone in the Barbary Coast.

"No meaner cutthroats exist than in that part of town. . . . And it's in the middle of that nest of thieves where I'll be going when Jeffries makes his move.

"Chi Lin, and someone else he knows, are watching Jeffries, and they'll get word to me when he leaves the ship. I plan to catch him in the transaction; I want to see it with my own eyes, for he's been too good a sailor to eliminate if not guilty."

"I'll go with you," I told him, wondering about his word, "eliminate."

Malone protested. "No, it's too dangerous, Sean. It's a one-man job. If you were to go along I'd be concerned about your welfare, and I don't need that on my mind. I want to concentrate on nothing but my own well-being."

"Is he stealing part of the cargo, too?" I asked.

"No . . . he's smarter than that — I've checked the lists of lading. It's the opium I'm concerned about. I realize he can make a lot more money smuggling the stuff than being Captain of a ship, but all my Captains and their crews have been warned about bringing it in, and I won't stand for it."

Malone had certain rules in life, where he stood firm on principle, and apparently drugs involved one of them. Other things that might skirt the law didn't seem to matter. But if he'd told the skipper of his ship "no opium," then there'd be hell to pay if the man was smuggling it.

Eight o'clock that evening had come and past before Chi Lin came rushing into the house. He told Malone that Jeffries had left the boat with his First Mate, and they were heading for the Barbary Coast district. They were armed, Chi Lin added, and Jeffries was carrying a large package.

Malone grabbed his coat and followed Chi Lin out the door. I waited until I was sure Malone wouldn't notice me, then trailed close behind them.

They'd reached the warehouse in time to see Jeffries and his First Mate enter the large frame structure. I watched from afar as Malone hesitated a minute or two, and then slowly opened the door. He stepped into total darkness. Inside, his eyes searched in the pitch black nothingness, until he finally could discern the barest sliver of lamplight coming from beneath and alongside a door at the far end of the building.

He silently crept on, up to the door that hung slightly ajar. Through the narrow crack of the opening he could see inside the room, counting seven men, four of them scattered about. And it sounded to Malone as if his Shipmaster and Mate were in trouble. From the tone, he doubted the two would leave the room alive.

He'd heard Jeffries speak up, the anger evident in his voice. "Listen here! . . .Our agreement was you'd only have one other man with you. . . . I see four!"

The one who apparently was the boss, a large rumpled-looking man, sat at a desk, his thick jowls jiggling as he spoke. "Well, I changed my mind! . . . Now let's see the opium."

Jeffries, apprehensive and now obviously fearful for his life, handed over the package, and the thug laid it on the desk and opened it. The paunchy scoundrel was pleased. "Good! . . . Now let's see the diamonds," he demanded.

Jeffries spoke up. "What about the money? I want to see something on the table!"

The scoundrel reached into a lower drawer and pulled out a knapsack as he growled, "Don't fret. I have your money . . . right here."

Jeffries reached for the bag of bills. The large man shouted. "Hold on . . . not so fast! I want to see the diamonds before you take that!"

Jeffries laid a small leather pouch on the desk. The fleshy thug poured out the stones. He stirred the polished gems sparkling brilliant colors, even in the dim light of the lantern, and with a lone stubby finger he'd counted twenty. He muttered to himself, then put the diamonds back in the sack and pulled the drawstring tight.

Five minutes after Malone had entered the warehouse, I'd followed. Stepping into the darkness I quickly moved to the right. I knew I'd have to be careful that Malone didn't take me for the enemy, so I stayed still, getting accustomed to the dark.

After a time, I could make out a shadowy Malone maybe a hundred feet away. I was surprised that he was so intent on eavesdropping he was not aware of my presence — nor of the other man that I'd spotted stealthily working his way toward him, behind some boxes. I inched my way closer, and when the assassin raised his six-gun I threw my bowie, hard and fast, the way Henry had taught me. The thug made an almost silent short gasp, then dropped to the floor, the blade embedded in his heart. I could see that Malone had heard it, and he'd jerked around. He couldn't see me in the darkness, but he looked over at the cutthroat lying on the floor.

Shortly all hell broke loose as gunfire roared from the store room. Malone slammed open the door with his six-gun in his fist, and gunsmoke came rolling out. I rushed forward to help, grabbing my bowie as I went by the dead man. But by the time I'd reached the doorway, Malone was coming out, thumbing more shells into his chambers.

I looked inside the room. The fat merchant thief was slumped over his desk. The others lay in heaps, and surely dead.

Malone looked up after loading his gun. "Come on, Sean, let's go."

But before leaving, he'd grabbed a kerosene can sitting by the pot-bellied stove and doused the room. He quickly threw a match as we jumped out a side opening.

In the street, people were beginning to gather. Malone, carrying the knapsack, walked up to one of the bystanders and asked what was going on.

"I don't know . . . ," replied the onlooker, as he watched the gold then red and blue flames eat away at the wood-frame warehouse and boil skyward.

We could hear the clang of a fire wagon, as we began climbing the steep slope to Malone's house. I peered back into a night sky tinged with red. Malone never once looked back.

When we had stepped inside the house, he scolded me. "I thought I told you not to follow!"

"No . . ." I replied. "You told me I couldn't go with you!"

Malone produced his familiar smile, then reached over to pat my shoulder. "Well, I'm glad you did, lad. I knew it was you when I saw the knife. You saved my life, and I'm obliged."

We walked into the kitchen, but before sitting down, Malone reached in his pocket, pulled out the leather pouch, and threw it on the table. "Take any one of the diamonds you want, Sean. They belong to Jones Shipping, but you can have one out of my share."

I'd refused at first, thinking it wouldn't be right. But Malone insisted, and I said I'd accept if he'd pick the gem for me.

Back in my room, I sewed it into the cuff of my pants.

The next morning, after breakfast, I told Malone about Katrina — my love for her and the frightening circumstances of her disappearance.

I could see Malone's concern. "You're chasing a ghost, Sean. You'd best quit running around looking in every town between here and Cheyenne. . . . If she's alive, and she loves you, she'll find you. The problem is you don't know where to look for her, but she knows the way to find you. She has the key and you don't."

"I suppose you're right," I replied. "It's just that I think I should be doing something. I can't stand around helpless and useless."

"I understand," Malone acknowledged. "But you just keep on with your life, and when Katrina can, she'll contact the Statler in Denver, or Sarah in St. Louis. And if she's alive and she doesn't get in touch with you some way, then maybe you're better off without her."

I knew he was right. I'd thought then I would find a job there in San Francisco until spring. "But one thing I don't want is to be chained to a desk in an office somewhere. I need to be out and about."

The next day, I walked into Wells Fargo looking for work. After I had listed my experience, the manager told me nothing was available right then, but he thought he'd have an opening in March, riding shotgun on the stage to Sacramento.

As I left the office his shout followed. "Hey, partner, if you're around in March, come back. I'd like to hire ya!"

Twenty

IN EARLY FEBRUARY 1872 I stopped my blue-roan and looked back at the town of San Francisco. Genius had left the stables near the outskirts like a shot. He'd been cooped up so long, he wanted to run; and I just let him go. We were a good three miles from the bay town when I stopped to rest him. Pausing for a time, I rubbed him down, and as he cooled, I canvassed the scene with admiring eyes.

Words can't describe the beauty of that land by the sea. The lifting fog of morning had challenged the magnificent sun in the sky, but it had lost its quest, vaporizing into a vanishing death. A three-masted clipper and brig rode the Pacific with full white sails furled against the clouds, while north in the bay lay anchored ships with bare masts, rocking in the swells against a backdrop of stately homes and green-foliaged mountains. West, as far as eyes could see, out where the water and sky meet, rose a canvas that could only be painted by God. There, massing in the high firmament, cathedral clouds gathered, slowly swirling into shades of white and ashen blue.

But I was anxious now to be on my way, and I reined the gelding south, though still turning in my saddle to look above the sea, where it seemed God's throne shone gold, as angel clouds seemed to have gathered around in prayer.

Malone's work had been accomplished in San Francisco, and he had sailed in late January for Savannah. He'd strolled the *Dolphin* decks that trip as its Master.

John Allison, the ship's Second Mate, was just twenty-three years of age, but he had sailed the seven seas some fourteen years, for he'd been nine when he first went to sea. And by the time they had berthed in Georgia, Malone had figured the seaman could well handle the ship's command.

"He no doubt could take the *Dolphin* now," Malone had said before he'd left, "but I want to show him a Captain's task firsthand, and what I expect of him when he becomes her Master."

Allison going to sea at nine reminded me of when I was seven and had sailed with Pa. We rode the swells for over ten long months, a time in my life I'll never forget — a time I got to know my father, who before then had been like a stranger, always at sea and rarely home. Those days seemed to me like yesterday, as I thought back to that April day of 1858.

Pa had shouted to me up the stairway at Mosswood. "Sean! . . . It's time to go!"

I took another look out of our second-floor window. She was there all right. Pa's clipper ship, the *White Swan*, lay up in the bay, looking majestic with her bare masts beseeching a pure blue sky. I was excited beyond belief at the adventure before me when I ran down the steps, and yet somewhat sad, with Ma standing there crying.

Pa was consoling her as best he could. "All will be well, Elizabeth. I'll look after the lad. You know this will be good for him."

Ma's tears spilled over as she nodded her understanding. "I know . . ." she'd acknowledged, holding me close before turning loose. Then Ma kissed Pa, and kissed me again.

"Sean . . . you take care," she told me as I went out the door. It broke my heart to see her so melancholy, but I knew Pa and I had a job to be done.

Pa and I walked to the coast, not quite a mile away. As we began to plod across the deep sand near the beach, I could feel a homesick loneliness at leaving Ma. I stopped and peered back to Mosswood. I could tell, even from the water's edge, that she was still standing on the high ground southwest of the house, watching with her hand above her eyes to shade from the morning sun. She waved one last time, and I waved back.

When we neared the breakers, eight of the ship's crew dropped the longboat to the sea and headed for shore. We waded water out to the beached boat, and I scampered up the ropes into the craft before Pa could lift me. Pa smiled and quipped, as the crew took oars to return to the ship, "Sean, me boy, it looks like you'll take to the sea just fine — you'll do all right!"

The *White Swan* was one of the fastest ships afloat, her frame made of white oak timbers and five-inch yellow pine planking. For strength, she was held together by metal straps.

The minute we'd stepped aboard, Pa gave orders to "*Sail ho!*" At the command, the men rushed to their stations, and in minutes sails were hoisted up the foremast, mainmast, and mizzenmast. Trimmed, Pa's clipper ship was slim and built for speed. And he was confident that in full canvas, no other ship afloat could catch her.

Once aboard, Pa had me drop my seabag in our cabin, then sign the articles for the run. I officially became a seaman.

We'd pulled anchor and set sail south, then ruddered southeast as the ship's hull split calm seas, clipping twelve knots through the water. Right off, that first day, Pa taught me how to figure the speed we were traveling, and it became part of my duties. I would toss off the stern a knotted line stored on a spinning reel. The line had a small, flat, wooden piece attached perpendicular to it — a piece I'd heard them call the log or drogue. The line flowed out as the bow of the ship raced on, splitting the rolling sea, until the sandglass at my side ran out. Then I would count the knots, already tied at measured intervals on the line, and the number that I'd totaled was our nautical speed. It was Pa that then recorded the knots in his log book.

My second morning aboard ship was nothing but oceans of water and sky, as far as eyes could see, with the ship gliding through the swells in a dipping and rising motion. But before that day had dropped its curtain of light, I'd had my sea legs.

Pa'd introduced me to his First Mate, Turk Nelson, then thirty years of age. He was a nice-looking man, but with a deep scar slashed across his jaw that gave a rakish efffect. He'd carried a long knife at his left side, behind a wide-wrapped sash around his waist; on his right rested his large flintlock pistol.

Turk enlightened me about the ship, since Pa was busy at the wheel, and I'd discovered that at midship, the clipper was armed with six Saker cannon, three starboard and three port. They fired a nine-pound ball that carried some four thousand yards, and an experienced gunner, Turk said, could wreak havoc to an enemy ship and crew. He showed me as well the various shot that already had been made up — case shot for spraying decks, chain shot for bringing down rigging, and hot shot to set enemy sails afire.

Pa's *White Swan* had a crew of thirty regular men, but also aboard that first leg of our journey were some twenty others, men passengers who would work off part of their six hundred dollar fare from Louisiana to San Francisco as extra hands aboard. I could tell that most were down and out vagabonds, expecting to hit it rich in the gold fields, and after looking over the tough, ragged lot of them, I figured they probably didn't care how they got rich — by finding the gold themselves or taking it from some poor miner at his claim, or in the alleys of town.

We'd sailed from Breton Sound into the Gulf of Mexico, to the Caribbean Sea, and past Cuba, Jamaica, Haiti, and the Dominican Republic, about which I'd heard so many amazing tales from Pa — small countries with bountiful yields from their lands, but seemingly at constant war with themselves or their colonial masters. We berthed for a day at Santo Domingo, the sights of which lit up my young, impressionable imagination. From there we sailed out beyond the South American coastline, far from any sight of land. Two days later we crossed the equator, where I was initiated with the seamen's ritual for crossing that mighty divide. The Crossing the Line Ceremony I was told would make me worthy to enter King Neptune's domain.

Needless to say, my eyes lit up with anticipation, but I was taken aback when, out of the ranks of the seamen, large buckets of salt water were poured onto me, almost stealing away my breath. Small ocean fish from the buckets hit me on the head, and one was placed into my gasping open mouth.

Two able crewmen then took hold of me, one at my head, one at my feet, and swung me back and forth, as if in preparation to tossing me overboard. I was at that point wondering if, indeed, they might deliver me to the deep, but when I'd caught Pa's eye on a swing back toward center deck, I had seen him wink at me amidst his laughter. I knew I'd be safe from actual harm amidst the seamen's jovial rites.

In all, I survived the raucous ritual and became a humbled member of the Order of Shellbacks. Pa gave a short speech, welcoming me to Neptune's League, and the men all raised a cup of ale to my new milestone. I, too, was given a cup of the brew, but could barely tolerate its bite. And from the conversation I'd heard thereabouts amongst the men on that momentous occasion, I knew I had received but a token of what they usually put forth in such events.

Things soon got back to normal aboard ship, and Pa and Turk worked with me on the different sailors' knots. In no time I was tying the splice, figure eight, sheepshank, bowline, reef, and clove hitch.

At times, our sleek craft, with her sails straining aloft, her hull leaping crests of waves, skimmed the seas at fourteen knots, our canvas full and set, in strong currents. East of Argentina, we'd had two separate storms; then off the Falkland shores, which the Argentinians call *Las Islas Malvinas* — the Malvinas — we found some especially rough seas, into west winds blowing. My fear was only mitigated by Pa's calm and reassurance.

Nearing Cape Horn, however, Pa had ordered me below to our cabin, as he'd lashed himself to the deck chair, with his hands on the shrouds and the wheel. I had wanted to stay by, but he'd refused my request.

It was impossible to see anything but splashing water out of my porthole. Ferocious winds and freezing rain buffeted the ship, and for seamen hanging to the hurricane deck, it was like riding a bucking steed. Sailors came below caked with ice on near frozen hands and feet.

Pa hadn't left his station during that storm for two full days, and it had worried me. But on the third morning, when there came a short lull, and while the gale abated somewhat, I'd managed to reach Pa at the wheel by holding onto anything nailed down that I could grab. When Pa saw me on the spar, I handed him a cup of hot coffee, though much had spilt as I'd struggled on my way. Nevertheless, he downed the remainder but sternly added, "Lad, I told ya to stay below deck!"

I pleaded my case. "I know, Pa, but how can I be a sailor and stay below?"

Pa never said a thing; he just grabbed hold of me and strapped me to an eyebolt in the deck. The tether was ten-foot long, to where I could stand or sit as I pleased, with Pa some five feet away.

It wasn't long and the storm worsened again. Pa was forcefully wheeling the ship from crashing into perilous shores, forever weighing the odds as to the sails, always shouting orders and listening for Mates on watch. He noted every lurch . . . and every roaring wind change in the rigging, for I knew he had the lives of the crew in his hands.

I had tried to stand amidst the force of the gale, releasing my hold, but was swept tight to the end of the tether. Winds tore the breath from my lungs, and all I could see were topsails and enormous waves of water.

It was then that Turk, hanging on for dear life, came aft. Not more than ten feet away, he'd shouted to Pa, but to no avail. Coming closer, he cupped hands around his mouth.

"Cap'n . . . winds blow north-northwest. Shall I take down the skys'ls?" he screamed in sharp winds that carried his words quickly away almost before they'd left his mouth.

"Mr. Mate, can ye see the head sails?" Pa shouted back.

Turk moved fore, leaning into the wind to the mainmast, barely visible in a maze of roiling sea and sky and buried lower sails awash. Turk slowly returned to the spar.

"Aye, Cap'n, she's there like a shadow and in place," he shouted above the din.

"Then let her be, First Mate . . . the winds blow right!"

The morning brought calming seas and sunshine. We'd past the Cape and sailed on north-northwest. Crews cleaned the deck and assessed the damage. Two men had been killed as we had rounded the Cape — one when he'd gone up the foremast to check on the skysail. The sail had blown out of its boltropes, knocking the lad loose, and he'd fallen to his death from the topmast crosstree. The other hand we'd lost the following day, when a gust of wind had fish-tailed the craft, as a gigantic wave had hit the ship, and he was swept helplessly overboard.

It was but two days later that we'd docked at a native village along the coast of Chile, another colorful and exciting adventure for any young lad. And while there, we'd bartered our trinkets and tools of various kind to the locals, in exchange for their sea otter pelts.

A hundred days from home, we harbored again, in San Francisco. It was there that we sold the merchants our hold of miners' tools, sugar, flour, boots, and clothing. And from the northern trappers and traders we bought their pelts of beaver and mink.

Two days later, we sailed from San Francisco Bay with a hold full of the pelts, heading for the South China Seas. My excitement was etched on my face, and Pa chuckled as he told me, "This'll be the time of your life, Sean."

After forty days crossing the Pacific, we docked in a deep water port at Canton, China. Pa'd told again how proud he was of me — that he'd feared many times on that voyage I might be sickened by the seas — yet I'd never once become ill.

"You're made for the sea," he told me.

Ashore, Pa and I'd gone to the merchants' warehouse, arranging to stay the night. A week later we had sold our pelts, and with money in hand, for our return voyage we bought tea and the delicate Canton cups and saucers much-prized back in America. After a fortnight in Canton, we pulled anchor and sailed from the harbor on shortened canvas.

From there we took the winds south-southwest, making ports of call at Danang and Saigon, the major commercial ports of ancient Viet Nam. Danang's harbor had been a large and safe haven, though in 1858, the year we were there, French and Spanish ships had entered the Han River port and had let loose their cannon on the proud city, as part of an ultimate plan to take over that country.

The South China Seas held more danger for us, however, for when we'd left the port of Saigon, again on shortened canvas, we were attacked by pirates, rampant in those waters. A two-masted brig and two sloops had tried closing on us. Then in an instant, shot from the closest brig hit our foremast, near the topsail, where it hung precariously to the mast.

Pa had shouted orders for me to go below deck, but, out of fear for his safety and unquenchable curiosity, I'd stayed near the ladder to watch.

Six men were quickly sent aloft to fix the damaged skysail, and then, instead of heaving to, as demanded by the threatening pirate ship, Pa barked out more orders and wheeled the rudder sharply right for the open sea. The First and Second Mates were rushing men to their stations while Pa called for full sail, followed by the Second Mate's own shout of encouragement.

"*Haul away lively, lads!*"

The crew, fast to it, unwound line from the spools, as the enormous canvas billowed. In short order the foremast had been repair-rigged spliced with another piece of mast, and the skysail again blossomed in a South China Sea west wind. In our race to safety, the pirates fired several more shots that blessedly hit water fore and aft, but they'd never had a chance in catching us, for we had pulled farther and farther away from the slower rigs into the open sea.

It was time, then, to relax, to celebrate our besting of the would-be plunderers. We'd traveled on through glorious seas to the Malay peninsula area, making port at Singapore, the small island off its southern tip. We moved on to the old fortress city of Batavia, on the island of Java, and finally far west again, through the Indian Ocean, to Madagascar, off of southeast Africa. There we were forced to surreptitiously trade far offshore with the few foreigners allowed by the renowned Queen Ranavalona to deal in commerce with her country — some few privileged European merchants.

I knew I was but a mere child in years, but I felt that I had experienced more beautiful lands of enchanting pasts than grown men five times my age. And by then, after our dealings at Madagascar, our hold was overflowing with the added coffee, pepper, sugar, and spices we had acquired.

From Madagascar we eagerly set full sail once again, around the Cape of Good Hope at the south of Africa's tip, on westward. We had been at sea two hundred forty-five days. Many a time we had breasted typhoon and gale with sails whipping in the wind, but we'd made it through thus far without additional loss of life.

Days from our last stop at Madagascar, after crossing the South Atlantic Ocean, we'd finally lowered sails and pulled port at Rio de Janeiro, Brazil, to freshen our supply of food and water. Two days later, we trimmed sail and pulled anchor, on our way again, in what turned out to be surprisingly cold winds and angry seas. Then forty-nine days out of Rio, on our way north-northwest, we had sighted Barbados, at the far eastern end of the Caribbean.

"*Land ho!*"shouted the Second Mate from his perch atop the mainmast spar of thc main skysail.

We were just three days from home, and Pa never made a move to berth at the port. Then around noon, as we plied calm seas, came a shout from aloft in the main mast.

"*Sail ho!*"

We rode the seas with shortened sail as Pa studied the horizon with his glass, and Turk stood by for orders. A short time later, with his decision made, Pa excitedly shouted, "*Full sail ahead! All gunners to their sta-*

tions! . . . All fighting men armed with pike, sword, and musket!"

My heart seemed to stop its rhythms at the moment. I had thought we were safely on our final leg of the journey home. The deck looked like a confusion of bodies rushing about, but I discovered it would turn out to be a well-organized placement of men at their posts. All during that rush of feet, the First and Second Mates were shouting armament orders as the crew quickly prepared for action.

I felt the ship's movement as Pa'd turned the wheel and ruddered the clipper toward the approaching vessel. The intruder, heavy with cargo, lay low in the water. She was a three-masted bark, but we could see she was immediately filling her sails to change course. Yet the security of the deserted coastline was too far for her, and in half an hour our faster ship had the curious vessel cut off from shore.

It was then that she ran up her colors — as Pa had well known — the skull and crossbone of the dreaded Barbary pirate. Our brave and adventurous seamen held their stations for the fight, and I could see by the horde of sailors aboard and manning the bark's decks that we'd be outnumbered two to one. I later learned that the bark had been a merchant ship lately taken and commandeered by the pirates. Its cargo had been sold in the islands of the Caribbean and replaced with captured treasure, valuables then on their way to North Africa — a hold full of plundered loot.

We heaved to and shortened sail as Pa shouted to the gunners. "*Fire at will!*"

My heart was racing as the breath was nearly forced from me by the concussion. Outsailing the pirate ship, we raked her decks with three cannon broadsides, causing mayhem as the marauders tumbled to the deck. Their main and foremast were soon toppled as our cannon roared, and screams had filled the smoke-layered air. Grappling hooks had locked the two warring vessels together, and our sailors leapt to the stolen bark's deck into furious hand-to-hand fighting.

As the violence continued, I remained beneath piles of canvas and ropes on the deck, too frightened to leave — almost too frightened to watch.

Then, finally, to my relief, the Captain of the stolen bark, knowing he'd been completely defeated, struck colors.

We'd lost seven men in the fierce battle, the bark twenty-nine. Of the bark's twenty-six remaining men, ten that had been originally shanghaied by the thieves had signed on with Pa's clipper.

After an inventory of the captured ship's hold, we transferred the valuable cargo to the *White Swan*. But while the two ships had been grappled together during the heat of the battle, they both had drifted closer and closer to the reef along the shore. When we finally cut the bark and her crew free, with her rudder and masts shattered, she continued to drift helplessly toward her ultimate destruction. When she'd finally hit hard, it gutted her hull, and she slowly broke up and sank.

As to any remaining sea dogs aboard her, I figured some surely must have made it ashore.

The golden sun arched high that early March day of 1859 when we'd unfurled sails and dropped anchor in deep Gulf water. I could distinguish Mosswood in the distance on high ground. The house, wrapped in purple shadow, looked as majestic as I had remembered.

We had spent some three hundred days at sea. It would not take much to convince me there was no place like home.

Twenty-One

KATRINA CONCLUDED in January of 1872 that the Carson Butte area was nothing more than a country silenced in buried snow. With the passes drifted high, there had been no freight in and out since early November, and the wagon roads probably would not open again until late March. Folks had earlier stocked up on supplies, with the hope they had enough to carry them through the winter months.

In a normal season, however, she'd been told, life in Carson Butte wasn't all that active either. The only news in and out of town was the freight line run by Jacob Miles that traveled to Ogden on Mondays and returned Thursdays. What news Miles brought back was about the only contact the townsfolk had with the outside world.

Local businessmen like Pete Landry and others had Miles's wagons and mule teams bring in needed supplies once a week. The Wells Fargo stage hadn't rolled across the bridge into Carson Butte since '69, back when the town was in its heyday, and gold was plentiful. Wells Fargo had come to town then and opened shop; but now their office was closed, and from what Katrina had heard, they probably wouldn't start up again.

The two saloons in town were some of the busiest places, of

course. The Sluice Box was run by Rock Jensen, a rather unwholesome boor of a man, not too particular who frequented his establishment. It was where the undesirables settled in for drink. The bar cornered across the street was the Gold Dust, owned by Pete MacArthur, a red-haired, jovial man of large stature, a no-nonsense guy who put up with no funny business. His was a place where decent townsfolk would go, along with the local countryfolk wanting a presence of respectability.

It seemed inevitable that the two different establishments would survive in Carson Butte, for it was certain that people are not all alike, and the habits of one were not that of another.

Not long after Katrina had settled there, she'd stepped the boardwalk looking amongst the mostly deserted shops. That day, she slowly strolled by MacArthur's saloon, noticing that the corner section of his large building was empty. As she'd looked through the dingy glass pane, she could see that once upon a time it had been connected to the Gold Dust.

For three months Katrina had been speculating in her mind about that empty portion of the structure on the corner, with its wide double doors angled at forty-five degrees to the main and side streets. She'd thought that if what she had seen inside through the window could be cleaned up, she had some ideas — things she might pattern after what she had found in her travels through some of the West's larger cities and towns.

It was nearly noontime when Katrina, bundled in heavy clothes, plodded a world of stark white as far as eyes could see, amidst a haze of blowing snow. A narrow scooped pathway over two feet deep wound its way down the three blocks of buildings. A flurry of wind lifted the powdery snow from the walkway and showered Katrina as she opened the door to the Gold Dust Saloon.

She wiped her feet on the gunny sack inside the door and hesitated a bit on entering the establishment, though she knew that MacArthur also served food, and the place was regularly frequented by women with their husbands. Though she had no man with her, she'd thought she should be at ease, for she had heard nothing but good about Pete MacArthur.

He had a pleasant smile on his face as she'd walked up to the bar.

"Good morning, Mr. MacArthur. . . . May I have a cup of coffee, please?"

"Sure, lass," he replied. "And what brings you out on a cold, dismal winter's day?"

Like all other natives of Carson Butte, MacArthur was charmed by the lovely Katrina. "*What man's heart wouldn't skip a beat*," he'd thought, "*just lookin' upon her beauty*."

"Well, it's a business dealing I have in mind, and I was told you own the corner building adjacent. I would like to talk with you about renting that corner, for I think it's what I've been looking to find."

MacArthur turned and nodded toward the dining area. "Let's sit at a table, young lady."

Katrina took her coffee, walked the few steps, then pulled back a straight chair and sat down.

"I indeed own the corner," MacArthur said, and continued. "What I have here and what's there were all one building when I put it up in '65. Every night for three years the place was packed — and then the bottom fell out in '68. . . . I've closed off most of the corner area now, its width and length near fifty by a hundred fifty. I'd kept open the bar area here, but still had not been makin' ends meet until I put a kitchen in the back and the Mrs. and I started sellin' meals."

MacArthur confessed that his wife Susan did most of the cooking.

Pausing in thought, Katrina then asked, "Do you mind if I look at the building? It would let me know if it would meet my needs."

"Well, sure," he replied. "Look at whatever you want. There's a door there in the kitchen area to the closed-off part of the building."

Pointed in the right direction, Katrina first walked toward the back, to a stairway that went up along the south wall, stopping at a balcony overlooking the saloon. Two short hallways and seven sleeping rooms were up there, though the seventh was really two. The balcony and the seventh room protruded into the vacant corner building some ten feet, above the empty room below. Everything inside was covered with dust and hanging cobwebs.

Back down the stairs, Katrina went to the kitchen. From there she opened the door that led to the main floor of the corner building. Halfway along the south wall was a large twenty-foot arched doorway, with two steps down into the vacant room; the opening, now partitioned shut, connected the two buildings. A counter east of the doorway went to the front of the building. North of the counter were dust-covered tables and chairs.

Katrina walked among the tables, and as she examined the room, at the rear of the building she could see a stage, framed with what looked like purple velvet curtains beneath the film of dust. An old upright piano, ornate and imposing in the silence, graced the front of the stage. To the right, and below the balcony and seventh room above, Katrina found a wall partitioned, with a closed door. Peeking inside, Katrina saw what must have once served as dressing rooms.

After almost an hour, Katrina walked back through the kitchen, into the saloon. The place was empty, and MacArthur awaited her at the table. She sat down, still deep in thought, as he poured her another cup of coffee and waited for her to speak.

"Mr. MacArthur," she finally said, "I want to rent the empty building!"

He stroked his chin, considering her words, then cautiously warned her, "You know it would take a lot of money to fix up the place."

Katrina nodded. "Yes . . . it could. But it needn't. What the place really wants is a lot of elbow grease. . . . I can do that. My problem is I have but fifteen dollars to my name. I could, however, clean and fix up the upstairs room to live in, where the balcony overlooks the empty building, if you could wait for a while on the rent."

"What is it you want to do with the building?" MacArthur asked.

Katrina leaned forward and looked him in the eye. "In the front part, it was my thought to put in a small baking establishment, much like those in the large cities. I know how you men love pastries, and cakes and pies. The tables and chairs are already there. Also, I've had experience acting in plays, and after a time I'd like to put on some small productions — even have the community, the audience, become involved in them, perhaps with townsfolk singing."

MacArthur was skeptical. "You'd have the expense of putting in an oven — maybe two — for your goods." But he couldn't dampen her spirits.

". . . Not if I started out by using your oven in the kitchen, and in exchange, I'd help your wife with the cooking she's been doing. Then we could take down that ugly partition between the two buildings."

MacArthur figured it would be an opportunity for him to help the young lassie, and maybe improve his own property, in addition to giving Susan a hand in the kitchen. He pondered whether it might indirectly help his own business as well.

"Well, young lady, you know it just might work. I do like the idea. But you can't handle it alone," he mulled. And then he hastened to add, "Tell ya what I'll do. We'll go partners, split the profit on your business after expenses, and I'll put up the cash to get it started."

Katrina was surprised; she knew she had just heard a once-in-a-lifetime offer.

"You have a partner, Mr. MacArthur!" Katrina replied, and held out her hand. They closed their arrangement, with no signatures required.

Walking back to the General Store, Katrina's thoughts were running apace. She'd reasoned that she might ask the daughter of Julius McBride, the blacksmith, to help in the shop, for Sharon was about Katrina's age and they had become close the past few months. And Sharon had confided that she would some day like to try her hand at acting as well.

Before Katrina stepped into the General Store, she said she'd quite suddenly thought again of me. She knew she needed to get word someway that she was safe; but now, with snowdrifts still some twenty feet in the passes, that was impossible.

A week later, Katrina resigned her position at the General Store, to the great regret of Mr. and Mrs. Landry — though they were pleased with her spirit and enthusiasm for the new venture. Anything that might keep customers close in town, and bring new ones in, was a welcomed plan.

Katrina moved into the upstairs room at the Gold Dust after she had scrubbed and cleaned the accumulated dust. She'd determined that the following day would be time enough to start working on her baking area and theater section, which by then she had decided to call "The Showcase."

Three days out of San Francisco, I rode into Sacramento and boarded the train for Cheyenne. I had loaded Genius into the stock car, where I'd covered his shoulders and back with a heavy blanket.

When Malone had left by ship for Savannah, I'd first thought I might stay the winter in San Francisco, but I soon became restless. I knew February was not the time to travel across the high ranges of the Sierra, Wasatch, and Rocky Mountains, but I'd talked to a kindly merchant on Montgomery Street who'd told me the trains were hauling freight that direction every day. And the railroads in the Sierras, he'd said, had built up to nearly forty miles of snow sheds to protect the tracks, at places where there'd been seventy-foot drifts in years past. In other areas, the railroad was using Bucker plows, clearing out drifts as deep as thirty feet, each plow at times pushed by as many as twelve steam engines.

The trip wasn't pleasant, for the train had simply crawled its way through the mountains. Many times we'd be stopped for hours, waiting for crews to clear tracks of the drifted snow where no sheds had been placed. It took what felt like forever to reach Cheyenne, and as we had passed through Utah Territory, I'd felt a hollow emptiness, a helplessness I couldn't explain. During that trip I'd spent many an hour checking on Genius in the stock car, covering him with additional blankets to keep him warm, and breaking ice to see he had adequate water.

Then, once I'd finally reached Cheyenne, I again was simply restless, and decided to continue on right away to Denver, as the tracks were said to have been cleared.

Late the following day I arrived. I rode Genius over to the Statler Hotel and took a room. I'd inquired, but no letter was awaiting me there from Katrina.

In all, I spent a month rambling about the city, hoping beyond hope that Katrina might suddenly appear, or send word, before reluctantly boarding a train once again, for St. Louis.

It was early April when I rode up the lane to White Oaks, my way heralded by battalions of still bare-limbed trees, just budding out at their edges. Henry greeted me at the door with surprise, but evident joy. We shook hands and walked together into the spacious entry.

"Miss Sarah not here," he told me. "She in Savannah awaitin' Malone's ship to dock." After polite conversation, Henry wanted to know all about San Francisco and the far West. I told him a little of what happened, but not everything, explaining that maybe Malone might want to tell fill him in on all our adventures.

Henry grunted. "No, Malone, say nothin'. He be tight-lipped what he do. He a good, tough man . . . good for Sarah; but he live a mystery. You tell me, if you will; I be wantin' to know."

I told Henry what had taken place in the city by the bay, and, predictably, he simply shook his head, as if in disbelief.

"I thought so," he said. "I met Jeffries one time there in Savannah, 'n told Sarah then he no good. . . . I see shifty in his eyes; he couldn' hide it from me. . . . And I think Malone had know'd it too, but he'd not be wantin' to change her father's favorite Cap'n.

"Mr. Jones, bless his soul, he always be a poor judge o' men. . . . But Malone wouldn' make that mistake, except for Sarah's plea to keep Jeffries on with the fleet."

Henry finished with his evaluation of Ring Jeffries, then smiled. ". . . So you saved Malone's life?" he asked with both amusement and pride.

"Yes . . . but I wouldn't want it known," I replied.

Henry chuckled. "Don't ya be worry, lad; no one hear it from me. But I proud of ya. The knife blade right through the heart to the hilt . . . and in the darkness of a warehouse! Why, you'll do, lad; ya might even be better'n Malone with a blade!"

"Well, I don't know about that," I told him. "But I'll never be your equal, Henry . . . that much I do know."

Henry asked to see my bowie knife, so I'd reached to my back and pulled it from its sheath. He studied the blade and grinned.

He hefted it for balance. "I see you honed the thick of it. . . . I like it! It steady," he summed up.

Henry pulled out his blade and compared the two. "I think your be some lighter than mine. It give more speed."

I told him I had tried to shape it like his. "Do you think I've honed it too slim?" I inquired.

Henry was certain. "No! . . . it sound like it must air perfect."

Henry added, "Tomorrow, I'd like a throw or two with th' knife, if that be all right with ya."

The following day, after hurling my knife at a fence post, Henry acknowledged, "I think I hone my blade a little more."

A month passed, and on the 1st of May I received a letter from Louis Dumont, my attorney in New Orleans. He'd wanted to see me — soon, if possible — business he had not wanted to write about by mail. I'd wanted to wait for Malone and Sarah to come back, and in my return letter told Dumont I would try to be in New Orleans by early June.

I still had heard nothing from Katrina, and melancholy ruled my hapless days.

On the 10th of May, Malone and Sarah rode up the lane to the house beneath arching trees covered with new oak leaves turning a deep green along the darkened limbs. What was it the pundits often said? . . ."*Good things come in sets of three*."

I figured it must be true, for that very day I'd received a letter from Katrina. I could almost not contain my excitement and, yet, my trepidation.

My Dearest Sean,

I have been unable to contact you because of the dire circumstances I have of late been through. But now, be assured that all is well.

I am in the town of Carson Butte, near the northern border of Utah Territory, where I have remained since a very distasteful end to the situation with my stepfather — but I will tell you more of that later.

I have a business, now, running a pastry shop — a small bakery — and am putting on plays, as well, for the dear folks in this area.

In a month or two I will have saved enough so that I can come to you, if that is your wish — though I would rather you came to Carson Butte if possible. The townsfolk here have taken me in without a question, and have been so kind, dear Sean, that I would not feel right in leaving here yet for another year. I hope that you can understand that sense of obligation I have to them.

I await your letter, and worry you may feel differently about our understanding. But I want you to know I am yours forever.

With My Love, Katrina

I was so happy to receive Katrina's letter that I had trouble thinking clearly, until I remembered my necessary trip to New Orleans on the following day. It was then that I'd become despondent again, realizing I could not leave for Carson Butte until I had finished my business with Dumont.

Malone had found his chart of the West, though I could not locate the town on the map. But that night, I wrote to Katrina, explaining to her that my love had never waned, and that I would happily come to Carson Butte as soon as possible. I'd put the letter in a small packet, and had decided to enclose, as well, the diamond Malone that had given me, with the explanation that she should sell the gem if she needed money.

The next morning, as I prepared to leave for the docks along the Mississippi, I gave the package to Henry to mail.

Twenty-Two

IN LESS THAN a month, Katrina and her helper, Sharon McBride, had washed, cleaned, and scrubbed MacArthur's old corner building until it looked like new. With his help, they removed the partition between the two businesses, and people around could hardly believe how attractive the old vacant interior now bestowed itself.

During that time, Katrina had helped Susan MacArthur in the kitchen with the cooking and dishes. Mrs. MacArthur was a plump, jovial lady, and she'd mothered Katrina like she was her own.

Katrina opened the bake shop in late February, during a blinding snowstorm. Her first customers were the Landrys, McBrides, and Bentleys. Then later in the day, she saw Jacob Miles stomp snow from his boots before coming in to have a plate of the Showcase's special fried doughnuts. And while Miles was there, Grace Shore came in, from the dress shop, and had a pastry as well.

At eight that evening, Katrina was in the course of preparing to close the shop when Rock Jensen, from the Sluice Box Saloon, stormed in and ordered a piece of cherry pie. Katrina had never liked the man, who'd always seemed to devour her from head to toe with his piercing beady eyes. But she'd looked up through the wide archway into the saloon, and felt safe when she saw MacArthur washing glasses at the bar.

Jensen had toyed with his fork as he watched her every move. Then, much to her relief Marshal Clayborne showed up for a bit of dessert and coffee, and before long, Jensen left, with an indifferent nod to the Marshal.

When Clayborne had sat down, he'd expressed his concern to Katrina, having seen the disreputable Jensen cross the street.

"I figured I'd just check on ya. The man's no good, and I'm just waitin' for him to make a wrong move, so's I can run him out of town.

He could see the tension on Katrina's face. "But don't you worry, young lady, I don't suppose there's a man in town who won't see to it that you're safe. I'd pity anyone who bothered ya."

Katrina thanked the Marshal, relieved and grateful to hear that so many kind souls were watching out for her.

That first day she had taken in just under four dollars, and she'd sunk down in a chair, discouraged, realizing she would definitely have to do better to make the place pay. But she knew, as well, that it had been a late winter day when neither man nor beast should have left their shelter.

As the weather brightened, so did Katrina's business. Before long, the placer miners from the north, along with ranch hands from the Bear River country, started coming to Carson Butte.

In March, Katrina began rehearsals on a play she'd recalled from her own acting days, that would need only a cast of five. Shakespeare's plays, she knew from trekking around the West with her mother, were out of the question, for that might require some twelve to forty performers.

With her cast of locals and herself, the play opened the first Friday in April to a packed room. The flyers Mr. Charlton had printed for her, which had been distributed around the countryside, had accomplished their goal. The performance turned into a festive occasion for the town, and a success for Katrina's small theater and bake shop. In addition, Pete MacArthur did a booming business that day as well. The locals had been kept inside too long that cold winter — they were more than anxious to get out and see something new.

Spring had come late that year in Carson Butte, and before the countryside had prepared for summer, it was almost May. In the past month, the town had seen four new business tenants move in, though some forty other vacant buildings still remained on the street from the early boom days.

In the meantime, gold had been found nearby on Kitten Creek, some ten miles north, at a site where granite stood on end with long escarpments and deep canyons — not a big discovery, but enough to bring in new placers, scratch-panning for the precious metal.

Katrina's plays were by then performed each Friday and Saturday night, with a ticket price of twenty-five cents for adults and ten cents for the children. And they continued to be a success, as were her community singalongs after the performance. Many a tear was shed at most every performance when the audience harmonized the tunes of days gone by, songs that stirred memories of home and family long and far away.

On the third weekend in May, Katrina's play had sold out and Carson Butte was overflowing with miners and cowhands from as far as forty miles distant. All had heard of the beautiful girl at Carson Butte who could act and sing like heaven itself, and they flocked to the town in high country. By mid-June, ten more of the vacant buildings had been rented or sold, and up the slope, just north of the Katrina's Showcase, a church was in the process of being framed. And Mr. Charlton was now putting out a bi-weekly newspaper on his old foot-pedaling printer.

Then suddenly, in late June, Wells Fargo returned to its old space along the street, with a stagecoach arriving every other day. It surprised no one that following Saturday when Andrew Brown blew into town on the afternoon stage. He'd come to see what was actually happening in Carson Butte, after hearing Wells Fargo had resumed its operations to the village. Two years earlier, Brown had operated the hotel in town, but void of business and broke, he'd been forced to lock the doors, pack his wagon, and rumble off to greener pastures.

When Brown stepped down off the stage that day, he was amazed at the number of people, mostly families, crowding the boardwalks, moving in and out of the shops. Astonished at what lay before his eyes, he walked to the General Store to talk to Pete Landry, for if anyone knew what had transformed the place, he surely would. When Landry had finally finished with his customer, Brown pulled him aside and queried the mayor.

"Good golly, Pete. What's goin' on? . . . What's happened with the town? I can't believe what I'm seein'! . . . Did the miners make another strike hereabouts?"

Andrew Brown couldn't stop asking questions.

"Whoa!" Landry answered. "I know it's hard to believe that the village is growing again. But it's true. It's like the old days — except a more reliable class of people has come to town — steady, regular folk; not so many n'er do wells."

Landry told Brown about the small find on Kitten Creek, and how it had brought in a few placers working their claims.

"Then what else has happened? Where'd everyone come from?" Brown asked. Landry smiled, then paused for a moment.

"Well, it's like this, Andrew. It all started the day young Katrina came to town."

"Katrina? . . . Who's Katrina?" Brown asked. Landry rubbed his stubbly chin and mused to himself that he'd need to shave before going to the theater that evening.

"Well, . . . Katrina Thornton," he replied. "She runs the Showcase down on the corner, and if you think I'm busy, you should go down there. I'll guarantee you it'll be standing-room only at her bake shop. And don't forget to see if you can talk someone out of their ticket to the play."

Brown's face showed his disbelief. "The play? Bake shop? . . . You mean the corner building next to the Gold Dust?"

"That's it! Katrina and MacArthur went partnership in the Showcase, with a bakery in the front. In the back, the stage area, on Fridays and Saturdays, she puts on plays.

"She's the lead in the show tonight, and after the last curtain she'll direct the sing-alongs with the audience. We've been practicin' a couple hours a day in the mornings for a week. I've got a small part in it too."

Brown was amazed at the entire conversation. He simply shook his head as Landry added, "I'll tell you right now, Andrew, if Katrina hadn't found her way to Carson Butte, we'd still be a ghost town."

"What about the old hotel? . . . What's happenin' with it?" Brown asked. "I might be interested."

"I'll rent it to ya cheap," Landry told him. "Fifty dollars a month."

Andrew Brown decided he couldn't pass up the offer. The men shook hands to close the deal.

It was the last day of June when Wells Fargo had dropped off my package for Katrina. The clerk had walked down to the bake shop with it, then waited while she examined the packet and immediately broke into a smile upon seeing it was from me. He'd decided to order a piece of pie and coffee, hoping Katrina might relieve his curiosity and give some hint at its sender. The clerk had seen the St. Louis return address in what looked to him like finely detailed script.

But Katrina simply thanked him for the delivery and hurried off to Susan MacArthur's kitchen as the clerk ate his pie. She'd asked Mrs. MacArthur if she would keep an eye on the bakery just for a short time while she went upstairs. Katrina knew she had to be alone with the package.

In her room she sat at the table and carefully unpeeled the wrap, admiring my writing, as had the clerk. Inside she found the interesting small leather pouch and the letter, which she slowly unfolded and read.

> *My Dear Katrina,*
>
> *I received your letter today, and became the happiest man in the world. I was beginning to think I had lost you. I've missed you so much. I would start for Carson Butte this minute if I could. But I'm to leave tomorrow for New Orleans, to take care of pressing business matters there. I will do my best to make it to Carson Butte by some time in September.*
>
> *Please look in the leather pouch, dear Katrina. I thought you might have need for some money in the meantime, and if so, I want you to sell the diamond for cash. If not, hang onto it and we'll have it put in a brooch or necklace for you, as it's much too big for a ring — and for our engagement, Katrina, I would like you to have my mother's diamond ring, which I have also enclosed.*
>
> *Everyone here is well. Malone and Sarah are anxious to meet you in future days, and they send their best regards. Malone seemed a bit shocked that you ended up in Carson Butte. We had looked on an older map, but the town was not listed on the parchment, though Malone had heard of the place.*
>
> *He did show me about where the hamlet should be located, however.*
>
> *I look forward to seeing you as soon as possible in the fall.*
>
> *Forever Yours, With Love, Sean*

Katrina opened the pouch. The large diamond was the most beautiful gem she had ever seen — a clear, blue and white diamond, sparkling with all the other colors of the rainbow. Then she'd looked at my mother's ring, which in truth was itself an amazingly stunning stone, with the setting anchored by two smaller diamonds, one on each side of the band.

But what meant the most to Katrina, she'd later told me, was that I had wanted to give her Ma's ring, which she knew must have meant the world to me.

She slipped the lovely token on her finger, and when she'd held it out to admire the beauty, her blue eyes began to mist and she couldn't hold back the tears of joy.

By July, Carson Butte had settled in hot at mid-mornings, but the nights were often cold, so that a body felt comfortable under cover. Things could not have been much better for Katrina and the townsfolk. Business remained brisk, and to the surprise of everyone, four new establishments were being built, one of them the Carson Butte Bank.

Jacob Miles's freight line had hauled in the new ovens for her bakery, and Katrina had by then hired Sharon McBride on a permanent basis, to help with the baking and waiting tables. The Landrys had hired Bentley's son in the store, and it seemed like every businessman in Carson Butte was adding new help. Jacob Miles had even built onto his barn and hired two more hands for hauling freight.

The Carson Butte residents now believed their town would survive after all.

It was some time in mid-July when Katrina had talked with Marshal Clayborne. She long had carried with her the fear that the authorities might be looking for her, and so told the Marshal all that had happened the past year — the murder of her mother, Shane kidnaping her, her killing of the man, and then her escape and arrival at Carson Butte.

The Marshal was sympathetic. "Don't you worry yourself, child. You did the only thing you could. I'll see that nothing happens to ya." Then he mulled, "I know the area of the cabin. . . . Folks call it Robbers Roost. There's so many outlaws thereabouts that most the time authorities stay clear of the place. It's some forty crow-fly miles from here, but by road it'd be at least double."

Katrina said she'd felt better after their talk, but for some reason concern continued to nag at her. It was a few days later that Marshal Clayborne got on the stage for Ogden, leaving his newly hired deputy to look after things. Three days passed, and when he came back to Carson Butte, he'd gone straight to Katrina's Showcase. He ordered coffee, then asked Katrina to sit a minute.

"I've good news for you, lass. . . . No lawman's lookin' for ya. I've talked to the Sheriff in Ogden, and when I asked if there'd been a killin' last fall in outlaw territory, he seemed surprised that I'd mentioned it.

"The Sheriff affirmed a report of a man killed by a girl, which he'd said he'd doubted at the time, for they'd put a posse together to ride to the hideout. They found the cabin empty, looked around, and saw a freshly filled, oversized grave. They'd figured the corpse had to be a giant to fit in a grave that size, and when they'd started throwin' out dirt to uncover the victim, they were surprised to find not one body in the grave, but four!

"The Sheriff said it looked like maybe the outlaws had been at war, killin' off each other.

"Anyway, the Sheriff says they didn't much care what'd happened, as it appeared to be good riddance. And since then, he's heard no one will go near the cabin. . . .They think the place is cursed!"

Katrina questioned. "Four cadavers? I don't understand how there came to be four dead bodies."

Clayborne replied, "Aye, and the Sheriff didn't either; but somehow four outlaws ended up in that grave."

Katrina was relieved to know she was not wanted by the law. Then, as she sat and thought about it, Clayborne's account had struck her oddly amusing — the justice of it all.

Twenty-Three

I'D BEEN IN New Orleans for two months in the early summer of 1872, and at the time it seemed to me that my attorney, Louis Dumont, had accomplished all that was necessary. But he disagreed.

It seemed Lucia Champlain had taken a new tack in her attempt to gain control of Mosswood by filing suit claiming my affidavits, as son of Robert Sinclair, were forged and false, that Sean Sinclair "was dead," she'd stated, and that she, as the closest kin to Robert Sinclair, was rightful owner and heir of his estate. In May, after reading the filing written by Lucia's attorney, Dumont had felt my presence in court was necessary to settle the charge once and for all.

With the help of witnesses found by Dumont, who had remembered seeing me with my father and mother, Lucia's claim was finally dismissed, and I was declared the rightful heir to all of my parents' properties and goods. My courtroom meeting with Lucia was no more pleasant than any other I'd had with her. At no time did Lucia and I lock eyes, nor did she even look my way.

Back in Dumont's office, I'd thanked him for his handling of the case. He was a pleasant man, small of stature, beginning to bald at forty, and very smart. He sat back in his leather chair and nodded his acknowledgment, then laid down the papers he'd been looking at and peered up at me. He had changed my will as I'd wished, noting Katrina to be my first heir.

"At your death," he stated, "she inherits all your earthly goods. If anything should happen to her, it will go to Sarah Jones. . . .Then Malone is next in line."

But in a fatherly voice, Dumont added, "I would strongly suggest, Sean, that you and Katrina have children — blood heirs closer than Sarah and Malone . . . and when you do, we can make a new arrangement."

Dumont was to have the proper papers ready for me to sign in a couple days.

"One other thing," he added. "I've had transferred to your Wells Fargo account the forty thousand dollars your father had on deposit at his New Orleans bank."

I was amazed at the amount of money, and I silently offered a prayer of thanks for my Ma and Pa, who had never ceased to love me and provide for me — even now, when they were gone. It was a somewhat sad moment in the midst of the triumph I had felt at the court's decision.

I figured I would be on my way to Katrina in Carson Butte in just a few days, early and ahead of time — until Dumont suggested one more thing to consider.

"Before leaving town, I would recommend you locate your father's treasure — *your* treasure now — and turn it into cash . . . or at least a good part of it. It does you no good buried somewhere. If anything happened to you, no one would ever benefit."

I realized he was surely correct, and when he said he could handle the arrangements for disposing of the valuables, I agreed to think about it. An intermediary's fee would be ten percent of the gain and Dumont's five percent — well worth the arrangement. And Dumont figured that the coins and most of the jewelry were no doubt antiquities that could easily be sold to collectors.

That night, back at my hotel on Bourbon Street, I'd thought more about the treasure and knew for certain that Dumont was right. What he'd told me only made sense. And I knew in my heart that Dumont was honorable; he had never done anything to prove otherwise. He had looked after my welfare from the beginning, ever since Malone had directed me to him some ten years before, up until this time, and for but a modest fee — and all done without his knowledge of Pa's treasure until in recent weeks.

I was disappointed, however, that to retrieve the treasure would delay my leaving for Carson Butte and Katrina. My heart ached to see her again. And thinking about Mosswood touched sensitivities in my heart, evoking feelings again of both joy and sorrow. It was where I had last seen Ma and Pa, on that bitter day when both were taken from me.

I remembered back and wondered . . . if not for Malone finding me, where might I be? I had been a sad and hurting boy on this very street some twelve years earlier, trying to deal with an often brutal world as if I were a man.

I lay back on my bed, filled with melancholy, and yet with hope for my future. When all was said and done, I knew in my heart that I wanted to see my boyhood home again — or what remained of the burned-out shell and timbers. I knew I needed to touch back to where this all began. And I'd concluded that most surely unearthing Pa's treasure would not slow me down for more than a few weeks, so that I could leave New Orleans at the first of September, and make it to Utah before October.

The following morning I walked into Dumont's office and told him, "I'll do it. . . . I'll bring in the treasure. I believe you're correct; it is the right thing to do."

After a bit of conversation, I left and walked the short distance to my hotel. I would have liked to have seen Terrill while in New Orleans, for his house was not over two blocks from my hotel. Though I had gone there a couple of times, his male domestic had said he had not as yet returned from Colorado.

That evening I felt encouraged, with a new sense of enthusiasm, and dressed in my best clothes to enjoy a special meal, a sort of turning point. I lit the kerosene lamp on the table, bathed with the water from the white porcelain bowl, and put on my black suit, white shirt, blue string tie, and ebony boots. I looked in the dresser mirror, and was pleased at what I saw — a blue-eyed, ruddy-complexioned young man with straw-blonde hair, a man some had said was handsome.

I checked my six-gun, spinning the loaded cylinder, listening to the familiar click as the chambers raced by. I put it behind my belt on the left side, covered by my coat. Before stepping outside my room, I made certain my sheathed bowie lay in place at my back.

I dined across the street from the hotel, in a dimly lit, elegant place with gold decorative lamps on each white linen-covered table. Along the far wall were luxurious arched cubicles, with curtains for private dining, and I sat in the middle of one of them, where I could see the entranceway door. Five couples also shared tables, and another pair occupied a niche across the way, much like the one I had.

I'd ordered a dinner of shrimp and white wine, and as I looked about, I realized that the place reminded me of Lucia — maybe it was the elegance, maybe the dark, mysterious setting. I had been careful in my movements and actions around town for the past two months, never going to the same place twice or repeating anything that might set a routine — so careful that I'd felt hostage to her voodoo. And I knew that I'd have to be even more wary than ever, once I started retrieving Pa's hidden treasure. Yet I also knew I could not continue living that way, on the edge, worrying every moment about the Champlains. I was determined to come up with some solutions.

As I waited for my dinner I considered going to see Lucia at Blackstone, to try again to find some common ground, some way to appease the woman. Then, as those grand thoughts went tumbling through my mind, Lucia walked through the archway to the dining room. My breath felt as if it had been taken from me.

She paused a moment, looked around, spotted me in the cubicle, and came over to where I sat. Every eye followed her across the room — which I understood, for if I allowed myself, I too could become enchanted with her beauty. It amazed me to observe how the woman affected everyone that laid eyes on her.

"Good evening, Sean . . ." she purred. "May I sit down?"

I nodded. "Yes, Lucia," well aware that I should have said "no," and that I might end up going to my grave in an effort to broker this odd family peace. I thought I must surely be a fool, as she slipped into the chair across from me.

The attendant appeared to take Lucia's order, and Lucia looked up into my eyes, as I poured her wine.

"What are you having, Sean? I'll just have the same thing . . .whatever it is."

I was always amazed at how Lucia could be so charming outwardly, so smooth as silk, yet under that facade, she harbored the evil of a woman of amazing violence. I felt like a helpless fly caught in the insidious trap of a spider. I could almost imagine its long, jointed, hairy legs bearing down on me.

Lucia was indeed making me nervous, and I had a difficult time masking it. She smiled in her winning way that could melt the resolve of any adversary, then cooed her offer.

"Sean . . . let's do make peace. We're really family. . . . I believe I've been wrong in treating you as I have. Please, come see me at Blackstone where we can become better acquainted."

My mind kept spinning . . . *the spider and the fly. . . .*

I was desperately wanting to believe the woman, but her invitation muddled my mind and made me more on edge than ever. I'd thought I simply had to figure someway to totally change the workings of her heart and win her over.

Then reality set in. "*No,*" I rationalized, ". . . *I ought to kill her! What am I thinking? After all she'd had my own Ma and Pa murdered.*"

But like a fool, I'd agreed to a visit. "How about tomorrow evening?"

The voodoo priestess was delighted with her accomplishment. "Wonderful, Sean dear! . . . I'll be so happy to have you out to the plantation. It will make a perfect day!"

I'd smiled weakly. The day certainly would not be perfect for me; and I'd wished she could communicate with me normally, without attempting to conquer mind, heart, and soul.

While we ate, I'd noticed that an unusual-looking man — a suspicious sort — had entered the room and had moved into the darkness along the wall. He remained there seemingly studying the place a moment, then after a time slipped between the tables and into the niche at Lucia's back. Once inside, he'd pulled the curtains shut.

Again, my heart seemed to stop. "*She's hired an assassin to kill me!*" I thought.

My mind raced almost uncontrollably, trying to figure out this new situation. Lucia had just convinced me that the following day would be when she would make her move. She apparently had cleverly entrapped me into letting down my guard. I was certain the assassin would shoot or knife me in the back as I left the restaurant.

But, I'd determined, she'd fail again, now that I knew her plan.

The curtain moved in the shadows behind Lucia. I could barely make out the man's figure, and Lucia sat in the way, so that I could see little. I hid my suspicion of the man's presence by continuing to look at Lucia, but I followed his calculated movements from the corner of my eye, my hand at my side.

I watched amazed as he slowly and silently raised his six-gun . . . but when he did, my own came up, and I shot him, directly between the eyes. The gunman had fired before his weapon had come on target, and his bullet hit harmlessly into the wall.

Lucia heard the explosion of the bullet, looked at my gun, and let out a scream as smoke filled our cubicle. The man fell out onto the floor, pulling the curtains down with him.

It was a horrendous moment for everyone in the room. Lucia continued to gasp, thinking her own life was over — as well it should have been if I had had any presence of mind by then. But when she saw the assassin dead behind her, lying on the floor, I'd thought she finally remembered her game, for she'd grabbed me and gave me a smothering hug.

"Thank you, Sean!" she breathed, holding my face in her hands. "You've saved my life! I cannot thank you enough!"

The look in my eye should have told her I didn't believe a word of the tripe she was passing forth, and I was about to tell her so, but I'd hesitated, thinking I'd better see how things played out.

To my complete amazement, at that moment Terrill walked through the archway, as some diners were rushing out of the room and others continued to mill around, examining the body and speculating.

"*Terrill!*" Lucia called in her most dramatic voice. "Sean has saved my life! *He has killed Roberto!*"

I'd stood next to Lucia almost in shock myself. However, doing some quick thinking upon seeing Terrill once again, at a most propitious time, I realized she was right! The man's intentions had been to kill Lucia, not me!

Terrill shook my hand. "Welcome to the family, Sean. We are all indebted to you."

Lucia sank down in a chair with her head in her hands, seemingly mumbling to herself.

From that day forward, everything appeared to have changed between Lucia and me. The authorities called the shooting self-defense, and all I had to do was stop by the Police Commissioner's office the following morning to verify the report.

My mind and my feelings were still in a conflict, however, for I'd kept thinking back to how it had been Lucia who had been the cause of all the grief in my life. It was she who was totally to blame.

I knew I would have to search deep within myself to do what God had long commanded, to somehow forgive this woman and her ways.

The next afternoon, Terrill and I rode to Blackstone, and Genuis was happy to stretch out the several miles after being cooped up at the stables. Riding along in the shade of leafy oaks, I'd asked Terrill, "Who was this Roberto?"

He took a moment to respond in his typical, concise way. "Roberto was the brother to Manuel Perez. Manuel and Lucia were married for nearly a year before he mysteriously died. She inherited his estate and the Perez family, mostly Roberto, never forgot their anger."

I was treated like royalty at Blackstone. I met Daniel and Julia in a social role for the first time, and amazingly both treated me with respect, as if we had been close all our lives. I could hardly understand it all. But it seemed that the code of blood and honor certainly held forth now.

In time, a Creole domestic set the table for us all, and brought in the elaborate platters of food. Lucia had indicated that I should sit next to her, she at the head of the table. Once seated, they bowed heads. I was taken aback, not knowing what to expect. Then Lucia spoke in words I could not understand, a sort of chant I'd heard many years earlier, when the Creoles at Mosswood would sing an incantation to their gods.

I peered at my food and hesitated with an obviously audible deep breath. Lucia was watching me and smiled, this time not a deceptive, enticing smile, but what would seem to be genuine.

"Sean," she said, "I want to make a toast. I want all to know that Sean Sinclair is family now; and no harm must ever come to him henceforth."

The room was somber. It was like a commandment.

After the toast, Lucia asked if I would like to sit at the head of the table.

I was overwhelmed. "No, Lucia," I replied. "This is your home."

That evening, as Terrill and I rode back into New Orleans, we talked about Lucia. Terrill acknowledged that he had not approved of her ways, but he'd thought that in the past two days he had seen a change — a transformation of sorts — which he'd hoped would be permanent.

I certainly agreed with him.

They next day I'd rented a buckboard from the hostler at the stables, hitched up two blacks, and took off for Mosswood. It was late when I pulled into the plantation yard, and so I settled in for the night by fixing a crude bed in the old horse barn.

In the morning, when I awoke, my pocket watch read six o'clock. I stretched, and walked outside. I could see in the light of day that the place hadn't changed, except for the weeds growing across the yard, and the ugly debris of the burnt-out house.

But there was also the obvious stark loneliness along the plantation grounds that was not present there in happier times. My eyes suddenly filled with tears. I felt an overwhelming sorrow that I hadn't allowed myself to acknowledge for years. As I walked over to Ma and Pa's grave beneath the oak, the early morning sun glistened across the mist of the bay, and for a moment I could see a ghostly ship in the blue waters, a ship that had set a deep mooring back in 1858.

I remembered how Pa had anchored the *White Swan* after we'd been at sea for ten months or so, and eight seaman had lowered the longboat to fetch Ma waiting ashore. On deck, she was so happy to see us. She'd grabbed me and Pa, covering us with her hugs and warm kisses.

We'd gone below deck to talk, then, and right off Pa had asked her, "Elizabeth . . . what would you think of me quitting my seaman's ways?"

Ma was overjoyed.

"Well . . . now I can. We have just taken on a bounty of all we'll ever need."

Pa then turned to me and asked me to locate Turk for him. I found him on the main deck.

"The Master wants to see you, Turk."

The First Mate followed me to the cabin, and Pa smiled at the young sea dog when he entered the room. Pa had explained to me earlier that on past voyages when it came to any plunder taken by the *White Swan*, he had kept half, gave Turk fifteen percent, the Second Mate ten, and the balance split among the lower officers and crew. They all knew they would be paid well.

Pa ordered Turk to load three trunks of the treasure into a longboat and take it ashore.

"Pack it to the house, and put it in the east room, if you will."

"Aye, sir," Turk replied, and jumped to it.

Three hours later, Turk was back and reported to Pa, his mission completed.

Pa was pleased. "And now, Turk, I've a proposition for you." It was the first time I'd heard Pa call the Mate by name, and I think it surprised him.

Pa motioned to a chair, where Turk sat down. Pa then asked the seaman, "How would you like to own the *White Swan*?"

Turk's eyes lit up. "Aye, Master," he replied."I'd like it for sure."

"Then you listen to my proposal, and see how it sets.

"I will take one more trunk of treasure, and you will keep the remaining two. Then you will deliver the cargo in the hold to Savannah for me, and afterward, the *White Swan* and remaining booty will be yours.

"What think you, First Mate?"

Turk was so surprised, he could hardly speak; but knowing he'd been handed a generous gift, he quickly accepted.

"I thank you, sir, and you needn't fear, I'll well take care of the crew."

The next afternoon, with the four trunks in the house, Pa handed Turk the ship's documents of ownership. Later, I watched the *White Swan* sail out of sight, as I stood on the high ground near the house.

As I recall now, it had taken Pa two weeks and some fifteen trips into the swamp before the trunks were safely hidden. And looking back on things, I don't think Pa really wanted to give the ship away, but knowing it would make Ma happy, he did it for her.

It took me two weeks as well to deliver the treasure cache to Dumont, and another week to hire a contractor to rebuild Mosswood.

A week short of October, I loaded my blue-roan onto the Mississippi riverboat moored along the docks in New Orleans, and four days later, after a short visit with Malone and Sarah, I was at the Union Pacific depot in St. Louis, where I stepped up into the passenger car for my trip to Carson Butte.

Twenty-Four

AUGUST OF 1872 found the high country town of Carson Butte to be the busiest place in northern Utah. A new schoolhouse was being built and would be ready for the local children in October. Optimism ruled everywhere along main street, the town blossoming like a springtime flower. At least most folks were optimistic that day — all except maybe Pete Landry. But it was probably his job to worry, if anyone did, inasmuch as he was the mayor.

On the warm late summer day, after reading for Katrina's new play, Landry sat at a Showcase table with a mug of coffee in his hands. He looked to be thinking deeply and somewhat discouraged, so Katrina had walked over and sat down with him. She'd asked him if something was on his mind.

"No . . . nothing really I guess, Katrina. I just worry sometimes; it's my nature. I should be the happiest man in the world right now, watching the town grow as it is. It's doing what I'd prayed for." Then continuing on, Landry admitted, "Well . . . I think what's been bothering me is that we need to be looking how to provide for all these here folks now . . . with our town services, and with provisions, year 'round."

Katrina was surprised. "Do we have a problem?" she asked.

"Well, yes, Katrina. Say we have a long, bad winter this year — snowed in for several months. Why, I've been hereabouts where we've been marooned close to five months! Not even Miles's freight wagons could get through. And with no way in or out for staples . . . it could be a disaster. . . . It's just something we need to start thinking about as a town," he added.

Katrina could understand his concern, but hastened to add, "Now don't you worry yourself sick, Mr. Landry; the good Lord will provide. He always does."

Landry nodded, "Aye, maybe you're right, young lady."

He smiled at Katrina, and his mood seemed to improve, as it always did when he was around her. She was his real success story. No one had forgotten that he and Mrs. Landry had given Katrina her start — her first job — when she'd first appeared in Carson Butte.

He finished his coffee and left the bakery to return to his store.

Katrina thought about their conversation. She knew that Landry was certainly right. Providing a source of provisions for the number of families that had now settled in the area might be a serious task in harsh conditions. What they'd really needed, she'd thought, was a slaughterhouse thereabouts; but that was a big venture for the locals to get into.

Then Katrina thought of the diamond I had sent her, turning over in her mind the possibilities. . . .What if she'd sold it, and invested the money in a slaughterhouse, and maybe even a butcher shop? That would surely take care of any future concerns — except, of course, for finding the live animals. The area around Carson Butte didn't seem to have any cattle-raising operations large enough to provide for a slaughterhouse, yet some of the lush grassy plateaus were certainly accessible to herding cattle on the trails.

Never one to get discouraged, Katrina tried the idea on Mr. Landry the following day.

Landry was amazed — but no more amazed than he'd been when she started up the Showcase theater and bakery.

"I guess it'd surely work, " he said, "though we'd need a warehouse to store enough perishables for a winter. And I guess you could add an underground cave to store winter ice and keep goods all summer."

Then he mulled, "I could probably build a warehouse to store the staples. . . ." But just as quickly as his enthusiasm rose, reality set in.

"I don't know, Katrina . . . it's a nice idea, but it'd take a few thousand dollars to put in an operation like you're suggesting, and myself and Mrs. Landry, why we just don't have that much to venture right now."

Katrina leaned forward across the table. "Mr. Landry," she smiled. "I can get the money!"

"*You* can get the money?" he replied. "Where in the world are you gonna get money like that, Katrina?"

Katrina smiled, and in a quiet voice told him, "I have a very valuable diamond that I could sell, which would bring at least two times what you're talking about! . . . My only problem is, who could I get to run the operation?"

"Wait a minute, young lady. This isn't something you just jump into. We need to think about this."

Katrina shook her head. "I've thought about it, Mr. Landry. I just need you to help me find the right people and get it going."

Landry could tell Katrina's mind was set.

"Well, I know someone who I think might be the man — Bill Thorson hereabouts. He's not involved in anything major right now, and I think he'd jump at the chance to handle it."

Landry began to get excited at the thought of the project; but his excitement turned back to practical matters. He realized it would take time to sell Katrina's diamond and begin construction. The building work alone would take at least four months. And everything being considered, there was no way the work could be finished that year, before winter, with the early freeze but a month away.

Nevertheless, Katrina urged him to find someone he could trust to turn the diamond into cash. And so, on the tenth of September, Pete Landry stepped onto the stage headed for Salt Lake. A week later, early in the day, he'd returned to Carson Butte with a smile on his face and six thousand dollars in his money belt.

That afternoon, Katrina walked into the Carson Butte Bank and deposited five thousand of the money. She'd decided to loan five hundred of it to Landry, to build the warehouse, and she paid off her debt to MacArthur with another five hundred.

The following week, Katrina hired Bill Thorson to build the slaughterhouse and butchering plant just northwest of town on a ten-acre plot of ground — a spot large enough for corrals and holding pens. And when Thorson would finish the construction, he was to manage the whole operation.

It was past mid-September when Katrina had received my letter confiding that I had some unexpected and urgent business to attend to, and that it could be into October before I reached Carson Butte. She was disappointed, she'd acknowledged, but she'd thought another month could be managed, as long as she had the assurance that I would be there soon.

It seemed as if life would for certain take another new turn for both of us. Katrina was as happy and excited as I was. The serenity of Katrina's life, however, would soon be challenged.

Late that month, close to noontime, she felt the dark eyes of a tall, slim cowhand, packing a six-gun, following her around the room. She'd thought he looked familiar, but was sure he hadn't been in the bakery before.

In the midst of wiping her counter and straightening her goods, she suddenly realized where she had seen him. Her throat tightened and her heart raced as it all came back. He was one of the outlaws at her stepfather's cabin the first night she had been there. He'd stopped with another outlaw that night, but they'd left early the following morning.

Katrina thought hard to recall his name . . . *Brigg Dalton!*

No doubt he had recognized her too, she was sure.

She left the counter for her helper to handle, then hurried to her room. She needed to be alone, to think this through. But inside she felt almost ill as the memory of those horrible days griped her. Marshal Clayborne had reassured her that no lawmen were looking for her in Shane's death, but Dalton could clarify the story for them and report her as having been the girl at the cabin who had actually killed Shane.

Katrina wondered if she should tell the Marshal about Dalton, but decided she'd best go back downstairs and see how things evolved. She was relieved when she saw that Dalton was gone, and wondered if maybe she'd been worrying for nothing.

A week went by before Katrina saw him again. She'd been on the street, talking to Grace Shore in front of her dress and yarn shop, when he rode up and dismounted at the Sluice Box. He'd tied his horse to the hitching rail, then disappeared into the saloon.

A chill went through her at the sight of the man, and Grace asked, "What's the matter, child, are you cold?"

Katrina tried to smile. "Just a bit, Mrs. Shore. Seems even the nights are getting brisker — and I saw a flock of geese flying south this morning."

The two women parted and Katrina walked on, turning into the Showcase.

When I finally arrived in Utah, I'd unloaded Genius at Ogden from the Union Pacific stock car and bought a pack horse from the hostler at the stables. The clerk at Wells Fargo gave me directions to Carson Butte, and an hour later I was putting supplies from the General Store onto my packer. By nightfall I was on the trail northeast out of town.

That next morning I rode the gravel wilderness path heading higher and higher into the mountains, covered with a dense green forest of trees. I camped by a mountain stream that night, bringing back memories of Colorado. I loved the West, almost as much as Malone's White Oaks and my Mosswood.

I fixed a small fire of dried wood, thinking there was no need to alert anyone thereabouts to my presence with a heavy trail of smoke, then cooked a supper of bacon and beans.

On a bed of pine needles, I lay under my blanket and thought of Katrina, not more than a day away. I could hear the nearby mountain stream gurgling its sweet lullabies to me, and with only good thoughts in mind, the warm blanket, cold air, and rush of the water put me to sleep.

I thought I was dreaming when I felt the wet of what turned out to be a snowflake settle on my face at first light. Then wide awake, I knew it hadn't been a dream. But I lay there, under a thin cover of white snow, not wanting to get up.

After a quick meal, the night's overcast had dissipated, and I mounted my gelding, riding a trail where God must have swept the snow clear with a simple movement of his hand. It wasn't long before the day warmed, as sunlight filtered down through vistas of golden aspen and heavy pine.

Around midday I breasted a ridge that looked down upon the most beautiful sea of grass I'd ever seen. I paused there not ten feet from where Katrina had stopped a year earlier. I could see Carson Butte nestled far below, and I was anxious to be on my way. But something held me as my eyes canvassed the scene. Higher distant mountains peaked above the timberline and ranged east, west, and north. Miles upon miles of high country meadow lay in between, and at varying elevations, east and north behind the town, rolled slopes of undulating hills. West, a purple mesa graced the landscape, catching my attention. I figured it was ten miles to the butte, though maybe more, for distances can be deceiving in high country. I couldn't see the south end of the butte, so it might not have been a true mesa, but it must have been where the town had gotten its name. It was a beautiful sanctuary.

I reined my gelding, pulling the pack horse, down the steep trail to Carson Butte.

Katrina had gone to the bakery an hour early that morning to do some record keeping, and had left the door unlocked behind her. She heard it open as Brigg Dalton walked in.

"I been wantin' to talk to ya," he said, as he sat at the nearest table. "Sit down," he ordered.

"The place is closed. You tell me what's on your mind, and then you'll have to get out."

"That's pretty big talk for someone wanted for murder," he drawled, looking up at her.

"Murder? . . . I'm not wanted for murder!" Katrina shot back. "Now get on your way!"

"Not so fast, sister. I know you killed Floyd Shane."

Katrina said she'd fought hard with herself to keep calm. Her heart was pounding.

"I want you to leave, right now!"

"Why, you're a little fireball, aren't ya?"

Katrina looked around for MacArthur, but he hadn't come in yet, and probably wouldn't until ten.

"Now listen," Dalton said, "let's try to get along. You treat me right and I'll forget about your killin' Shane. I didn't like him much anyway. You come with me, and I'll develop a sudden case of amnesia."

Katrina was furious at Dalton's proposition.

"You're barking up the wrong tree, mister. . . . The Marshal already knows all about Shane! . . . *Now get out of here!*"

Just as Katrina was ordering Dalton out, I'd walked through the door. I'll not forget the look on her face.

"Sean!" she called, with a look of shock and relief in one, and she ran over, tears spilling down her cheeks.

Dalton was nearly beside himself with anger.

"Ain't that a pretty picture!" he snarled.

Then suddenly, he stood up, six-gun in hand, giving us an order.

"Both of ya, with your hands up . . . and little lassie you come to me, or I'll take care of yer boyfriend."

If the truth be told, Dalton had never expected things to go this far. He'd simply gotten himself in too deep, and he was not about to lose this round and turn back. He should have just walked out and ridden away when he saw me — but a fool doesn't always think right, at least not when they believe they have the upper hand.

And Dalton had no idea who he was facing across the room.

Katrina was trembling; she did as she was told, slowly walking over to the outlaw. He grabbed her arm, then turned the gun to her head and challenged me.

"Okay, cowboy, now you lay yer gun on the table . . . with fingers on the butt."

I did as I was told, but when he picked up my gun I swore to him, "You know you'll not walk out of here alive."

Dalton laughed. "Who's gonna stop me? . . . And she's goin' with me, right out that door."

While he was talking, I was figuring that sometime before he'd leave, he might lower his gun from Katrina's head, and when he did, I'd take him. But I could see Dalton was jumpy, and I didn't want anything to set him off while he held Katrina.

The next moment, I heard something from the back room — a brush of air or a movement ever so slight, maybe even a mouse scurrying across the floor. Dalton, nerves on edge, swung around with his gun in that direction.

It took but a split instant for me to grab my bowie, and it flew like a shot into the outlaw's chest. His eyes widened as he looked at me and gasped for air. He tried to bring his six-gun on line, but couldn't do it. Dalton slumped to the floor.

Katrina seemed frozen in fear against the frame of the door, then softly began sobbing as I took her in my arms.

"It's all right, Katrina. . . . Everything's going to be all right."

November of 1872 rolled into Carson Butte with a blizzard, and where the wind couldn't get to it, the snow piled up in six-foot drifts. Katrina, then eighteen, and I, twenty-one, had married in mid-October, united by the Reverend Hawthorne in God's presence, in the church a block north of

Main Street. Katrina was so loved by everyone that I think all of Carson Butte was there, crowding into the new building.

For the time being, we lived in the place Katrina had fixed up at the Gold Dust, the two rooms she had made into a sitting room and bedroom.

Shortly after I had arrived, she'd told me about selling the diamond, and what she'd done with the money. It sounded like a sensible move to me.

"That diamond was yours to do with as you please," I told her, "and I think helping the town that took care of you when you needed it was the right thing."

Katrina took me over to where Bill Thorson had just started to build the slaughterhouse before the weather had forced him to stop.

"Next year," Katrina said, "it will be finished, and we'll have our provisions stored." But we both considered the coming winter, with the early weather blowing so cold, wondering if that would be the year Carson Butte might not make it through those long winter months for lack of food.

"That's just what Mr. Landry had been worried about," Katrina told me.

I had reassured Katrina that I would try to work on the problem, talk with Landry, and find some solution. "And I'll talk to Jacob Miles in the morning, as well, and maybe between the three of us we can come up with something. He travels a lot of country hauling his freight, and he might know where we could pick up some cattle, not too far away."

"You mean drive cattle in here?" Katrina asked. "Why, I don't think you can, Sean, not with winter coming on so fast."

"Well, you may be right, but I'll look into it."

The next day I put on my heavy wool shirt and socks, and warmest boots, and threw on my sheepskin coat and hat, with a scarf up around my ears as I went outdoors. The snow was cleared from the street, where the wind had blown it away, and I walked a hard frozen ground with not a soul in sight.

I found Miles in the barn, breaking ice in the tank. I helped him bring each of the horses from their stalls to drink, and my own gelding was glad to see me, nuzzling my arm. The barn was a bit warmer than outdoors, but not much, with just a small amount of heat coming from a pot-bellied stove Miles had near the store room. It was passable up to maybe ten feet from the stove, but in another ten it was bitter cold. The old building had just too many open cracks streaming air to hold back the winter.

Right off, Miles didn't know of any cattle herds in the area, at least not of any size that could be bought.

"But you might ask Landry," he'd suggested as an afterthought. "He's real tight with Washakie, the Chief of the Shoshone. If there's any cattle in the area, that Indian would know it."

Miles had informed me that Washakie and his clan of followers liked to summer over by the mesa, along the natural lake below the plateau, but winters they moved to the lower elevations along the Bear River.

I asked the freighter how the town had protected itself in the summertime when the Indians were close by.

He seemed surprised. "Well, Sean, the Shoshone are friendly. And Washakie, while once a warrior, has become a bridging force between the white man and the Indians. He's a man of knowledge and leadership — why he speaks French and English as well as other Indian languages."

Half an hour later, I was talking with Pete Landry, explaining what I had in mind. Though he knew of no herds of any size in the area, he agreed with Miles that the Shoshone might. It came to me then that it had been Washakie that Landry had gone to when he'd traded off Katrina's horse.

I asked Landry if he knew whereabouts the Chief might be camped, and he'd acknowledged that Washakie was over past the mesa, maybe twenty miles beyond, but through some pretty rough country.

"The last six miles," he'd added, "is nothing but switchbacks and drop-offs into a meadow along the Bear River in a grove of aspen." Landry confirmed that Washakie liked to winter there.

Landry tried to give me more specific directions, then said, "It's easy to spot the trail from the lake by the mesa. The beaten way'll take you right to the camp . . . but I wouldn't advise it this time of year. The last few miles are pretty hard traveling."

I thanked Landry as I walked out the door to find Katrina at the Showcase.

Twenty-Five

THE TEMPERATURE overnight had dropped to zero, and the fact of it was that the morning outside was bitter. By the time I'd walked to the stables, I was almost numb. The only thing saving the day was that there was no wind.

Genius wasn't any happier than I was when I rode him out of the barn and into a gloomy white countryside. But I'd made up my mind to locate the Shoshone, and so I centered my horse on the mesa as he plodded through the six inches of powder. Not a tree was seen between the town and the butte, only a rolling white blanket of land with blades of grass sticking out of the snow.

As I neared the plateau, I could see a timber of aspen and portions of a lake fringed with cottonwood and willow. To my left, the mesa showed a connection to the shoulder east and the high mountainous ridge that I had breasted when I'd first seen Carson Butte. The saddle of the land, some seventy feet higher than the basin floor, and maybe fifty feet lower than the plateau of the mesa, connected the butte. In the saddle and the east shoulder slope were areas of pine, aspen, and spruce. In the lower areas were timbers of lodgepole pine. The spruce trees held patches of snow in their branches, like elegant ladies dressed in furs of ermine pinned with emerald brooches.

The sun struggled through the mist of morning and swallowed up an overcast sky, slowly dissipating fine particles of frost that floated in the air. An hour later I rode by the lake and took the trail around the butte, then turned west. The next four hours I rode the undulating high country of snow-covered grass before starting the grade down to lower elevations. Though dropping fast, the trail didn't seem so bad until I hit the rimrock of escarpments and cliffs that fell into a valley far below. There I could see some forty lodges in the Shoshone camp.

I'd looked down the steep path and felt a sweat at my neck, even though the temperature was nearly zero. I had no choice but to rein my horse down that perilous way. I knew I didn't like it, nor did Genius. Gingerly the gelding stepped out, lifting his legs high above the snow. I really admired the horse; he just accepted my judgment and put his trust in me.

About halfway down, we came upon a five-hundred-foot stretch of hanging cliff, not over eight feet wide, that had a drop-off of maybe two hundred feet. Genius and I never looked down; we went on like two fools who didn't know any better. At one stretch, I could feel his sure footing beginning to slip where the snow was packed and icy. Though he'd slide no more than a foot or so, it was enough to scare us both. For a short distance, where the trail was extra slippery, I got off and walked.

It wasn't long before we were past the treacherous section, and I could see that the edge of the drop-off along the trail was now securely lined with aspen. Though it still ran along that deep canyon, I felt like I'd been spared disaster.

When we'd finally reached the bottom, I led Genius across an open riffle on the river, and at the same time I was trying to halter my apprehensions, for I was about to ride into the Shoshone campgrounds. I reined the horse up to the largest lodge, which I'd figured housed the Chief. As I had thought, the old warrior Washakie immediately appeared outside to greet me. Another warrior came up and took my horse.

I was invited inside the lodge, and I sat close to the floor, the place to which I'd been directed. I introduced myself and gifted the Chieftain with a special bowie knife that I had honed down to what I thought was Henry's and my own special liking.

Washakie was so pleased that it was doubtful I could have given him a better gift. I began to feel more confident, and happy that I had given him something he would value.

We soon talked about the plight in Carson Butte. He'd confided that his people, as well, would need supplies through that fast-coming winter, for the buffalo were now becoming scarce.

I'd asked the Chief if he knew of any cattle in the area that the town might buy, and with apparent genuine apology he'd acknowledged he did not — though he'd offered the possibility that his nephew, Moon Bear, might have some information.

I was shocked at how well Moon Bear also spoke English. I felt somewhat embarrassed that I could not match their skill in their language, and after a time of polite conversation, I'd asked the warrior where he had learned to speak my own so adeptly. It was at a mission in Salt Lake, he'd said, where he had attended as a youth. I thought, at that moment, that the white man had at least given something of lasting value back to these people.

Moon Bear knew of many sources of small numbers of cattle, but the only large herd, he'd said, was miles to the south and east on the Strawberry River, one hundred fifty miles from Carson Butte. It was there that a rancher from Oklahoma Territory had brought in the cattle from Texas two years before, and he was certain the man would be willing to sell.

That information was all I'd needed to hear, and I'd then asked Moon Bear if he would go along with me to the Strawberry River, to help drive the herd back to Carson Butte. I could see he was skeptical of success at that time of year, but when I told him the Shoshone could have a share of the cattle, he accepted and offered to bring four other warriors for the drive.

I stayed that exciting night with the Shoshone, and was treated like an honored guest. The next day, by an easier route shown to me by Moon Bear, I returned to Carson Butte.

Katrina had not wanted me to travel, even to the Shoshone at that season of the year, and I could tell she wasn't too happy that I had made the arrangements with Moon Bear. But she eventually realized the need for the immediate trip in light of the potential catastrophe that could face all of us without a supply of meat for the coming months.

It was a cold, clear day when I left Carson Butte, leading a pack horse, with five Shoshone and three of our own townsmen, all heading for Strawberry River country. I rode out of town with the city's four thousand dollars in gold coin in my money belt. As for failure of my mission, I had never considered the possibility.

We rode a week in sub-freezing temperatures, bucking tall drifts of snow, before we reached thc ranch on the Strawberry. Back of the barns I could see some of the longhorns along the fence, munching prairie hay where it had been scattered.

When I walked up to the house and knocked on the door, a husky man, graying at the temples, answered. He was wearing a well-used six-gun in a tied-down holster, and when he'd seen the five Indians and three white men sitting on their horses in the yard, he'd instantly reached for his weapon.

I quickly reassured him. ". . . They're with me, and friendly."

Though hc was at first relieved, I could tell he was wondering if he should believe me or not. But he must have trusted my word, for he'd removed his hand from his six-gun. It was then that I'd told him why I was there.

To my dismay, I learned that though the cattleman indeed had a thousand head on his spread, he wasn't ready to part with them, for he'd already sold enough steers that fall in Salt Lake. I looked over at Moon Bear and could see the disappointment and distress in his eyes as well. But I did not give up my quest that easily.

Over the course of the rest of that day I managed to buy a hundred head from the man, convincing him how important it was to Carson Butte and to our Shoshone friends. He was a good man. He'd finally agreed to sell me the mostly full-grown young steers for thirty dollars a head, and though ten dollars over the going price, I had no choice, for he would take no less.

Still, I was happy the old rancher did not ask for more, as I was prepared — at a last resort — to go forty dollars, if that was what it would take to buy the steers. In addition to the cattle, I got him to throw in three good pack horses.

It was ten days later when we'd reached the town of Echo, fifty miles south of Carson Butte. Although the hundred miles had been a cold trip, it had been fairly easy going compared to my cattle drive north from Texas. I was no stranger to trail life or its hardships, and realized the true test would come once we'd started up the mountain to home.

We stayed in Echo for two days, loading up on supplies and giving the cattle a rest. We'd found a good meadow nearby a creek, and it wasn't long before the herd had brushed the grass free of the snow. The longhorns were eagerly filling their bellies, and it turned out a good thing they did, because the days ahead proved to be many without ready forage.

It was a sunny 7th of December when we'd started the herd north. That first day, to the satisfaction of everyone, we'd pushed them a good ten miles, leaving us only forty more to Carson Butte. Moon Bear and two Shoshone riders had split off from us then, headed north with their ten head and a pack horse. The other two warriors stayed with me to help with the tough miles ahead to Carson Butte, and I was grateful for Moon Bear's consideration.

As we traveled higher into the mountains, the slim wagon road constricted. The narrowed way strung out the cattle and made for slow going. By evening, we'd covered but five miles.

That night snow began to fall, and I cannot describe the worry that took over my mind. The morning showed a foot of white cover, with flakes still coming down. By nightfall, I'd doubted we had made over a mile, what with the cattle slipping and sliding, many on the ground at times, thrashing to get back on their feet. I was nervous, but I prayed that God would carry us through this final passage, for if we didn't make it, I knew that one or the other of us — the cattle, or the good people of Carson Butte — would be the victims of the elements.

From that time on we had intermittent good and bad days. On a good day we had managed to maybe travel three hard miles, yet we'd trudged on, determined to clear the pathways through drifts of fifteen feet in places.

It was impossible to find forage by then, and the cattle had eaten nothing for two days. Time was escaping us, as it was difficult keeping track of it; but we'd figured we'd been on the trail for at least two weeks. And surely, we'd thought, Carson Butte could not be far off.

The following day dawned too calm to be true, for the sky had taken what I'd considered an ominous haze. An hour later, snowflakes fell in ever thicker patterns. A north wind picked up and swung down the mountain, carrying what seemed like a flash-flood of snow. Winds whipped and the woods we traveled vanished; our visibility had dropped to but a few hard-earned feet. Nevertheless, we would not be deterred. We moved on into the storm with the cattle bawling and, in truth, all of us quietly wishing we could stop.

I'd burrowed farther down into my sheepskin coat, but still I rode nearly frozen with the gusting winds tearing at my clothes and lungs. We continued on, leaning into the bitter wind.

I suddenly realized that the trail had leveled off, and so with renewed energies I rode on ahead in a swirling white-out world. I soon came upon the rimrock, and I can't explain the feeling of relief — the joy. I bowed my head and thanked God right there for this reassurance that we were indeed almost home. Though I couldn't see the town, I knew that Carson Butte was just below.

We soon made camp, for I wasn't about to go down that icy slope in the blind. I looked at my pocket watch; it showed twelve, but I'd lost bearings in the white surrounding us and couldn't remember for certain if it was noon or midnight, though it seemed to be the night. We huddled down to rest while the storm continued to rage.

When I awoke, the sky was clear and the storm had passed. After a quick meal, I rode to the rim and looked down on Carson Butte covered in a blanket of snow. Smoke fingered into the sky from the buildings. At first I could see no one. Then a dark speck of a figure moved in front of the stables, as did others on the boardwalk. It appeared that they were digging their way out from the storm.

Looking back on what we had traveled through, I was thankful that the rancher had longhorns instead of herefords, for those short-legged, heavy animals would never have survived the drive.

It was nearly noon when we'd checked on our herd and started down the mountainside. Horse and cattle plowed through eighteen inches of snow, on to the bottom. Halfway down, I could see a steel-dust mare plunging through the drifted wagon road toward us. I knew it had to be Katrina.

She was there waiting for me at the bottom of the steep slope. Her loving welcome made my trip worthwhile. An hour later we drove the eighty-eight head of cattle into the holding pens west of town, and after warming up at the stables, I gave the two Shoshone each a gold piece and the thanks of Carson Butte. Then I went by Landry's, just before going home, and counted out eight hundred dollars in gold coin left over from the trip.

That evening, Katrina and I were in our quarters at the Showcase, and I was just getting ready to relax, when she said, "Come on, Sean, get dressed . . . or we'll be late!"

"Late? . . . To what?" I'd asked.

"The Christmas party at the church; it's Christmas Eve. Did you forget?"

I had indeed forgotten the date. We'd been on the trail sixteen days after parting from Moon Bear — sixteen days for just forty miles.

I dressed, then hurried to the stables to invite the two Shoshone to join us, but they had already gone. It was nearly eight o'clock when Katrina and I walked into the church. The small one-room place of worship had stood out in the glow of night, surrounded by a sea of snow. Its lamplights shone warmly from its windows in patterned squares of gold.

Inside, the townsfolk came around to shake my hand, as if I were some kind of hero. But I'd announced that I could not take the credit for the success of our drive, for if Washakie and Moon Bear had not been the guiding partners, the outcome might have been very much different.

Nevertheless, Pete Landry kept up the praise, insisting, "There wasn't a man in Carson Butte willing to do what you did under those circumstances, and I for one won't forget it.

"Katrina has helped us to make the town what it is, and now you've helped to give us security."

I appreciated his words, and finally we all relaxed to enjoy a spread of food put on by the ladies of the town. In time, the room was cleared for a Christmas dance, with two spirited fiddlers and a piano player providing the music.

The old frontier town was enjoying a very special holiday that year.

The day after Christmas, with holiday festivities quickly behind us, I was enjoying coffee at Katrina's bakery when Marshal Clayborne walked through the door. We'd greeted each other, and once again spoke of the cattle drive. It seemed to be a topic that wouldn't be put to rest for a while, but I knew how much the town had appreciated the venture.

The Marshal filled me in on town business while I'd been gone, and I'd learned that the disreputable Rock Jensen, owner of the Sluice Box, had finally been run out of town, having been tied to two thefts in the territory.

"We had no real proof, and a lawyer might have got him off the charges," Clayborne added, so we gave him two days to get out of town or face two years in jail.

"He left the next day in a huff, and we're better off without him and his kind."

I'd acknowledged the Marshal was right, adding, "I'm sure it made Katrina happy, for she's said she's always been a bit nervous of the barman."

I laughed as I told the Marshal, "I thought maybe I'd have to go over to his place and read to him from the Good Book. . . . Now I guess it's not necessary."

It seemed that Carson Butte was well on its way to becoming the peaceful town it had longed to be.

Twenty-Six

IN EARLY MARCH of 1873 a spring wind blew through Carson Butte, and making its way across the low rolling hills, it melted the snow. The warmer weather brought new life into town, with a buzz of activity. Pete Landry was back to working on his warehouse, and Bill Thorson was finishing the slaughterhouse and butcher shop, which he'd located west of Landry's General Store. The townsfolk worked at their tasks as well, realizing the respite in the weather was probably temporary, for spring snow squalls were not uncommon in those parts.

But now through the hardest part of winter, Carson Butte still had thirty longhorns in the holding pens. In January and February, Thorson had cut ice and hauled it by sled to store in a side cave, back of the new meat market. It would house and keep all the perishables needed through the heat of summer.

Later, when he had completed his enterprise, and all the costs had been totaled, Thorson determined the construction had run to just two thousand dollars — less than Katrina and Pete Landry had initially considered.

The question then became where Katrina and Thorson could find a regular livestock supplier, as they needed a steady purchase of cattle and hogs for their venture to succeed. When I'd heard them going over the problem, I knew the opportunity was ripe for me to present my plan.

I had lately been giving thought to buying good grazing land thereabouts, and had checked with the clerk at the land office, finding that most of the country around Carson Butte was for sale. The land could be made to work for some good ranching, if I'd improve the access trails between the grazing and the town.

I looked at Katrina. "I've long wanted my own ranch, and perhaps this was the time to start it."

"But where're ya gonna get the cattle?" Thorson asked. There's just none available in this part of the country. Even that rancher over on Strawberry told you he'd part with no more."

I'd acknowledged he was correct, but added, "I've got contacts in Texas, and I've been thinking I could go and bring in a herd."

Earlier that past fall, after I'd arrived in Carson Butte, I had written to Tex Dobson at Uvalde about the possibility of buying some cattle, in the event that my plans worked out. I told Katrina and Thorson that Tex had a mixed herd of at least a thousand head, available that spring.

I'd quickly peered up at Katrina to register her reaction, but to my surprise, her face showed nothing . . . it was unreadable. Then I could see she was working my idea over in her mind, and she hesitatingly asked, "Do you think you could make the drive before winter?"

"Yes . . . I think so, Katrina," I told her. "If I left for Texas right away, I could travel by rail as far as Council Grove, in Kansas, then by stage to Uvalde. I should be able to make the trip in ten to twelve days. And if I could get a herd together and started back in early April, we should be able to return here some time in September."

Katrina was a businesswoman and a realist. "Sean, it seems like you've given us hope again where we had none."

I was excited. I relished a new challenge, and I offered to wire Tex before the day was out, to tell him I could be in Uvalde at the first of April.

Later, alone with Katrina, I'd checked with her again to be certain that my plan for a ranch, and then being gone again, for six months, were what she'd really wanted as well. I was reassured.

The very next day I rode into Washakie's camp to see if he would let me have the same four warriors that had been wranglers on our winter drive. But the Chief hesitated, for the Shoshone's arch-enemy the Sioux were on the warpath to the north, in Montana Territory, apparently fighting both the white man and each other. Finally, however, after I'd told the old warrior the arrangement I would give him in exchange, he agreed.

Upon hearing of the venture, Moon Bear spoke up, for he'd wanted to ride with us as well, much to Washakie's reluctance. I was pleased, of course, and it would turn out, across the markings of time, that Moon Bear and I would evolve into fast friends for life.

That day, as I had traveled to see Washakie, and then on my way back to Carson Butte, I had studied the intriguing mesa and its surrounding territory. I had wished that there'd been more time to examine it firsthand, but I knew that I'd have days enough for that once we had brought the cattle to the ranch.

The land bank was closed when I rode into town, and the evening stars were beginning to twinkle like summer fireflies in the night. But by eight the next morning I was back with the clerk at his office, looking at the map before me, which had laid out the area into mile-square sections.

"What's for sale?" I'd asked.

"Just about anything, Sean, except for Carson Butte . . . and the land a mile north of the mesa. That's open range clear to Bear River."

I asked him to show me the location of the mesa on the map, and he dropped his finger to trace a line. "It's the dashed area here, and you can have all you want in there, up to within four miles of town, for a dollar an acre."

I studied the map further, then asked. "Where's the rim south of the mesa?"

He pointed, adding, "It's around a mile of moutainside."

From the rimrock south and to a mile north of the butte totaled six miles; and from a point four miles out of town to a mile past the mesa was also six miles. The area covered thirty-six sections, twenty-three thousand and forty acres that abutted six miles of open range land.

I wrote out a Wells Fargo draft for twenty-three thousand and forty dollars and handed it to the clerk for the thirty-six sections of land. He gave me a receipt and smiled.

"It'll probably be a few weeks before we have the deed, Sean."

I instructed the clerk that I'd be leaving town for a while, and that he should just give the papers to Katrina when they arrived.

That day, the Anchor K Ranch was born along the upper reaches of Utah Territory. The anchor was for me and my memorable days with Pa at sea. The K was for Katrina.

It was the 28th of March when the Shoshone and I stepped down out of the railcar at Council Grove. I had rented a two-seated buggy from the local hostler, and after buying a bowie knife at the General Store, and with the Shoshone piled in the rig, I reined the pair of grays north on the road that would take me to Chancy Sharp's ranch along the Neosho River. It had been a long time since I'd seen Chancy, and I was excited to have even a short visit with my old friend.

When I pulled the buckboard into the yard, Chancy'd recognized me through the front window and rushed out of the house to greet me. Behind him walked a pretty lady that turned out to be his wife. We were both somewhat taken aback at the reunion — I, figuring Chancy would always remain a bachelor, and him, seeing five Indians in my company.

But Chancy was cordial and took the Shoshone to the bunkhouse, where they could bed down and relax. That evening, Chancy's Mrs. fixed us all a hearty meal of fried chicken. But the Indians declined to eat inside the house, except for Moon Bear, and so we carried four meals out to them. Chancy seemed to enjoy his conversations with the well-spoken Moon Bear, and I was pleased that my two friends might likewise become friends.

Just before suppertime David Monroe, our trail cook back in '71, came in from riding fence, and joined us in the meal. The evening passed quickly, and before I'd realized it the hall clock was chiming nine. Chancy and Mrs. Sharp, as well as Moon Bear, excused themselves for the night, but Dave and I continued our visit through several more turns of the clock. He confided that he'd been considering heading back to Texas in the near future, as Chancy no longer had a cook's need for the wrangler now that he was settled with a wife.

It was then that I'd told Dave about my plans for the spread in Utah and the drive I'd soon be making. His eyes seemed to light up as I described the challenging adventure that lay before me.

"Gosh, Sean, I'd really like to ride along with you, but I've said nothing yet to Chancy about even thinking of leaving, and I don't want to up and run off just when things are starting to get busy with spring calving. Chancy's treated me right, and I owe him."

It came to me then that Dave would be just the man to work into managing the new Anchor K, and I told him what I'd had in mind. If he'd wanted it, he had the job.

Dave whistled. "Twenty-three thousand acres, plus open range — that's a lot of grass."

He shook his head and looked at me. "I do want the job, Sean, and I'm ready for the challenge, but what about Chancy?"

I reassured Dave that I would talk to Chancy in the morning. "I'm sure he'll want what's best for you."

After breakfast the next day I'd told Chancy my plans and my conversation with Dave the previous night. I was relieved to see that Chancy was pleased at Dave's opportunity, and in truth wished him well, though he'd acknowledged he would surely miss the reliable hand. By nine that morning we were rolling down the wagon road back to Council Grove to pick up the stage south.

By the time we'd reached Texas, I had finished honing the bowie knife I'd bought, and I gave it to Moon Bear. The gift surprised the warrior, and he sincerely thanked me, admitting, "When I'd seen the knife you gave my uncle . . . I had wished for one just like it!"

On the 3rd of April, Dave, Moon Bear, four Shoshone, and I got off the stage in Uvalde along the Nueces. As my feet touched the ground, I felt for the six-gun along my right leg and then for the bowie at my back. I was reassured, and stepped up onto the boardwalk.

We walked to the stables to check on the horses that had been purchased for me by Tex Dobson, and the hostler had remembered me from when I'd been there a couple years before. He'd had my twenty head out back, in the holding corral. While at the stables, I made arrangements with him for the Shoshone to bed in at the barn.

Uvalde came back familiar to me as Dave and I paced along the boardwalk; I couldn't forget it was one of the roughest towns in Texas. As we walked into the Corral Saloon, we were met by a familiar smell of dust, stale beer, and smoke. But I was pleased to see Butch Calhoun still behind the bar, and he remembered me right off.

An hour later, I'd thought about checking in at the hotel, then reconsidered, deciding I'd stay at the stables with the Shoshone. The hostler was pleased to oblige us all in the haymow half full of new hay.

We spent a restful night there, and the next morning, after we'd found a meal at the General Store, I'd roped out a well-formed strawberry-roan gelding for my mount, then told the others to pick out any one they'd wanted. It wasn't long before we readied to head northwest out of town to find Tex Dobson. But just as we'd climbed on our horses, he rode up to the stables. We greeted each other and caught up a bit on the past couple years, then he told me about what I really had come for — the cattle were held a day's ride west.

At nine we rode out of Uvalde, with the Shoshone herding thirteen horses. On the way, I asked Tex if he was still gathering up strays. He'd acknowledged that after he'd bought his ranch over on the Pecos, he'd gathered a herd for himself and hadn't done much since. He admitted he'd gone into debt on some rangeland, and once again had been in the process of rounding up a sizeable herd to help pay that off.

"About then I'd received your letter, Sean, and decided I needed the cash right then more than I needed those cattle for myself. I figured I'd just have to round up more later — though I must say it's been harder to find 'em."

The herd Tex had for me was a mixed bunch of some twelve-hundred head, in a holding area of grass along Devil's River. Arriving early the next day, all seemed well. Tex had bought me a used chuck wagon fully equipped, including staples and perishables, and a remuda of thirty more horses to add to the twenty we'd picked up in Uvalde. He'd also hired six riders for me, who would make the drive to Utah for two hundred dollars each.

As the men prepared to pull stakes, Tex and I rode the herd. Immediately I noticed all the cattle had been burned with my Anchor K brand — twelve-hundred head of a mixed bunch, mostly cows, with maybe two hundred steers and two dozen bulls. Included in the herd, but not the count, were at least three hundred calves, and along with that many more yearling bulls and heifers.

I had some concerns right off about the calves still with their mothers, for I knew a lot of them wouldn't make it to Utah, and not only that, but as I had learned earlier with Chancy, they were probably going to make trouble in the herd. I could see they were all a wild bunch of cattle, only recently pulled out of the brush, and it would take some doing before we got them accustomed to the trail.

Nevertheless, all in all I was well pleased, and I'd thanked Tex for his work in getting things ready and for providing more than the number of animals he'd been asked to get. I handed him a pouch filled with $15,000 in gold, nodded a good-bye, then shouted to my men.

"*Move 'em out!*"

By mid-morning we were chasing an angry bunch of longhorns all over the landscape. They didn't want to be pushed. Fortunately, once again, to our rescue a big old bull with the scars of many a fight moved into the front and led the herd. We made our own trail through the arroyos as the wranglers whooped and hollered the cattle west across a dry-as-bone land of brush, cacti, and yucca plant.

Five days later we crossed the Pecos River, and then we crossed it again south of New Mexico on the last day of April. From there we followed the river and hit the Goodnight-Loving trail that had been cut in '66 to New Mexico and Colorado. On the 28th of May we stopped for a day at Fort Sumner, New Mexico, then we left the Pecos and crossed the Canadian River six days later. On the 20th of June we trailed into Denver.

I was relieved to reach that point, for we'd already experienced a Comanche skirmish in Texas, where the Indians got off with a hundred head of cattle, and then during a flash flood along the Pecos, we lost another twenty head. Our worst problem had been the calves falling behind and bawling for their mothers, and then their mothers doing everything possible to turn around and get back to them. We had stopped at every house we could along the way to rid ourselves of the youngest animals that couldn't keep up, and, finally, by Denver those that were left — maybe a good hundred or more — were finally staying right with the herd.

We lay over in Denver for three days, and on the second, as we rested the herd north of town, a drover stopped by.

"Ya wantin' to sell?" he'd asked.

"No," I politely refused. "We're heading for Utah with this bunch."

"Well, I wished you'd sell," he stubbornly pressed again. "I'd give ya twenty-five thousand for the cattle, horses, and all your appurtenances."

I acknowledge the gravelly drover that it was a fair offer, adding, "If the cattle weren't promised in Carson Butte, I'd take it."

"Well, if ya bring any more this way and ya want to sell 'em, look me up," the man drawled as he handed me his card.

In time, we passed through Cheyenne, Wyoming Territory, in a cloud of dust, and without stopping. But west of town two days we had a running fight with a party of Sioux, and a few days after that it was the Cheyenne and the Arapaho. With no more than twenty enemy warriors attacking us, they were no match against our Shoshone and wranglers with Winchesters. Nevertheless, in all these latest assaults along the trail we lost maybe fifty more head, and four horses.

A month after leaving the Cheyenne area, we drove well over a thousand head of bawling cattle into Green River, Wyoming.

On the 26th of August, we hit Ogden, and camped in a large meadow north of town. I was encouraged and relieved to finally be back in Utah. I knew we could make the distance now.

On the 3rd of September I breasted the summit of the rim and saw Carson Butte off below. I was pleased at our success and proud of my men who had faithfully stayed the course for the long drive across country.

The town shone its colors of roofs and barns, like a welcoming quilt on a wind-chilled night, lit by a sinking golden sun past its zenith, painting pink trails onto far western clouds. A feeling of home came over me, and with a lump in my throat I shouted to the men, "*Move 'em on! . . . We're headin' home!*"

After stringing the cattle down the slope, we drove them through the town as men, women, and children watched in delight along the dust-clogged street. It was a celebration parade, as we then moved them west the four miles to the Anchor K and let the cattle slowly spread out into knee-deep grass.

Twenty-Seven

THE FOLLOWING MORNING I went to the stables, anxious to ride out and explore the Anchor K. Genius was glad to see me after the five long months, and he took off through the double doors and down main street like a shot. I let him run for a mile, then we settled down to a fast walk. We looked over the ranch, checking on the lay of the land and exploring.

A few days later, as I was riding through the deep grasses, I was more impressed than ever with the property. I'd decided to build a house on some high ground, in a scattering of aspen and pine. North from that eminence you could see the dark-blue, clear-as-crystal lake. Beyond, as far as my eyes could reach, they canvassed across the Anchor K and into the range-free grasslands for miles and miles. And distant from the range land, purple mountain peaks graced into the sky above the timberline.

Eight miles northeast from where I rode, and easily seen, lay Carson Butte. That morning her townsfolk were silent, except for the occasional ring of the blacksmith's anvil coming across the grasslands. A quarter mile to the south was a heavy growth of lodgepole pine to the slope of the mountain, rising up to the rim and the peaks far beyond. Five hundred feet west of the bench were more of the heavily forested pine, and then for a quarter mile of nearly flat incline began the steep slope to the top saddle of rock connecting the mountain to the mesa. The beauty of the land was to be seen everywhere.

On September 10th I'd received a letter from my attorney in New Orleans telling me Pa's treasure finally had been sold — except for the one trunk I had asked him to deliver to the Champlains at Blackstone. Dumont wrote:

> *I must tell you that the three sold trunks of treasure, after fees, have made you a very wealthy man. The total amount I'll not put in this letter. I did, however, deposit $100,000 into your Wells Fargo account, and a sizeable portion at the New Orleans bank to draw interest. The bulk I invested in local building, shipping, and state bonds for a better return. The bank will be sending you an accounting in the near future.*
>
> *Your plantation house at Mosswood has been completed and is ready for your return. I have paid all the construction bills, $119,210, before making your deposits. I have leased the thousand acres of land at Mosswood to a reputable planter, to be farmed on a 50-50 share basis. I have also hired male and female domestics to care for the house and grounds, their pay to come out of your account at the bank.*
>
> *I might note that your gift to the Champlains seemed to baffle your stepsister Lucia; I could see it was something she had never expected.*
>
> *I look forward to seeing you when you return to New Orleans.*
>
> *Your Obedient Servant*
>
> *Louis Dumont, Attorney at Law*

I pondered Dumont's words, somewhat overwhelmed at my sudden wealth, but grateful once again to Pa and Ma, and to God, who had always watched over me through the darkest times of my life's journey.

Back at the Anchor K, the ranch was making progress. Dave had hired Moon Bear as his assistant, as well as three other of our riders — two of the Shoshone and one of the Texans that had wanted to stay after the drive. And once the cattle had settled down, Dave made a final count reporting seven hundred twenty-two cows, two hundred fifteen steers, twenty-one bulls, one hundred twenty-one calves, one hundred twenty-eight yearling bulls, and one hundred eighty-two heifers, for a total of one thousand three hundred eighty-nine bovine. He'd also counted, incuding his own mount, forty-two horses.

By mid-September of 1873, Katrina and I had hired a carpenter to build our house. We'd decided we didn't want a big place like awaited at Mosswood, but something that was comfortable and more suited to the area. We did include a library, however, as we both spent time with the written word.

Meanwhile, downstream north of the lake, we had built a house for Dave that included a separate place for his assistant and outside foreman. Across a wide open yard to the north, we planned for a bunkhouse, large barn, and holding corrals.

The carpenter had hired eight of the local men and immediately went to work on the two houses and bunk. By late November, the bunkhouse and Dave's house were completed. Then Katrina and I moved into our new place on the 10th of December, in a blinding snowstorm. The barn and corrals wouldn't be finished until late spring.

Before Christmas, however, we moved back to our rooms in town at the Gold Dust, as Katrina needed to be at the Showcase most days and was concerned a storm would keep us from reaching town.

That winter we sold a hundred Anchor K steers to Bill Thorson for his slaughterhouse operation, and the Shoshone took twenty as a part of my agreement with Washakie.

February of 1874 came in with a blizzard that lasted two days, and I wondered how Dave was doing at the Anchor K, for Katrina and I were still at the Gold Dust. But I turned that care over to God, and somehow felt all would be fine. Dave was a capable man, and he knew cattle, so I determined to worry about it no more.

It was in March, after a warming wind had blown across the ranch, that Dave and I were able to ride out to look at the cattle. They were pawing loose the remaining snow to get at last year's grass.

"They look good," I told Dave, despite the fact we'd lost some thirty head to the sub-freezing weather that winter, and we may have lost one bull to a grizzly. I'd thought a grizzly, because no cat or black bear would have had a chance bringing down a longhorn bull. Fortunately, the zero temperatures had by then abated, which had saved us from losing any more.

Dave and I'd decided a fence was needed along the six miles of the ranch's east line, to keep the cattle out of the grass between the Anchor K and Carson Butte, and we'd determined pole fencing would do best. I'd suggested using the lodgepole pine in the area.

"You could selectively pick your timber, and that would leave a good thinning of the trees," I'd told him.

We agreed that only the east line would need enclosure, as the south and west had their natural barriers of cliff and timber, and to the north was open range.

In early April, Katrina and I finally moved back to the Anchor K. Then on the 10th, a Saturday, we'd gone to town on errands, and as we approached Carson Butte, we could see a flood of people filling the boardwalk. It was an amazing sight; in only two years the town had grown to four hundred. Each new business brought in another, and each hired more help. The old-timers around town didn't hesitate to tell anyone who would listen that the progress was all due to a slip of a girl named Katrina. She had brought hope to a place where hope had vanished.

I certainly could understand that, as she had changed my life as well.

While I stood in front of the Showcase, searching my eyes toward the Anchor K, I could see specks of our cattle in the distant grasses now turning green. It, too, was a picture of hope for the future.

The day before, I'd been riding my blue-roan along the mesa, where up out of last year's leaves the wildflowers were blooming and waving their silent praises to God. The total portrait of the surrounding landscape was one of unlimited promise.

That next Monday, when the air blew cool and the sun felt warm, I rode the Anchor K alone. I wanted to see it all up close, to hear its rhythms and melodies in the springtime wind. I'd remembered Pa telling me that most people see the beauty of land and sea to some degree, but hardly any ever listen.

"Those that do," Pa'd said, "learn to love the songs of the land and sea as God's gift."

Pa had felt that nature was something you needed to experience on your own, in solitude, for it would bring a new understanding and peace to your life. I think I knew what he was talking about, even back then as a child. And the many years when I'd been on the move, I still knew the songs of the land, though there were times I would forget, until I'd stop by God's gardens and listen.

As my ears searched over the Anchor K, I heard the whisperings through the trees, and I shouted back with a full heart, my voice echoing, ". . . *Hello, wind!* . . ." I felt a joy inside that only God can gift a man.

That day I rode along an icy stream that roared its way down from the southern slopes, to where below it ran into the glacial lake above the barns and Dave's house. Along the saddle, south of the mesa, I'd searched for a path to the top and, finally, after hours of looking, I'd found a game trail that wound me through boulders and trees, in and out, almost like a needle stitching a pattern.

When suddenly I breasted the slope, I was in the mile-wide saddle thick with trees and brush growing out of the barren rock. Along the southern face of the mesa were patches of aspen, spruce, yucca, cacti, and manzanita. The mesa plateau glaring ominous above me looked to be some fifty feet of cliff.

Where I could see through the foliage, I had a view east to Carson Butte; to the west there ranged a vast acreage of grassland that traveled many miles, to what appeared to be a deep canyon. And beyond the gorge rose a range of mountain to the height of the rimrock south overlooking Carson Butte. Past the far upper rim were several tree-barren snow-covered peaks.

I'd found no way to the top of the mesa from the saddle, so I spent a peaceful day out of the cold wind in a grassy area surrounded by spruce trees. As I sat back in the tall dry grass, Genius was off trailing his reins and searching out clumps on his own. For a time I remained, eyes shut, catching the sun warming my shoulders. I watched a ship-like cloud sail off to the south, only to disappear where I'd reckoned it had moored at some foreign port of call.

Suddenly my eyes fixed maybe fifty feet off. I took notice of an old, dry stream bed, and as I'd looked it over, good sense told mc it shouldn't have been there, as it would have taken a great amount of runoff to cause that extent of erosion. There was no doubt that the ditch at times carried an enormous amount of rainfall.

It was chocked full with Manzanita brush, and appeared to go to the base of the escarpment's rock face. I couldn't resist, so I began exploring the gully. Some fifty feet farther west, in a narrow clearing of the manzanita, I saw a trail up to the rock face. Along the cliff, a gravely path three feet in width turned east between the rock and the manzanita. By the signs, dccr and other game had probably been using the trail for years.

At the waterway, I could see a tunnel entered the rock, it's opening covered from the south with manzanita. The dark, yawning cavern was some seven feet high, and appeared forbidding, almost ominous. But my curiosity would not let me stop, and inside, amidst the darkness, at an upward angle I could see a small square of daylight.

The floor of the cave, scored smooth from runoff erosion, slanted an easy grade for nearly four hundred feet to the mesa top. I could see right off that the cavity fell in a low spot of the mesa floor that surely drained several hundred acres. In ancient times it was probably a natural lake that had found a crack where water worked its way down to the saddle. Years of pressure runoff, with freeze and thaw, had eaten away the cavity to its present size.

It was a tunnel large enough for horse or bovine to reach the mesa plateau. But I knew one thing was certain — neither man nor beast would want to be in the cavern during a rainstorm.

After having walked the enclosed waterway, I rode Genius to the tunnel entrance and dismounted, figuring that the first time I'd better walk him through the cavity. He didn't want to go, but with some urging entered into the darkness and moved right along with me to the top. By then, dusk was settling across the countryside, and we didn't get to see much of the mesa.

I had no trouble taking Genius back through the dark enclosed waterway.

By seven the next morning I was on the mesa again, riding Genius. I think the gelding was as excited as I was. What a wonderful unexpected surprise it was to be able to ride my horse across what seemed like the heights of the world. And it was like entering into another land — beautiful and isolated.

The mesa, according to the land office map, was around four miles long and close to a mile wide. If so, it covered four sections of land, making twenty-five hundred and sixty acres of island sanctuary.

From a distance, the mesa top had appeared flat and treeless, except for the scatterings of cliff-hanging wind-worried pine trees, but in reality the top was like a park of undulating countryside, grassy hillocks and valleys of native grasses, large yucca cacti, and areas of aspen, pine, spruce, and Douglas fir. The highest eminence on the plateau covered at least two hundred acres of ground, an area graced with the beauty of far-reaching rolling hills as high as twenty feet, looking down on valleys of grass-covered meadows. Near the center of the mesa a good fifty acres was scattered with islands of tall red-rock pinnacles that plunged skyward, one a good sixty feet.

I walked the area with an understanding that this was what it must be like in Paradise — pure, untouched by human hands. My thoughts could not help but grow melancholy as I thought of God's Heaven, wondering how Ma and Pa would have enjoyed this place with me, and saddened that we did not have the chance to share these things together through the years.

As Genius munched grass nearby, now and then glancing up at me, I looked down at Pa's ruby ring on my finger. In truth, I knew that I still had a part of them with me, deep in my heart and soul — and that was worth more than all that money in the New Orleans bank or Wells Fargo combined.

After a time, with my eyes and heart at peace, I looked at my pocket watch. The day was moving on, and I was surprised to see I'd been on the mesa nearly eight hours. From where I sat, to the south along and below a red escarpment, I could see several large cottonwood and a chartreuse greening of willow. I mounted my gelding and rode to the pinnacle. In the massive rock's north shade was a pooling of cold sweet water. I drank long, as did Genius.

I could see that the pool, covering a good two acres, lay deep and disappeared underneath the overhanging rock. As I mounted up, I considered how I could bring the cattle up there, but just as quickly decided against it, for I knew they would tear up the pristine beauty and muddy the reservoir of water. A few horses might be all that I would want to put on the mesa.

I mounted Genius and reined him south, and he went back through the tunnel like he had traveled it a hundred times. Minutes later I was riding the slope to the house, anxious to tell Katrina about our sanctuary in the sky.

The next morning I took Katrina to the mesa top, and she shared the same joy as I did. From then on, we spent many a happy time together in our mountain haven.

A few days later I rode the range with Dave, and was pleased at how well he'd had things running all across the ranch. I could see that the Anchor K was taking on the air of a first-class cattle operation.

Twenty-Eight

MAY WAS ABOUT as close as one could come to Heaven. That's what Ma used to say, and I know why; she loved spring flowers. Well, it was the 1st of May, 1874, in Carson Butte; the wheel of time had simply kept moving along, never stopping, never waiting.

It was Saturday morning, and I was hitching the buckboard to a pair of white-blazed roans. I'd slapped the reins, and the team trotted the buggy up to the house, where Katrina stepped out into sunlight gleaming on her dark hair as she gave me a smile. I thought she was the most beautiful woman in the world, and everybody I knew in Carson Butte would agree.

Katrina was with child and had long started to show, with the baby due sometime in June. We both could hardy contain our joy, and the town was thrilled at the news as well. I'd needed to travel back to New Orleans, but it was decided we would wait until the fall to make the trip, maybe in September, when the baby would be at least three months old.

Carson Butte was buzzing when we pulled into the stables. After unhitching the roans and turning them loose in the corral, Katrina and I walked out the double doors into the bright mid-morning sunlight. We looked down the street to a town full of people, then over at George Bentley who sat on a straight-back chair, leaning against the barn's clapboard siding.

I asked George what was going on. "I didn't know there were this many people in the whole county," I'd told him.

Then I figured to myself it must have been the warm weather that once again had brought everyone out, after having been cooped up most of the long, hard winter.

Bentley allowed that he didn't know we had that many people either, adding, "But just last week three more families came to town . . . that Richard Thompson, the attorney . . . and Ralph Johnson — him and his wife are openin' another cafe. . . . and then there's a man that's a carpenter, who just went to work for Larson at the lumberyard."

Katrina and I continued down the boardwalk to the Showcase, as she had wanted to visit with Sharon McBride; and so I'd left her there, then walked the two blocks to the edge of town.

I'd put my right hand above my eyes to cut the glare, and searched the mesa top from the distance. It looked just as I'd thought it would — flat as a table top from those ten miles. Straining to see the pinnacles, I at first made out nothing; but then, almost invisible to the eye, was a pale blue of intermittent shapes, like misty clouds, toward the middle of the mesa. They appeared like protruding rock, and though I wasn't certain, I was fairly confident they were the tall angled formations.

The Showcase apparently was running well, and Sharon had no problems. Katrina and I loafed the day away, spending part of our time in our room at the Gold Dust. Katrina was in a play that evening, and so we ended up staying the night in town.

The next day, on the way back to the ranch, Katrina and I talked as we traveled. Katrina was thinking of selling the Showcase to Sharon.

"She's capable, and would keep it going," she'd acknowledged.

I supported Katrina's plan, believing she was making a good decision to be free of the responsibility of the place, now that our baby was on the way. But I'd asked, "Shouldn't you offer it to MacArthur first, since he'd originally put up the money and he owns the building?"

Katrina agreed. "Yes . . . I suppose you're right; though I don't think he'll want it. He never did like having to provide food in his own business. . . . But I'll talk to him."

Katrina pondered some. ". . . Maybe I should sell the slaughterhouse and butcher shop too. Bill Thorson now has them showing a decent profit; and, in fact, it was last week that he'd said he'd like to buy it some day."

With a morning sun warming our backs and gleaming down the road, we could see our new entrance gate maybe a mile ahead of us. The handsome structure was molded into an archway, and at the top, in bold, black, iron letters read Anchor K Ranch. North and south from the gate was the six miles of new pole fence.

Surveying our own property as we approached always seemed to cause my heart to miss its rhythms. I was deeply proud of the beautiful paradise we had created.

That next Monday morning at daylight I was at the barn to catch Dave, and after he had lined out the men, we went to his house to talk. He'd pointed to a chair at the kitchen table, and I sat down amidst the top strewn with papers. I glimpsed at what looked to me like hand-scribbled poetry, as he gathered up the sheets, and put them into stacks. He took the coffee pot from the stove top and poured me a cup, then sat down across from me.

"Well . . . what do you think, Sean? How do you like the way things are shaping up on the place?"

"I couldn't be happier," I told him. "You've organized things better than I believed possible. . . .

"But that's not what I'm here for, Dave. . . . I wanted you to know that Katrina and I will be going to New Orleans this fall for the winter. I feel assured that the ranch is in your good hands. But I'll need to ask you to start keeping books for me while I'm away."

Dave smiled. "I already have," and he pulled a ledger out of a cupboard drawer. "The only thing I don't have is a bank account."

"You will," I replied. "I'll set it up in town with a ten thousand dollar balance for you. And I'll have a letter, giving you power of attorney, so that you can handle all the ranch business while we're gone.

" . . . And there's one other thing that's been on my mind. . . . I believe we're going to need to find more buyers for our steers before they start to get too big. Carson Butte can't take half of what we need to sell this year."

Dave had thought of that too. "You know, Sean, around forty miles north is an Army camp. I rode over there last week, and the Major in charge said they'd take as many steers as we could supply."

I was pleased and impressed. It seemed like Dave had thought of everything, and so with the cattle business off my mind, I could relax. We sat back and talked of many things, some business, some personal. I asked him what he was writing, pointing at the papers stacked on the table.

"Oh, that's just my poetry, Sean," he'd replied. "Writing is something I've stayed with through the years; it keeps me sane in an unpredictable world."

He'd pointed to a stack of boxes in the corner. "Those two are full of twenty years of my frontier life. After I'd gone to Texas, I didn't have much time for it, though I've managed to write a few unpublished novels — they're in the bottom box; the top one is full of my poetry."

I was taken aback at the tenacity — and the complexity — of the man. He'd long ago told me he had studied literature in his college years, but I'd thought he'd left all that behind when he came West.

I asked if I could take a look at his verse — the one there on the table. He pushed it over to me.

New Orleans

'Twas a springtime day in New Orleans,
When he came to town from yonder hill.
He saw her there inside a courtyard gate
In the hue of afternoon shading and still.

She sat alone, in a green hibiscus bower,
Among crimson blossoms, before a wall
Of emerald foliage scented with jasmine,
By a fountain, cascading in a waterfall.

She began to sing, her voice melancholy,
Had baptized the territory of her retreat.
Then he vaulted the wall dappled in light
And dropped to her solitude on airy feet.

Now paired, they sat in the leafy canopy.
He wore a fine garment feathered in blue
Alongside her matching and lovely attire.
Then when I coughed, the bluebirds flew.

After a stunned moment I said to Dave, "It's a very nice poem, but the ending was a surprise."

"Well, it's supposed to be just that," he acknowledged. "It's called an allusion poem."

It was ten o'clock when I left Dave and mounted my blue-roan gelding. I heeled the horse south, expecting Genius to head for the shed when we reached the house, but he pulled to the west and I let him go. That horse and I must have had similar thoughts, for he made a line for the mesa. At the tunnel he eagerly went into the darkness and up the cavern.

I rode the plateau, amazed at how nature had molded the place in spring. It was a country of greened aspen, spruce, fir, and stunted pine. Lush grassy meadows with blue blossoming chicory, and ever-present manzanita, watercress, plantain, stonecrop, evening primrose, even wild raspberries filled the draws, amidst the other wildflower growths. A man could survive for a time, if marooned on the mesa, with the edible greens and berries there in abundance.

I watched the chipmunks play in the orange gravely soil, before they'd raced to where they homed amidst the rock. Deer tracks were plentiful, as were large cat tracks nearby. I'd considered it might take some effort to rid the place of the cougar, for I really didn't want them on the mesa threatening the horses and game.

There was no way for me to see the entire twenty-five hundred acres of the plateau, unless I had a year or two to stay right there. But then I didn't want to see it all at once anyway. I knew it would make for many surprises in my trips to the refuge.

The places that stood above the rest in that amazing land of beauty were the soaring pinnacles, and I rode to them after several hours of exploration. Following a drink at what I'd come to call the natural water tank, I walked to what appeared to be the tallest of the towers. I'd found a way to climb at least halfway to the top, and I scampered up the escarpment fracture, topping out at a cirque. But there was no way to get higher than the hanging meadow that graced half an acre of grass, with a few scattered aspen and one lone gnarled pine along the cliff's edge. The tree had been pitifully twisted and distorted, and it appealed to my nature to wonder how anything could take the beatings of the elements and still survive.

As I moved west along the notch in the rock, a shallow cave, a safe natural shelter, layered back to maybe ten feet of overhead protection. Along the north cliff, a large rock tabled on the meadow. I moved a smaller flat stone near the table, in the shade of several aspen trees. Their hanging leaves, shimmering in a slight breeze, were whispering down sweet words to the delicate plateau.

I sat on the rock, my back against the bole of an aspen tree. Down below, from the mesa floor, I couldn't see Carson Butte, but from where I sat there in the cirque, it shone clear in the distance, as smoke once again drifted skyward from the blacksmith shop. I spent two hours at the retreat before making my way back to the mesa floor. I could see on the way down that with a little work on the rift, the climb would be manageable for Katrina.

On the 15th of June my daughter, Susannah Marcia, was born into our world. The mid-wife explained that for her first child, Katrina's labor had gone fairly well. But it took several weeks before she began to recover her energies and feel like her old self again.

Carson Butte went crazy over the child, and whenever we made it into town for the day, Katrina had to go in most of the shops along the boardwalk to visit and show off the baby.

That August, the 10th was hot, and a day I'll not forget. Katrina and I were in town for the weekend, and warm golden light streaming down from the sun had captured the countryside — except for where puple shadows reigned underneath the boardwalk and the long narrow spaces between the buildings.

Katrina had gone to the Showcase with little Susannah, and I was at the stables talking to Slim. He had pulled out another chair for me to sit, but the temperature was steadily rising, and we'd had to move the chairs to the shade of an aspen near the corner of the building.

We sat quiet as I listened to life around me. A screen door slammed at the butcher shop. An eagle screeched from the sky overhead. An unseen dog from down the street continued his bark at an annoyance; and two horses, in the corral behind, were intermittently slapping flies off each other. A sort of a low hum — the people in conversation along the street — came to my ears in a monotone.

But in an instant there came a thunder and rumble from the wagon bridge. The stage clattered by the barn and squeaked and rushed to a stop at Wells Fargo down the block, amidst the driver's repeated calls and shouts to his horses. The clouds of dust that followed the coach into town slowly settled over the stage, the horses, and the boardwalk.

From my distance, I could see a beautiful blonde-haired lady step off the stage, with her long flowing white dress, flapping wide-brimmed hat, and delicate gloves and parasol. She was a picture to behold. Behind her, from out of the stage, stepped a nice-looking man in a dark blue suit and elegant cream-colored vest. They appeared to me as if they'd stepped straight out of an Eastern fashion catalog, and I couldn't believe that anyone would have that many clothes on in the August heat.

But heedless of me and my opinion, they'd hustled themselves across the street and down the boardwalk, turning many a head as they went. From where I sat, it looked to me like they'd gone directly to the Showcase . . . and I wondered why, for it was as if they'd known exactly where they were headed.

My instincts would prove valid much later, when I would learn that the handsome John Culberson and his stunning wife Jenny had been run out of almost every town of any size west of the Mississippi. Towns like San Francisco, Denver, and Kansas City had put up with the pair until they'd finally been caught with stolen goods in their possession.

High-class thieving was their specialty, particularly easy-to-apprehend jewelry. And word had it that if not for the beautiful, demanding Jenny, John Culberson would no doubt have gone the straight and narrow. But besides being beautiful, Jenny Culberson had a unquenchable larcenous streak in her bones and wanted a life that poor John could not easily afford.

Jenny knew no other way than to take what she'd wanted; and if John wished to be with the woman he loved, he had no choice. It all had started, it was said, some fifteen years before, when the two had been left homeless and running the hardscrabble streets of New York. It was a scene all too common for youngsters those days, children on their own when parents had succumbed to the inescapable yellow fever epidemic of 1850. The disease had raced through America's large coastal cities, leaving tender young lives hanging in the balance.

I'd felt some compassion for the pair when I'd heard that, for well I knew the terror of the orphan's life. And I'd been told so many times by Pa of the eight thousand who had died not far from us, in New Orleans, the summer of '52, from the same dreaded disease.

John Culberson had been eighteen and Jenny sixteen when they'd first met, and ever since that day they had traveled a lawless trail. Cheyenne had been their last stop before arriving in Carson Butte. Riding the train on their way far west, a chatty old-timer had told the pair of the town — "The fastest growin' place in the west," he'd said. "And, word had it, with lots of old money!"

He'd been telling the pair just what he'd thought they'd wanted to hear, embellishing his tale, and not really knowing the truth; but the two thieves eagerly took the bait.

"I've told no one," he'd said, "but they say the real action in the town is at a place called the Showcase, and the Gold Dust Saloon. The owners of the Showcase are rumored to be the wealthiest young folks west of the Mississippi!"

The pair had been headed for Virginia City, in far western Nevada, at the time, for though the law had told thcm two years before never to come back, they'd learned that the city now ran rich and had decided to take a chance.

And as for Carson Butte — they had never heard of the place until the old storyteller had bent their ears. But it was then they decided they might cash in on the mountain town.

Twenty-Nine

I WALKED INTO the Showcase and Katrina was sitting at a nearby table with the couple from off the stage. She'd seen me enter, stood up, and waved.

"Sean! . . . Sean, please come over here! I want you to meet the Culbersons."

When I strolled over to the table the man stood up.

Katrina introduced us, explaining that the pair were in town to see if Carson Butte was the kind of place they were looking for, perhaps to buy a business.

My suspicious instincts were still operating, and I'd asked Culberson what he did for a living.

"Well, nothing right now," he'd replied. "We've mostly been traveling around the country."

The explanation certainly seemed shallow to me, and the idea of looking at Carson Butte made no sense, as they'd appeared to be the kind of people who liked the city life, not some quiet little mountain town. I'd questioned right off their wanting to settle in Carson Butte, but for some reason Katrina had accepted them, as if they'd been long-lost friends. I couldn't determine why that might be, as she had always been strictly level-headed and mostly on guard, especially in the past. But I'd thought perhaps she'd come to grow into the comfort of the surroundings, both in Carson Butte and at our home, and the causes for suspicion or fear were no longer prominent in her mind. Whatever the case, Katrina had apparently extended to them the warm hand of friendship.

That afternoon, the Culbersons had found nothing to their taste at the hotel and stopped in again at the Showcase to appeal to Katrina for help in finding a place to stay. Katrina had showed them the room next to ours, then available at the Gold Dust, but they didn't like the furnishings there either, apparently not suiting their finer tastes. Wanting to help, Katrina generously showed them some of our furniture, which she offered to let them borrow.

Jenny was obviously delighted. "And we'll be right next door when you'rc in town."

I had wondered how she'd known we didn't live in town, and it also seemed to me that Jenny was admiring Katrina's diamond ring a little too much for comfort — but then again, I thought maybe I was simply being too suspicious.

That evening, the Culberson's attended the comedy performed at the Showcase, and as a result, they were able to meet almost everyone in Carson Butte. I'd noticed, however, that they seemed only to cultivate the acquaintance of the most prosperous folks in town.

By that time, I had become increasingly cautious of the pair, and without being obvious I'd carefully watched their actions throughout the evening. Katrina had thought I was being especially silly, and unnecessarily distrustful — that is, until the events of that weekend, when Mary Carpenter, the banker's wife, had discovered she was missing two hundred dollars in gold coin and her two-karat diamond ring.

I'd recalled specifically noting John Culberson slipping out of the Showcase just after the lamps had dimmed for the second scene that night of the comedy show. But he'd been gone just twenty minutes, and I'd figured at the time that it couldn't be long enough to create any mischief.

Marshal Clayborne, however, had determined the theft had indeed occurred that same Saturday night, while everyone was preoccupied at the play, for it was on Sunday that Mary Carpenter had discovered the valuables were missing.

But the Marshal could come up with no suspects.

It was the next Saturday morning that I'd caught him at the bakery and after greeting the lawman, I'd asked him why he was looking so discouraged.

"Well, it's the Carpenter case, Sean; I just can't come up with anything." I sympathized, but decided it was time that I forthrightly told him of my suspicions. "Maybe I can help, Marshal. . . . I think it's John Culberson."

"Culberson? . . . Why, no, he has an alibi. Him and his wife had never left the Showcase during the time Jacob and Mary Carpenter were away from home."

I smiled at him, then explained the facts. "On the contrary, Marshal; John left the Showcase for some twenty minutes during the second act."

"You sure?" Clayborne asked.

"I'm sure," I told him. "I timed it, but figured later it wasn't enough to take the goods. But it's dawned on me that it'd surely be long enough if he didn't have to search and knew right where the stash was located in the house. The three blocks coming and going wouldn't take over seven minutes, and if he'd had a skeleton key, that'd leave a good twelve minutes alone inside, time enough to pouch up any valuables."

The Marshal nodded in agreement. "I believe you're right, Sean — except I've talked to witnesses who've said neither of the Culberson's ever left the Showcase."

That wasn't too difficult to figure out.

"That's because the pair were sitting on the back row, Marshal, and John had picked a time when the lamps were dim and eyes focused on the stage. . . .There's no doubt about it, they're a clever couple."

Clayborne peered at me, ". . . But, Sean, I can't arrest 'em if they've got this alibi. What say we set a trap for the thief, and catch 'im with the goods?"

Katrina and I rode into town early the next Friday, leaving little Susannah at home with Moon Bear's sister to care for the baby. That trip, I'd had Katrina bring some of her own jewelry, for by then, I had convinced her that the thieves were indeed the Culbersons.

In our room at the Gold Dust we'd placed the jewel box with the lid open on the dresser. Inside were Katrina's keepsakes, some worthless baubles, along with a few valuable pieces I had kept from Pa's treasure.

Needless to say, the large diamond necklace and emerald brooch lying atop the pile would catch anyone's fancy.

After stabling our horses, the Marshal caught me to tell me there'd been another theft that previous last Sunday. While Pete and Mrs. Landry were out for a walk, someone had entered their place and taken the store's Saturday's sales, some three hundred dollars. And, again, there were no suspects.

We'd no sooner straightened our room at the Gold Dust when there was a knock at the door. It was the Culbersons, and Katrina graciously fixed a pot of coffee.

We sat at the table in small talk, and then John stood up and stretched, asking, "Do ya mind my standing for a while? I've been cooped up too much lately."

He walked around the room, stopping by the dresser as Jenny tried to draw our attention away from him with her gestures, telling an amusing story. Nevertheless, I could see him from the corner of my eye as he peered into the jewel box. From the look on his face, I was fearful he'd try right then to make off with the gems, and I would have to have a very unpleasant confrontation right there in our room. But he quickly walked back to the table.

"Did you tell 'em Jenny, that we might be leavin' next week?" Jenny appeared to be mildly surprised, but tried to hide it, and shook her head.

"Aye," he continued, before she could even think of an answer. "We have some business to take care of in San Francisco, but hopefully we can return soon to Carson Butte. We really do like it here."

"Sure . . ." Jenny took it up. "We plan to return soon as we can."

"But you'll be here this weekend?" I asked.

John acknowledged they would, and I told them I was pleased, for the following day I would be on the stage to Ogden and wouldn't return until Monday.

"Maybe you could keep Katrina company while I'm gone," I'd suggested.

"Wonderful!" John replied excitedly. "We'd love to look after Katrina while you're away."

I thought of the Old Testament verse in Proverbs: *Answer a fool according to his folly.* I thought surely that must apply here.

On Saturday morning I no sooner stepped into the stagecoach before the "All *aboard!*" As the team of mustangs rounded the bend out of town, straining for speed, I looked out the right side window just in time to see Culberson on the boardwalk, watching me leave. I supposed he'd wanted to make certain I was actually gone.

Two miles down the trail and out of eyesight, the stage pulled over and stopped, according to our pre-arrangement. From there I circled back and spent the day out of view at the stables. It was after dark when I finally surreptitiously crept to our room at the Gold Dust.

Thus far, the plan had gone well, and Katrina had done her job by making sure the Culbersons were at the cafe by half past six, keeping them there until at least seven. If things went as I'd suspected, John would attempt the robbery in the third act of Katrina's play, when things grew loud and rowdy on stage.

I looked at my pocket watch; it was half past eight. I'd figured Culberson would be showing up in less than ten minutes. I checked the loads in my six-gun and felt for the bowie at my back. I moved the chair to the rear corner of the room, away from the dresser and the door. Then I sat and waited in the dark.

It wasn't long before I could hear commotion from the stage far below; then I barely caught the turn of a key in the lock. Quickly the door opened enough to allow a shadowy figure to enter. The door was slowly and quietly closed, and a match struck. The flame flashed briefly on the face of the thief. It was indeed John Culberson. He had lit a small torch light, something I had never seen before, that glowed a halo as he moved to the dresser. I could see him filling a leather pouch with everything he found in the jewel box.

My shout shattered the thief's security.

"*Put the jewelry down!*" I ordered.

Culberson quickly dropped the torch, as if he'd been burned. He drew his six-gun and fired at the corner where I'd been, but by that time I had moved safely away. I aimed at the flames of his six-gun spitting fire from its barrel. I heard him crumple to the floor with a moan.

I couldn't be certain if he was playing possum or not, so I moved again in the darkness to hide my whereabouts in the room. But I could see his still figure lying on the floor, and after dousing the torch I snapped the head of a match to light the wick of the kerosene lamp.

Downstairs, at the Showcase, pandemonium had broken loose when the gunshots were heard. Some in the crowd came running up the stairway and were pounding at the door. Katrina, fearful that maybe things had gone wrong, had pushed it open, with Marshal Clayborne right behind her.

John lay dying beneath us, and softly spoke a thief's epitaph.

". . . It was for Jenny," he choked, as his life blood drained out of him. ". . . Life wasn't worth livin' . . . without her."

Jenny witnessed his last words as she stood in the doorway. But she never went to him, nor was there grief evident at the realization of his death. She simply stayed a moment, then caustically pouted.

"So that's how he made his way in life! . . . I didn't know!"

She turned and walked to her room, with the Marshal right behind her. He'd searched the place and found most of the money and all other articles that had been stolen in town. Then he put Jenny in jail, and all the while she cursed him from her cell, proclaiming her innocence.

The next morning I'd asked the Marshal what he'd planned to do with Jenny, and much discouraged, he replied, "There's nothin' I can do, Sean.

"He was the thief, and she claims she knew nothing. I have no way to prove it otherwise. I'll just put her on the afternoon stage for Denver, as that's where she wants to go. At least it's a long way from Carson Butte."

It had been quite some time since I'd had to kill anyone, and I'd told Clayborne I'd wished the man hadn't fired at me.

"I really didn't want to kill him . . . but he left me no choice."

The Marshal was sympathetic. "I understand, Sean; but Culberson said it all when he died, and I don't doubt for a minute it was for Jenny."

I couldn't help but feel bad about the whole happening. As people go, I liked John, and I was certain that underneath her uncaring demeanor Jenny surely had to be devastated, if nothing else for her loss of financial means. Yet I'd realized I had to be careful where I placed my sympathies, for the Holy Word teaches us that the man who lives by the sword shall likewise die by the sword.

On September the 15th Katrina and I were packing for New Orleans. We couldn't take much, so we'd selected judicially what we'd need, mainly our necessities, and things for little Susannah. I'd made arrangments for Dave to care for Genius and Katrina's mare while we were gone, and then instructed him, "Just let Genius have his way. Turn him loose when the weather's good and he'll go to the mesa; he loves the place."

I had told Dave that if he was on the plateau, he might keep and eye out for the big cat.

"Though you shouldn't see any tracks, for I killed a male and female that'd been scouting the area, and since that time I've seen none."

Katrina and I planned to be back some time in April, but I'd had no concerns. Dave was a good man.

"Don't you worry none," Dave affirmed. "I'll see to it that everything runs smooth while you're gone."

Before I'd left Dave, I'd told him I'd decided to prepare a contract giving him half of the profits made by the Anchor K. I'd come to believe it was only fair to share them with the person who was so primarily responsible for the success of our venture.

Dave stood speechless for a time, then when he shook my hand he managed to reply.

"I don't have enough words to thank you, Sean; you know I didn't have any idea anyone cared that much about an old cuss like me."

I smiled at him. "You're a valued part of this operation. We can't run it without you," I replied.

Katrina and I spent the following day in town, mostly at our attorney's office, taking care of business. Katrina had sold the Showcase to Sharon McBride, who in turn had made a deal with Pete MacArthur to rent the building under the existing terms. She had planned to continue the business just as though Katrina was still there, without changing a thing. And Katrina also had turned over the slaughterhouse and butcher shop to Bill Thorson, selling both for the amount she simply had invested, on monthly installments.

The day before leaving for Louisiana, we'd packed a lunch and spent several hours together on the mesa. I had mixed emotions when I made ready for the trip. I knew this journey would only be a few months, but I would miss Carson Butte. It had become home to us. Yet, I knew as well that there was always something exciting about traveling across country — the excitement of the unknown just over the horizon. And I would finally get to see Malone and Sarah again, when we stopped over in St. Louis.

It was eight o'clock the next morning when I'd pulled the buckboard in front of the house, and went inside to carry out the luggage. I had packed two suitcases, but I counted seven as I took them to the buggy. I laughed, thinking back on how Ma, too, always had taken along more than Pa'd anticipated. I remembered him chastising her when we went to Savannah, and her reply, "You ought to know by now, Robert, that womenfolk can't travel without takin' most the house with them." I chuckled at the recollection.

Finally fully loaded, I peered over at little Susannah, bundled in a blanket and quietly sleeping.

". . . *Git up!*" I called to the strawberry roans, as I snapped their stout leather reins.

We crossed the wagon bridge into Carson Butte at ten, in plenty of time to meet the outbound stage.

Thirty

THE ST. LOUIS DEPOT was a busy place when we stepped down out of the railcar amidst a hissing of steam and the rattling of the teletype inside the building. I looked at my pocket watch; it was close to noon. We ate dinner at a nearby cafe, and then went to the stables. The hostler had remembered me from being with Malone a few years back, and gave me a pair of black mustangs to hitch to the leased buckboard.

It was almost two when we'd entered the archway of trees at the White Oaks mansion. My heart felt as if it was pounding in my chest as I rode the familiar path.

I reined the horses around the house to the back door, as I had done so many times in years past, and as we alighted from the buckboard Henry came running out to greet us. He'd grabbed hold of me in a bear-like hug, and when I'd introduced Katrina, he gave her a hug as well, though gentler, welcoming her to White Oaks.

Knowing I was expecting to see Malone, Henry peered over to me and explained, "Malone not here, Sean; he and Missy Sarah in town for the day. He say it be late before they returned."

Katrina had hold of a suitcase and Henry said to her. "Must leave the suitcases, lassie. Come on in th' house with that li'l one . . . and see my family."

Katrina and the baby disappeared with Henry as I took the horses and buckboard to the barn. Once finished with caring for the animals, I went in the back door and down a hallway to the kitchen. Henry's daughter, Marie, and his granddaughter, Esther, were cuddling and cooing over Susannah, as Katrina stood watching with a proud smile on her face.

She suggested we had better get our suitcases, but when I looked around, Henry was missing. I'd figured we were probably too late. "I think by now Henry's probably already taken them up."

Katrina had asked the way to our room, as she'd wanted to refresh herself, and we passed through the main part of the house to the large entryway with its massive curving stairway to the second floor. She stopped and admired the magnificent passage, as she followed me up the sweeping stairs. Our suitcases had been placed in the west guest room, just as I had figured. And Henry had already put fresh water into the white porcelain pitcher.

Katrina settled Susannah in a small cradle that Henry must have quickly located, and then poured water into the bowl to wash her face. We spent the balance of that evening enjoying Henry's cooking and catching up on news with him.

White Oaks still felt like home to me — a strange feeling when I gave it much consideration, as our place in Utah now was where I'd put my roots.

The darkness before dawn the next morning came in with a cold rain, as the west wind gusted raindrops, like gravel, against the window of our room. I'd awoken early, as usual, mainly from habit, and went downstairs in the dark to the living room. An hour later, Malone and I were sharing old times, before Sarah came down to join us. Our visit was a welcome surprise to them, and I could see the pleasure on their faces.

Then when Katrina walked into the room with baby Susannah, it seemed as if we had a real family reunion, even though they had never met Katrina before. I couldn't remember a time when I'd been happier, or when I'd seen Katrina more taken with joy than at that moment. It gave me a wonderful feeling to have Katrina so lovingly accepted by those I loved. I recalled for just an instant the pain and fear I had felt when I'd thought I'd lost her.

Sarah was holding Susannah and making over the child with obvious joy, and as I watched I hoped that Malone and Sarah might have children of their own, for she was only thirty-two, and Malone but twelve years older.

We'd stayed with Malone and Sarah for a week, some of the happiest days either of us had ever spent. Two of those days I was with Malone riding the property, just like old times. Another day I spent with Henry, traveling to my favorite place along the Mississippi.

But the calendar days turned quickly and it soon was time to leave for New Orleans. As the darkness of night faded from the trees, an eastern sun rose golden that day above the waters of the Mississippi. Long shadows still ruled along the docks, as swells rolled along the hulls of firmly moored boats.

I helped Henry and Malone carry our luggage to the Alabama stateroom, as Sarah and Katrina talked along the railing, with Susannah sleeping peacefully in her bundle. But it wasn't long before the riverboat's horn moaned for visitors to leave the deck. Tears filled all our eyes as we said our good-byes.

While our boat pushed out into the river, we stood along the railing and waved until the three of them were out of sight. Then riding the swiftly changing currents of the river, the sternwheeler turned her paddles, gaining speed southward down the mighty Mississippi.

When we'd reached New Orleans, after departing the riverboat we'd rented a buggy pulled by a pair of roans we had picked up at the stables. On the wagon road a mile from town, the sunlight gleamed off the Mississippi waters, as if it had followed us all the way from Malone's White Oaks in St. Louis. The radiance seemed to stay with our little caravan, as did the serenading of the Louisiana songbirds, on our way to Mosswood. There we were greeted by our very kindly domestics hired for me by Louis Dumont. Once again we settled into new surroundings — new to me, as well as to Katrina — with apparent ease.

The following day, after a good night's sleep I walked the grounds above the bay and stopped to watch the sea gulls soar above the breakers, flashing white wings. The landscape, familiar to all my senses, assured me I was home, yet the house felt strange to me — not so much that it had been newly built, but perhaps because Ma and Pa weren't there to share it.

The last time I had been in our home at Mosswood was with them. But

I knew that the unceasing progression of time, which I so often had thought about, forced a person to move on to fresh new beginnings, to accept and adapt.

Mosswood simply would be one of our new beginnings. And Katrina and I would make it our home, at least part of the time.

We'd been wrong, Katrina and I, when we thought it might take a while to acquaint ourselves with the help. It looked like my attorney had chosen them wisely. The two hired were married, a pleasant older Creole couple that knew Henry Ducette, and before long they were like family to both of us — and little Susannah as well.

Four riding horses, along with a team, had been quartered in the shed, and I'd picked a chestnut gelding to ride. We liked each other right away, and before the week was out I was making trips, the thirty-some miles, into New Orleans.

Dumont had an endless amount of papers for me to sign again, and before I left his office he had, in addition, delivered a message to me from Lucia. She had asked that I come to see her when I returned to Louisiana and Mosswood — and that I bring along my wife and new daughter.

"Now how did she know I was married and had a daughter?" I asked Dumont. He shook his head. "It beats me; I remember only telling your domestics at Mosswood."

I figured she must have gotten word from them, though I'd wondered for a moment if besides being a voodoo priestess, Lucia was perhaps psychic. Nevertheless, I took her request in good spirits, as Lucia had not done a thing untoward since that day I had saved her life. I had even received a thoughtful note from her after Dumont had delivered the chest of treasure I had wanted her to have. I had no immediate reason to yet fear Lucia.

A week after we had arrived, we'd pretty much settled in, and Mosswood was starting to feel like home. That evening I brought up the possibility of visiting Blackstone. Katrina was hesitant about going to see the Champlains, and her concern was justified.

"I'm not sure I want anything to do with Lucia Champlain, Sean. It all makes me very uncomfortable, and from what's rumored and from what you've told me, she's responsible for having had my father killed as well."

But she very graciously added, ". . . On the other hand, since you want me to go, I'd feel guilty in not going with you. . . . I just don't know what I should do."

Katrina still wondered how I could embrace the Champlain family, with all their duplicity against me in the past. And I understood that. I pondered a moment before replying.

"I know how you feel Katrina. Lucia was responsible for the death of both my parents, and I too was bitter toward the Champlains and at one time ready to kill all of them connected with the deed. It's a part of my life that I know I've never gotten over completely.

"But I remember . . . when Pa and I were away at sea, we were clashing head-on with the brutal Barbary pirates off the coast of Barbados, and during the thick of the battle, the maimed and dead lay everywhere. Pa could see I was horrified and confused at such slaughter; and somehow he knew what I was thinking. He called back to me as the battle waned and before leaping to the other ship.

"*Sean!*" he'd shouted. "*The judgment is the Lord's!*"

I think what Pa was saying was that both sides would rationalize their actions that bloody day, and it's my belief that he strongly felt he had a legitimate reason to kill those pirates. What he did as a shipmaster, trading on the seas, was legitimate work, sanctioned by the laws, whereas the pirates took from others, by force — and in no way on legal grounds.

What Pa had said to me I'd later found in the Bible, and I'd asked myself what would our Lord do in my situation with the Champlains. . . . The answer I got back, Katrina, was to forgive. And that's the way I've handled it with Lucia. Even though deep down I had wanted something different, I knew there was no alternative.

". . .We really have no options, Katrina, if we follow God's Word. We have to forgive. It's not a chosen path; it's a commandment. And that's what I must do as a believer.

". . . But if you depict it differently, then you should act as to your understanding. Each of us has been given a will . . . and each of us must make a choice."

I looked over at Katrina holding Susannah and affirmed, "If tomorrow's a nice day I'd like to leave by eight o'clock. I want you with me, Katrina, but if your choice is not to go, I'll understand."

That night when I went off to sleep Katrina was still reading from the Bible. When I awoke at the crack of dawn, it lay on the bedstand next to her.

Katrina came down the steps just as I'd finished a hearty breakfast. She was dressed, but gave no indication as to her going with me to the Champlains. I sat at the table for a time, then told her I needed to ready the horses and buggy. I slowly walked to the shed where I harnessed the matched pair of roan mustangs and hitched them to the buckboard. After finishing my chores some thirty minutes later, I'd stopped the horses at the front door.

I had concluded by then that Katrina was undoubtedly not going with me, and I was on my way to the house to tell her good-bye when she walked out the door with Susannah bundled in a blanket. I smiled at her and kissed her cheek. I helped her into the coach, and directly had the horses trotting down the road to Blackstone.

We rode silently for a mile or two, neither of us saying a word. I'd figured when she was ready to speak she would; but then, when I'd peered at her sideways, she smiled at me, the kind of smile that says . . . *I love you, and everything will be fine*. She put her hand on mine and told me, "You were right."

With the baby in her arms she snuggled over against me, and I felt wonderful, like the day we had been married. By mid-morning we traveled down the lane into Blackstone. Someone had been fixing up around the place, as the mansion glowed with a new coat of paint.

When I pulled to a stop at the front door, Daniel and Julia came rushing out. Daniel was smiling, and shook hands with us both, then took the horses to the barn. I marveled that since I had saved Lucia's life, not a twinge of recrimination ever appeared in his eyes as a result of our gunfight a few years before.

And Julia, always more sweet natured than could be imagined of a Champlain, immediately took the baby from Katrina, cradling Susannah in her arms as we all walked inside the house.

Lucia was standing, waiting, by her favorite chair in the dimly lit parlor. I'd walked over and put my arms around her for but a moment, then introduced her to Katrina and Susannah. I stood back to look at Lucia. Never once in setting my eyes upon the Creole had I doubted that she was the most beautiful woman in the world. And though Katrina's beauty was also unique, in her very wholesome way, Lucia's musky milky skin, dark eyes, and black well-coifed hair were something to behold.

Still, despite the ameliorating events of the past, bringing Lucia and me together as family, her facade had not ceased to front mystery. One never really knew what lay behind her present mask, except a riddle of personalities. But that day, in her own way, I'd tried to reassure myself, from Lucia's actions, that she was genuinely pleased to see me and my new family. I'd realistically hoped I hadn't read her wrong.

Julia had taken the baby from Katrina again, and when she'd walked over to Lucia to show off Susannah, Julia purred, "Oh, Lucia . . . isn't she the most precious little girl in the whole world?"

Lucia looked down at the child, as at that moment Susannah cooed and smiled, and the baby seemed to capture even Lucia's heart. Who would have thought a tiny infant could enthrall even a voodoo priestess? . . . Or was it really something else? I could not keep from wondering.

Not many moments passed before Terrill came gliding through the door, in his ususal confident manner and announced, "I'm late Lucia . I'm sorry . . . you know how it is!"

His sister scowled at him. "I'm amazed you could even muster out of bed so early in the day!"

As the others were milling about, enjoying little Susannah's smiles, Katrina leaned over close. "Sean, I believe maybe Lucia *has* changed. . . . I couldn't have been treated better, and she really seems to adore the baby. She even wants Susannah to come over and stay with her when she's a little older."

I looked Katrina directly in the eye.

"No, Katrina. That cannot happen," I said. "You must be aware that though she has accepted us as family, and she loves to dabble with that beautiful little baby, she is still a voodoo priestess. She hasn't completely changed, Katrina. She has a lifestyle that our children must never be exposed to alone.

"Lucia can be extremely charming, and though she has made the covenant with me, after having saved her life, we mustn't forget that her voodoo religion might allow her to break that tie, should the necessary moment or opportunity present itself."

Katrina's eyes were wide with surprise. ". . . But what about your forgiveness, Sean!" It was almost an accusation.

I took her hand and held it in both of mine.

"I *have* forgiven her, Katrina, and I do not deny that I feel safer now, but we must always tread carefully with Lucia. Her life's rules are not ours, from the Holy Word."

It wasn't long before a servant called us all to what appeared to be an elaborate midday meal, and our conversation necessarily ceased there. In the dining room, Lucia sat at the head of the table, and I was on her right, with Katrina and the baby next to me. Terrill sat to Lucia's left.

But in getting seated, Katrina had dropped the baby's blanket. In an instant, Lucia was standing close by and retrieved it.

Once we all finally had been seated, Lucia held up her elegant crystal glass to make a toast.

"To the Champlains!" she enthusiastically proposed.

In but seconds, Lucia began to gasp for air, apparently choking on the wine she had just swallowed. She straightened up out of her chair, her eyes opening wide, and in a voice of anger she'd screamed, "*No! . . . Not me!*"

Lucia fell to the floor.

We were all nearly paralyzed, no one moving until I'd pulled Katrina to my arms and held her and Susannah close. Standing beside us, Julia was hysterical, crying and repeatedly calling Lucia's name. Only Terrill was composed. He looked at me strangely as I held Katrina, then he quickly moved around the table and asked if she was all right.

As she affirmed that she was, Terrill picked up something behind her, then went to the kitchen. He very directly returned and lifted his sister in his arms, carrying her to her room, across the hall, where he'd carefully placed her on the bed. He walked to the darkened window and pulled up the shade to let in the streaming sun. Then he looked around the room, and spoke in a firm voice to the rest of us, still standing.

"Lucia is dead. . . . I am the eldest, and now head of the Champlain house.

"Daniel and Julia, I want it understood now and henceforth *evermore*. There will be no more killings by the Champlain family.

". . . And, now, let's clean up the place."

Two hours later, after much sympathy and condolences amidst the shock, we were on our way home to Mosswood, with the late afternoon sun soft in the sky. Katrina, after a long time in thought, quietly asked, "Sean . . . what happened there today? Nothing makes sense.

Lucia seemed on top of the world. Why would she take her own life?"

I looked at Katrina before answering, and then laid out the truth.

"She didn't intend to take her life, Katrina. . . . The wine was meant for me."

I heard Katrina draw in her breath. I took her trembling hand beneath the carriage shawl.

". . . How can you be so sure?" she asked.

"Because, Katrina, I had switched my glass with Lucia's when Susannah's cover fell."

Tears filled Katrina's eyes, tears of confusion and disappointment.

". . . Even after all you'd done for her, and all she'd said, she still wanted to kill you! . . . I cannot understand such evil, Sean. Where does it come from?"

I tried to explain. "What I'd done for her, Katrina, apparently meant nothing, no matter what she'd said. I told you I had forgiven her; and I had. But I also was realistic enough to know that beneath her charming words she indeed *was* pure evil, as you have said. I had determined I would try to work around that, but never for a moment forgetting her true nature.

"Lucia's voodoo and the game of life were everything to her. She never gave up her lust for every piece of worth — the entire treasure — that my father had gained, and today I believe she had decided would finally be my last. That single chest of treasure I had given her had only whet her appetite for the rest.

I pulled Katrina close as we rode. "It was Terrill who had tried to explain that to me a long time ago."

"But what good would it do to kill you, with Susannah and me still alive?" she asked.

"Katrina!" I looked at her. "You were to die too, and it's my belief that she'd wanted Susannah for herself, to mold her as her own evil priestess."

I could feel Katrina's shudder.

"It gives me chills, Sean; my stomach almost turns at the thought. . . .Yet nothing happened to me; I wasn't the one poisoned. When was that supposed to take place do you suppose?"

I took a deep breath, and before I told her the truth, I thanked God that He'd been with me through the whole of that awful day.

"You weren't poisoned, Katrina, because you didn't drink the wine. Do you remember me holding your arm tightly, so that you couldn't get the glass up to your lips? And when Lucia had started gasping, you had set the wine down.

"I was watching Terrill at that moment, for he, too, had become suspicious of your danger. And that was when he had come from around the table, picked up your glass from behind us as we stood, and in an instant took it to the kitchen. I didn't have to be in there to know he had poured out the wine."

"Dear God in Heaven!" Katrina was devastated. "She meant to kill us both!"

Lucia's funeral was a stark and lonely affair — Katrina and I, the Champlains, and four others that no one knew. I figured they were probably curious enemies, checking to be certain that she had in fact been locked in her lifeless, chilling tomb.

Terrill and I at last grew to enjoy each other's company even more, becoming the close friends he had always hoped we could be. My apprehension toward him had finally reached its end with Lucia's death.

We often spend our time together reminiscing about our days in Kansas and Colorado; but never do we mention the name of Lucia.

Terrill had not asked if I had switched the glasses that night; but, in truth, I don't think he really wanted to know, for better to believe she had mistakenly killed herself, and not still be compelled, by an ancient family tradition, to eliminate her assassin.

As for Daniel and Julia, they were never really meant to wholeheartedly partake of Lucia's evil practice. Under Terrill's guidance Daniel made efforts to redirect his life from the hatred of Lucia's prodding. And it wasn't long before Daniel finally addressed our gunfight years before with his apologies, and his request for my forgiveness.

And Julia, a year after Lucia's death, had at last married — an honest God-fearing man.

In February of 1885, I visited Terrill at his home in New Orleans, and amidst our discourse he had asked if I would like him to return the ancient chest of treasure.

I looked him in the eye, and placed my hand on his shoulder.

"That chest was given to all the Champlains, Terrill, as a family gift. We are family, aren't we?"

"Yes, indeed we are," he replied with a smile. "As head of the family, I want to thank you for your gift, Sean. And may I do the same for you one day!"

I looked back at Terrill with sincerity as I spoke. "You already have, Terrill."

I learned that day that Lucia had never touched the treasure. Terrill had said it was at Blackstone, in her bedroom. "All she wanted was to have it close, to look at it."

I shook my head, amazed at another facet of that very complex woman.

"You might want to simply sell it all for cash," I suggested. "Dumont can get you top dollar, if you so decide. . . . It's pretty hard to spend a diamond brooch!"

We both laughed at the thought.

When I was ready to leave New Orleans that afternoon, Terrill handed me the deed to what had been the Thorntons' property.

"Give this to Katrina, Sean. I believe it's rightfully hers."

In early March, when we were still in Louisiana, we received an exciting letter from Sarah at White Oaks.

> *. . . I thought you both should know that I'm with child, due at any time. We couldn't be happier. James is quite excited about becoming a father — and Henry is near beside himself with joy as well.*
>
> *I might also tell you both that James has said he was planning to take Sean up on the invitation to visit Carson Butte, and we can hardly wait. All depends on the baby, of course — but in time we will be there!*
>
> *Love, Sarah*

I was truly happy for Malone and figured having a child of his own might finally be the thing that set deep the roots to his life.

The steamboat churned its paddles against the current of the Mississippi, as we headed north. We were on our way back to Carson Butte, and to our home along the sky in God's country. In the golden sunlight outside our stateroom I strode over to the promenade railing of the passenger deck, with my heart full. I peered over to Katrina and ten-month-old Susannah, each waving to me from deck chairs.

I stood there peaceful, with the family I'd always longed for nearby and safe, certain this time that everything would indeed be all right.

Cover artist . . . Tom Bookwalter, a nationally known illustrator and graphic artist, is currently a graphic design instructor at Kansas State University, Manhattan. Bookwalter's work appears in national magazines, annual reports, calendars, posters, and brochures. He has been honored by the National Geographic Society, the East and West Coast Society of Illustrators, the International Society of Business Communicators, and the Greater Jackson (Mississippi) Advertising Club. His clients include Rockwell International, 3M Company, Hewlett Packard, Ford Motor Company, VISA, IBM, United Technologies, Honeywell, Levi Strauss, AT&T, the National Football League, *The Washington Post*, and Miller Brewing, as well as the Department of the Navy, the Federal Reserve Bank of Kansas City, and the United States Information Agency.

Bookwalter attended Peru State University in Nebraska and earned his B.A. from Emporia State University, Emporia, Kansas. He attended the prestigious Art Center College of Design in Pasadena, California.

Bookwalter is represented nationally by the Neis Group, of Grand Rapids, Michigan; Munro Goodman Artists Representatives, in Chicago and New York; and the Image Mill, Des Moines, Iowa.

Also by Harold G. Ross

POETRY

Throughout My Passing Day

Where Eagles Fly

Along Golden Hills

Homage to the Gods

NOVELS OF THE AMERICAN WEST

Brannick and the Untamed West

Horizons West

The Emerald Prairie